MUTANT EMPIRE

BOOK 3

SALVATION

X·MEN

MUTANT EMPIRE

BOOK 3

SALVATION

CHRISTOPHER GOLDEN

ILLUSTRATIONS BY
RICK LEONARDI AND TERRY AUSTIN

BYRON PREISS MULTIMEDIA COMPANY, INC.

NEW YORK

BOULEVARD BOOKS, NEW YORK

X-MEN: MUTANT EMPIRE Book 3: SALVATION

A Boulevard Book
A Byron Preiss Multimedia Company, Inc. Book

Special thanks to Ginjer Buchanan, Steve Roman, Lara Stein,
Stacy Gittelman, Mike Thomas, Steve Behling, and John Conroy.

PRINTING HISTORY
Boulevard edition/May 1997

The Putnam Berkley World Wide Web site address is
http://www.berkley.com

Check out the Byron Preiss Multimedia Co., Inc. site
on the World Wide Web: http://www.byronpreiss.com

Make sure to check out *PB Plug*, the science fiction/fantasy newsletter, at
http://www.pbplug.com

ISBN: 1-57297-247-5

BOULEVARD
Boulevard Books are published by The Berkley Publishing Group,
200 Madison Avenue, New York, New York 10016.
BOULEVARD and its logo
are trademarks belonging to Berkley Publishing Corporation.

PRINTED IN THE UNITED STATES OF AMERICA

10 9 8 7 6 5 4 3 2 1

For

John and Lucy Russo,

who are always there,
with gratitude.

Acknowledgments

For their faith, the author would like to thank:
Connie and the boys (without whom . . .),
Lori Perkins, Keith R.A. DeCandido, and the
whole family. Also, much thanks to all those
who wrote or sent e-mail. It really helps.

"It's a long road, and a little wheel,
and it takes a lot of turns to get there."

—C. Daniels

Prologue

Manhattan island was coming back to life. It had, however, been resurrected as a vastly different entity. It was the middle of the week, but gone were the hordes of worker bees rubbing shoulders and elbows as they filtered in and out of offices. There were still plenty of people, but now there was breathing space as well. Estimates differed, but at least eighty percent of the island's human population had left their homes and most of their belongings in a mad dash for freedom.

The subway was dead on the tracks. There simply were not enough employees left to run it safely. On the street, the occasional city bus, private car, and enterprising cab navigated the now-abandoned skyscraper canyons. No more traffic. Vendors still toiled on corners throughout the city, though far fewer than the day before.

As the afternoon wore on, many shops, restaurants, delis, and small businesses opened their doors. After all, there were a lot of new customers. Mostly mutants.

The mutant known as Magneto, whose control over the Earth's magnetic field made him one of the most powerful beings alive, had declared Manhattan island a sanctuary for mutants. Magneto then declared the island a sovereign nation, and rechristened it "Haven." With the aid of his Acolytes, and an army of colossal pseudosentient robots called Sentinels, he then went about enforcing those declarations.

With the humans gone, and sanctuary assured, mutants poured in from across the country. The flood of genetically enhanced immigrants had not even begun to ebb. From around the world they came, and once they had gathered their strength into one place, Magneto would begin to enlarge his Mutant Empire. The tendrils of his power would spread across the globe.

For now, however, it was enough for him to watch the afternoon shadows stretch across the city. In less than a day, he had transformed one of the most important cities on Earth so that it conformed with his vision: a planet where mutants were the masters and humans were servants. It was the only way for mutants to survive human prejudices.

SALVATION

From the observation platform at the top of the Empire State Building, Magneto looked down upon his Mutant Empire and his heart swelled with triumph, happiness, and pride. The sun forced his slate-gray eyes into a squint, the wind whipped his silver-white hair across his forehead, and Magneto smiled.

It was a beginning.

*　*　*

Wolverine's return to consciousness was accompanied by a great deal of pain. He was not unfamiliar with pain. In fact, over the course of his long life, pain and Wolverine had become quite intimate. What surprised him, even as his eyelids strained to rise, was that the pain was there at all. He knew he had been unconscious for some time, likely several hours at least. Whatever wounds he had sustained should long since have been remedied by his mutant healing factor. They hadn't.

"Rise and shine, Logan," a deep, familiar voice said, just to his left. "Perhaps where intellect has proven ineffectual in providing a method of escape, righteous anger may yet prevail."

His eyes finally opened, but it took a moment for Wolverine to focus on the face behind the voice. No matter. It could only be one man. Hank McCoy, the Beast. One of the founding members of the X-Men. As Hank's blue-furred face gradually came into focus, Wolverine's mind seemed to clear just a bit. Of course he had not healed, he finally realized. He was wearing one of Magneto's inhibitor collars, a device specifically designed to negate the genetic x-factor that gave mutants their special abilities.

"'Lo, Hank," he managed to grunt, then cleared his throat. "What's the situation?"

"Bleak, I fear," the Beast responded, and gestured past Wolverine.

Logan turned to find that Storm and Bishop were still unconscious. The four of them had finally tracked Magneto and confronted him, intending to put an end to his "Mutant Empire" there and then. But things had gone terribly wrong. The X-Men had always faced difficult, sometimes impossible, odds. But four against a cityful of mutants was more than even they had been equipped to handle.

Now they hung suspended by their arms, legs, and torsos by clamps and cables forged of an adamantium alloy he had never seen before. Wolverine wondered how long the Beast had been awake, trying to work out a solution to their dilemma. He hoped Storm and Bishop would come to shortly, for a number of reasons—not the least of which was that he wanted to be certain that Storm, his old friend and the team's field leader, was not badly injured.

"We've languished in this fabricated dungeon for several hours. It's midafternoon, if I have made an accurate calculation," Hank elaborated. "How Magneto contrived to deploy this equipment so promptly is anybody's guess, but I suppose it indicates precisely how well prepared for the X-Men he truly was.

"Plainly, we are in either the basement or another sublevel of the Empire State Building, where Magneto has established his headquarters. Storm and Bishop are breathing fine, and ought to awaken presently. Otherwise, you'll all have to stop calling me 'Doctor' McCoy."

"What about you, Hank?" Wolverine said. "How are you feelin'?"

"Better than you, by all appearances," the Beast said, feigning a levity he clearly did not feel. "Although, if I could devise a plan of action, I would undoubtedly feel far better. It doesn't help to know that elsewhere in this structure, Trish Tilby is collaborating with the enemy."

Wolverine didn't respond to that. Over the years he had learned when it was better to say nothing. After a moment, however, he sensed that there was something else bothering the Beast, something haunting him even more painfully than the seeming betrayal by his old flame, Trish Tilby.

"Hank?" Logan asked.

The Beast hesitated.

"It's Bobby," he said after a moment. "If Magneto and company are to be believed, Iceman is dead."

Wolverine's entire body began to grow cold and still. His

SALVATION

lip curled back from his pointed incisors and his nostrils flared. Logan glanced around again at the apparatus within which they had been imprisoned, then turned his head to face Hank once more.

"We've got to figure a way out o' here," he growled. "We'll find Bobby, Hank. Don't give that a second thought. We'll find him, and we'll take Magneto down hard, once and for all."

*   *   *

Along a hallway lined with windows looking down on Haven, Amelia Voght walked with pride, excitement in her every step. It was really happening. Magneto and the Acolytes, Amelia chief among them, had forced the world to begin a fascinating metamorphosis. In her secret heart, she had always imagined that, once they conquered Manhattan, the island would be completely devoid of humans. Which would have been both triumph and failure. Yes, they would have their own government and security. But Magneto's intention had always been for mutants to rule humanity, not destroy it. Voght had privately doubted it was possible.

On this day she changed her mind.

Manhattan had been transformed into Haven, and there were still many humans in the city; humans prepared to live under whatever terms Magneto might dictate. Voght knew it was only a beginning, that fifteen percent would not be enough if the Mutant Empire were to spread across the globe. But when they began to see the inevitability of Magneto's rule, the other eighty-five percent would realize that obedience and death were their only options.

Of course, Haven was not yet secure. The United States was still on the fence, trying to decide what course of action to take. The only concern Amelia had was the potential for a nuclear strike. If they could sneak nukes in, catch Magneto unaware, the humans might actually destroy Haven. Aside from that, Voght figured they had it all wrapped up. And, after all, no matter what the threat, there was going to be an awful lot of resistance to the idea of turning Manhattan into Hiroshima.

At the end of the hall was a small reception area. Warm pastel-colored couches matched the prints that hung on the walls. Vertical blinds filtered out the glare of the afternoon sun, and nearly half a dozen potted plants drooped lazily, likely thirsting for the water which fortune had denied them that day.

Three men and a woman waited for her there. One of the men, an aging Latino, paced expectantly. Voght thought he must be the police commissioner, Wilson Ramos. The other two men, one white and one black, sat on a pale blue couch, whispering and gesturing frantically to each other. The woman stood, hands clasped behind her back, looking through the vertical blinds at the city, and the Hudson River beyond.

"Deputy Mayor Perkins?" Voght asked.

The woman turned to face her, and Voght was surprised at how unruffled she looked. Maxine Perkins looked great for a woman who was, at the very least, in her early forties. More importantly, despite the stress she was under—the mayor had abandoned his city without a thought; exit, stage left—Perkins managed to look more angry than frightened.

"That's me," she said. "Where's Magneto?"

Voght smiled.

"Something funny?" Perkins asked, herself not amused.

"Most people would not be so eager to encounter our new ruler," she said.

"Can't imagine why that would be," Deputy Mayor Perkins responded. "He's always so willing to compromise."

This time, Amelia laughed. This might actually turn out to be entertaining, she thought.

"My name is Amelia Voght," she said. "I suppose you could call me Magneto's lieutenant—or deputy, if you prefer. Now, if you are prepared, I will take you to him."

"Um," one of the men on the couch mumbled, as they all stood to follow her, "what do we call him?"

"Magneto," she said. "Lord Magneto. Mr. Lehnsherr. I

don't know, really. I don't think he's taken on a title of leadership yet.''

"I have a few things to call him," Commissioner Ramos hissed.

Voght stopped in her tracks, forcing the others to do the same behind her. She sighed and turned to face Ramos.

"Mr. Ramos, I say this as pleasantly as I can," she began. "You would do well to remember that, as of this day, Magneto is the only law this island knows. He is not in favor of the death penalty, but that does not mean he does not see its uses."

Ramos blanched, and said nothing more as they approached the massive oaken doors of the office Magneto was using as a meeting room. It was not nearly magnificent enough for the position he now held, at least not in Amelia's opinion, but it would do for now. The two other men, who Voght assumed were city officials under the deputy mayor's control, followed along in silence.

Before they reached the office, they passed a small conference room where Unuscione and several other Acolytes were working on a running census of Haven's mutant population. New arrivals were processed quickly, then asked to be patient as abandoned homes were found for them. Those with real power, particularly Alpha-level mutants, were moved into the Empire State Building temporarily and became novitiate Acolytes.

Unuscione stood in the doorway, a sneer of disgust on her face as Voght passed.

"Playing receptionist today, are we, Amelia?" Unuscione said. "That's appropriate."

Voght did not reply. Still, she knew that the final confrontation between herself and Carmela Unuscione could not be put off much longer.

Arriving at the office, Voght rapped twice, hard, on the oaken door, then pushed it open and stood back for the visitors to enter. Magneto stood with his back to them, a pose indicating how paltry was his concern that they might offer some threat. In one corner, Major Ivan Skolnick, the American operative who had revealed himself to be a mutant when he defected to their cause, stood vigilantly by.

Magneto turned, resplendent in his regal purple-and-crimson uniform and flowing cape. Without the helmet he wore during battle, his silver-white hair fell around his shoulders. He looked benevolently upon the newcomers and lifted his arms in welcome.

"Come in," he said. "Please, sit, make yourselves comfortable."

"Why are we here?" Maxine Perkins asked.

"Ah, a woman with little patience for small talk or courtesies," Magneto said, beaming at her appreciatively. "Excellent."

Voght was a bit surprised, both at Perkins's audacity and Magneto's amiable reaction. But the world had changed, hadn't that been what she'd been thinking minutes ago? Indeed. It was changing by the moment.

"Still," Magneto said, still smiling at his guests, "please do sit. We'll all be more comfortable that way."

The four officials settled into comfortable chairs arranged in front of the massive mahogany desk. Magneto stepped behind the desk, but did not sit. Instead, he leaned over it, palms on its gleaming wooden surface, and welcomed them warmly once again.

"I've invited you here because my sources indicate that Ms. Perkins and Mr. Ramos are the highest-ranking officials left in the city. I assume you other gentlemen are on Ms. Perkins's staff?" Magneto asked, and the pair nodded. "Good; time to get down to business, then. You all need to know how I wish this city to be run, now that I am its sole authority."

Voght could see from their reactions that Magneto's directness, and the truth of it, was a bitter pill for his audience to swallow. All but Ramos covered it well, but even he said nothing. Magneto's reputation was frightening enough, but his presence was significantly more imposing.

"First, Ms. Perkins," he began. "Since the mayor of this fair city has left, and you had the fortitude to remain, I appoint you the mayor of Haven's human population. You will continue to be responsible for the welfare of those of your people who have decided not to leave their homes. Answerable, of course, to me. You will work directly with my civic administrator, Major Skolnick, who will help me to outline the relationship between humans and mutants in Haven. For now, you may want to think of it as a class system, with all mutants as the nobility, or ruling class.''

The new mayor of Haven raised an eyebrow and touched a hand to her chin, apparently thinking hard about her new job description. She glanced at Skolnick before looking back at Magneto.

''You may appoint these others to whatever administrative position you wish. Keep in mind, however, that the faults this island had before I came to power will be eliminated. No more drugs. No more violent crime. We will clean up Haven, both literally and figuratively. Corruption will be a thing of the past.''

''How can you say that?'' Maxine Perkins asked. ''Corruption is inevitable in any system. Entropy rules.''

''No, Ms. Perkins,'' Magneto snarled. ''*I* rule. The corrupt are always cowardly as well. Therefore, reason dictates that the corrupt have fled Haven. And I will not countenance further corruption. In my ranks, or among your populace.''

''I suppose you expect me to enforce your laws,'' Commissioner Ramos said, no longer able to heed his own better instincts.

''That doesn't sit well with you, I can see,'' Magneto said.

Voght watched—fascinated as always by his unconscious ability to command absolute attention—as Magneto finally sat in the high leather chair behind the mahogany desk. He leaned back with his hands tightly gripping the arms of the chair.

''Mayor Perkins asked why she was here, Commissioner Ramos,'' Magneto reminded. ''Somehow, I sense that you have your own ideas about why you are here.''

''*Oh*, yeah,'' Ramos said, and Voght winced in anticipation of Magneto's eventual response.

Ramos stood and approached the desk, poking a finger in Magneto's general direction.

"I came here to tell you that I didn't stay behind to become your lapdog. I'm going to enforce the laws of this city, no matter who breaks them. New York's Finest are not going to be turned into your private army," Ramos said, nearly shouting.

Magneto smiled.

"Why, Mr. Ramos, I already have a private army. I don't need New York's Finest, and I most certainly don't need you," the mutant emperor said, lifting his hands in a gesture that indicated both amusement and dismissal.

He turned to Voght. "Amelia, would you mind?"

With a thought, Amelia Voght made Wilson Ramos disappear. With an electric crackle, he vanished from the room. Voght formed a mental picture of the pavement in front of the Empire State Building, and teleported Ramos there. If it had been up to her, she might well have simply teleported him out the window and let the others watch him fall. She was not a hardened killer, but she knew the value of an example. Still, Magneto would have been specific if he'd wanted the man dead. Her lord rarely sanctioned homicide. Much to the other Acolytes' disappointment.

"Good God!" one of the new mayor's previously silent minions shouted, standing and gawking in astonishment at the vacuum that had previously been occupied by an apparently suicidal police commissioner.

"Is there some problem?" Major Skolnick asked the man from his post.

Voght started; she had nearly forgotten Skolnick was in the room. That kind of an attention lapse could cost her her life one of these days, and she chided herself for it.

"No," the man stuttered. "No problem. None whatsoever."

"So, what do you expect of the police?" Mayor Perkins asked, as if nothing of concern had taken place.

Voght was more than a little impressed with the woman.

"The Acolytes, my elite mutant force, will police Haven's mutant population. They will also be tasked with enforcing my more radical mandates, including the elimination of drugs from the island," Magneto explained. "The human police officers will also deal with those mandates. Otherwise, they will simply enforce my laws, as Mr. Ramos described it."

"Which are?" Perkins pressed.

"Full employment, a fair wage, no homelessness, nor hunger, nor corruption. In essence, no crime. Courtesy. I want Haven to be an example to the world, so society knows what to expect when we begin our expansion. Haven is still the center of the Western world. We're going to improve it."

Magneto paused, and looked at the three people gathered in his makeshift office, apparently awaiting some kind of response. Voght was surprised when the black man stood, his demeanor grave.

"Mr. Lehnsherr," he began, "my name is Steven Tyree. If you're sincere about your goals, I'd like that commissioner's job."

Magneto raised an eyebrow. Voght wondered if he was as surprised as she that the man, who had seemed so tentative, had suddenly become so forward.

"Then, Mr. Tyree, you shall have it," Magneto agreed. "For as long as you fulfill your responsibilities."

Tyree sat back down, but not next to his still-unnamed associate. Voght understood. The man, whose name she still did not know, would not be welcome in the new administration. That much was obvious.

"You may go. Major Skolnick will be in contact with both of you sometime tomorrow," Magneto said, not even acknowledging the unnamed man.

As far as Voght was concerned, the man was just lucky to be leaving of his own volition rather than via her teleportation. She knew she wouldn't see him again. In fact, even as he turned for the door, she had almost forgotten his face.

Not Steve Tyree's face, though. He was handsome, for a human, and she admired his guts.

"Oh, Mr. Tyree, one final law we need to get straight," Magneto said.

Tyree regarded him warily, but said nothing.

"Bigotry will not be tolerated," Magneto said. "Bigots are to be dealt with most—harshly."

"You're the boss," Tyree said, and turned to go.

Voght was no longer smiling. First as a Jew, then as a mutant, Magneto had been persecuted his entire life. As a boy he had lost his family to bigotry. That loss, that persecution, had defined his life, had led, in a fashion, to the foundation of Haven.

But Voght was forced to wonder what Magneto would say if she pointed out that some of the Acolytes, the Kleinstock brothers and Unuscione chief among them, were rabid bigots in their own right. She doubted he would order them "dealt with."

But a woman could dream.

CHAPTER 1

Corsair was anxious. He was the leader of the Starjammers, and the captain of their ship, and it pained him to wonder if she was so badly damaged that he might never pilot her into space again. First things first, though: he had to drop off his passengers and then land safely before they could even think about repairs.

Behind him, Corsair's son, Scott Summers—who was called Cyclops when he led the X-Men into battle—appeared in the open hatchway.

"Corsair?"

"It better be good news, Scott," he grumbled. "I've had just about all I can take of the other kind."

"Good news for the X-Men, actually," Scott said, looking a little sheepish. "It's a bit selfish to be worried about this right now, but we were able to get the *Starjammer*'s cloaking system working again. That way, when you go to land her at the Xavier Institute, the military won't be able to connect you with the Professor."

Corsair could tell that Scott was uncomfortable making the X-Men's secrecy a priority, and he could understand why. As leader of the Starjammers, Corsair had already suffered far more than the X-Men on this journey. True, Gambit had been injured, but Corsair's entire crew had been hurt at one point or another. Raza, Ch'od, and Hepzibah, who was also his lover, all were in the main cabin, strapped to med-units. His beloved ship was barely flying. It was a lot to take.

But then, the other Starjammers had been injured rescuing Corsair himself from execution. The X-Men were in this predicament because they had gone on that mission. And the entire Earth, the world of Corsair's birth, was now in jeopardy from Magneto, something that might not have happened if the team had been at full strength when Magneto first tried to hijack the Sentinels.

No, Corsair couldn't hold Scott's priorities against him. Beyond the other circumstances, he knew that his son was not concerned for himself, but for Charles Xavier, the man who had founded the X-Men, the man who was the heart and soul and dreaming mind of the world's mutant population.

"All right, listen," Corsair said. "You guys are going to have to bail out over Jersey City. I'm afraid you won't be getting any help from the Starjammers on this one. I'm going to get this ship back to Westchester and nursemaid my crew back to health, and maybe then we can stitch her together. I'm sorry, Scott. I wish I could be there to back you up."

"Your team needs you, Dad," Scott said warmly.

There was a moment of silence, as the two men reflected on their relationship, which was almost defined by long-term separation and individual effort. Still, they were alike in many ways. Often that similarity brought them into conflict, yet just as often it was a reason to rejoice.

"Whoa," Corsair said, as an unwelcome thought entered his mind. "You're so worried about protecting Charles Xavier's secrets, what about explaining how the X-Men came to know of the situation in the first place, and how this ship contacted Val Cooper so she could give the word not to blow us out of the sky?"

Xavier and the X-Men's Jean Grey were both telepaths. The communication had been mind to mind, but that would be difficult to explain to the proper authorities without revealing that Xavier was a mutant, which was, to Corsair's way of thinking, one of the best kept secrets on Earth.

"Hey," Scott said with a shrug, "the army doesn't know our radio doesn't work. I won't tell if you won't."

Corsair smiled. It really was as simple as that. He needn't have been worried. But Scott was his son, after all. Worrying was a parent's job.

"Jersey City coming up," he said, after a glance out of the cockpit. "Better get your team ready to go."

Corsair took another look at Scott. It occurred to him that what was happening in Manhattan might really be the end. The odds were stacked incredibly high against the X-Men. It was conceivable that they might lose.

On the other hand, the odds seemed never to be in the X-Men's favor. It was something else the team shared with the Starjammers, other than the fact that both were led by a man named Summers. No, Corsair wasn't going to think about losing Scott.

During another moment of awkward silence, the two men, who had never been comfortable with expressions of affection, embraced warmly.

"You be careful," Corsair said. "Otherwise, who's gonna pull my butt out of the fire next time someone wants to execute me?"

"You're right," Scott answered. "Nobody else would bother. I guess I've got to survive this thing."

The two men smiled and in that moment, Corsair finally saw the resemblance others had always noticed between himself and his son. It made him proud.

* * *

"Let's go, people," Cyclops snapped as he entered the main cabin. "ETA in about three minutes. Let's not tax this old ship any more than is necessary."

The years had given the X-Men an instinctive rhythm of teamwork. In almost any combination, they moved together like a family of aerialists, there to catch one another in a pinch, always a heartbeat away from that fatal fall. This particular combination had functioned well, Cyclops felt. He had worked with Jean Grey and Warren Worthington III since the first days of the X-Men. With Rogue and Gambit added to the mix, they had made a formidable team.

Scott only hoped they were up to the task ahead of them. The odds were, to say the least, daunting.

You're worried, Jean's telepathic "voice" said, inside Scott's mind. *That disturbs me.*

"I'm always worried," he said aloud.

She walked across the cabin toward him, her smile a comfort as always. She wore the blue-and-gold uniform she had recently adopted, and it fit her snugly, flattering her. Even as the thought crossed his mind, Jean's smile widened. They shared a psychic rapport that put them in almost constant telepathic contact. Nothing was hidden between them. Not even the momentary whimsy that reminded him how long it had been since they'd had time alone together.

"Like an old married couple, aren't we?" Jean asked.

"I don't know about 'old'," Scott responded, granting her a rare smile. "But I get your point, and you're right. Something always comes up, doesn't it?"

"Let's make each other a promise," Jean said softly, sliding her arms around him and pulling him to her. "If we get out of this one with our skins, it's time for a long vacation."

"Hawaii?" he asked.

"Just what I was thinking," she said.

"Funny how I knew that."

Jean gave him a quick kiss, and they turned to face the rest of the team. Warren's biometallic wings, which earned him the codename Archangel, spread out behind him. His uniform had been damaged during their rescue of Corsair, and through the slashes, blue skin could be seen. His hair and eyebrows were bright blond, and it was a stark contrast to the sky-blue hue of his face. Scott could still not get used to it.

Rogue wore green and gold, as usual. Her auburn hair, skunk-streaked with white, tumbled around her shoulders in a way that was inevitably fetching. Still, Scott felt more protective of her than anything else. The woman had been through a lot. He wondered what was going to come of her burgeoning relationship with Gambit.

His real name was Remy LeBeau, but unlike most of the others, Scott still called him Gambit. He wasn't completely comfortable with the Cajun, not yet. On the other hand, Gambit was invaluable in a conflict. Even now, he had donned the floor-length brown duster that almost always covered his uniform. His eyes shone with a weird reddish energy, and even his most genuine smile was not without a trace of sarcasm.

"Good to see you've fully recovered, Gambit," Scott said.

"Cajuns are hard to kill, *mon ami*," Gambit replied with that slanted smile.

"Time to put that to the test," Archangel said.

Scott took one last look around at the injured Starjammers, laid out on medislabs in the cabin. He wished the X-Men could have done more, but Corsair and his crew were on their own. The future of the world was hanging in the balance. The X-Men were needed.

"Let's hit it," Scott said, and moved toward the back of the ship, where the airlock doors were already wide open to the sky.

The *Starjammer* skimmed along about five hundred feet above Jersey City. Without a moment's hesitation, Scott stepped to the open doorway and hurled himself out into the sky over the city. Without a parachute. In the distance, he could see the massive camp set up on the Jersey side of the Hudson River by the military, the press, and relief services. That was their destination.

He fell for several seconds more, his hands in the air above him. Cyclops didn't even look up when Archangel grabbed his outstretched wrists, slowing his descent and moving him toward the encampment in Exchange Place. The move had not been discussed beforehand, but it had been executed so many times that Scott never for a moment considered the danger inherent in such a jump.

Slightly above him, Rogue carried Gambit with her as she flew, a simple feat for a woman of such extraordinary power. Jean Grey floated twenty yards behind the rest of the team, held aloft by a crackling telekinetic energy field. She could have carried them all, if necessary. But it wasn't necessary, and Scott wanted her to conserve her power for the battle ahead.

Several moments later, Jean took the lead and, wordlessly, the X-Men followed. She was in telepathic contact with Professor Xavier, and led them toward him. Hundreds of cameras swung toward the sky when the first cries went up. They had been spotted. The military had been notified of their imminent arrival, but several of the officers and grunts swung their weapons skyward.

Scott, they can barely contain themselves, Jean said telepathically. *The hatred is flowing from them in waves. I feel like I might be sick.*

You're okay, Jean. I know it's hard, but try to ignore it.

SALVATION

I'd hate us, too, if I were one of them. It doesn't matter that we're here to help.

There was no response. In truth, Scott had not expected one. The situation was grim, there was little argument about that.

A moment later he spotted Professor Xavier, sitting in his wheelchair, waiting for them to arrive. By his side stood Valerie Cooper, the government agent in charge of X-Factor, the federally sanctioned mutant team lead by Scott's brother Alex.

As the X-Men touched down, Cyclops made the first move, a signal that the others followed. Rather than even acknowledge Charles Xavier at first, Cyclops approached Cooper directly. For the benefit of the cameras, and the federal agents who were watching their arrival closely, it was imperative that their contact appear to be Val Cooper.

"Cyclops, thank God you're all finally here, and all right," Cooper said. "I'd been concerned for your safety, given the dangers of your last mission."

Scott caught a glance between Jean and the Professor, and realized they were conversing telepathically. He probably could have eavesdropped, given his rapport with Jean, but that wasn't his style. Besides, he was playing for the audience now.

"We're all lucky to have survived," Scott replied. "Now we've got this fiasco to deal with. Out of the frying pan, I guess."

"Indeed," Cooper said. "I'm not sure if you know Professor Charles Xavier."

Cooper gestured to the Professor, and Cyclops exchanged pleasantries with the man. It was strange. Xavier was like a father to him in ways Corsair had never been. The charade made both men uncomfortable, and the rest of the team as well, Scott thought.

"Care to give us an update?" he asked, though he was certain Jean had already gotten the latest information through her psionic conversation with Professor Xavier.

"Magneto seems to be going about his business," Cooper began. "Mutants are pouring into Manhattan from just about every corner. The army has skirmished with some of them, attempting to keep them from joining Magneto's 'empire.' Mutants going into Manhattan are considered terrorists.''

"Dat don't include us, *oui*?" Gambit asked.

"Excluding the X-Men, yes, of course," Cooper responded. "While Magneto seems, at the moment, to be consolidating his power in Manhattan, we have no doubt that his plans are much broader. We've got to stop him here, or we might not be able to stop him at all. As more mutants arrive, his strength is increased dramatically."

"I don't guess he needs more mutants," Rogue said. "With all them Sentinels, and the Acolytes he has, he was pretty near unbeatable already."

"Any news of the rest of the team?" Archangel asked.

Cooper and Xavier looked at each other. Scott understood the look. Most of what they knew was from the Professor's psi abilities. The other X-Men had been captured by Magneto, they knew that. Iceman's whereabouts were still something of a mystery. The media knew they'd been captured from the video that had already come out of the city.

"Nothing new," Cooper said. "You five are all we've got."

"So, Valerie," Jean said, "are you going to tell us your plan sometime soon?"

There was a long moment where nobody spoke. Helicopters chopped the air above, the drone of many voices and the crackle of radios surrounded them. Cyclops saw that a nearby camera operator seemed to have focused on him, and wished he didn't have to wear the ruby quartz visor that controlled his optic beams, so that he might pull off an annoyed glare. That was one of the problems with having his eyes covered— it cut down on what you could communicate with a look.

"*Mademoiselle*," Gambit said, breaking the silence, "you don' got to tell us dis t'ing is pretty near suicide. Just us five little mutants gon' go up against a whole cityful. Dat's what we do. Let's just get on with it now. The longer we wait, de harder it's goin' to be."

"You're right, on all counts," Cooper said. "So here it is. The only way we're going to win this thing is to take the

SALVATION

Sentinels out of the picture. As long as Magneto can call them in, you guys haven't got a chance in hell.''

"How do we do that?" Jean asked.

"Two teams. One goes after Magneto and the other X-Men. The other hunts down the Alpha Sentinel, gets into its command center, and reprograms it with Magneto as priority target," Cooper explained.

"So the odds go from hopeless to worse than hopeless," Rogue said. "I'm not sure I like the sound of that."

"She's right," Scott said, finally speaking up. "It's the only way. We need to take the Alpha Sentinel down and keep Magneto distracted at the same time. The only problem I see in this whole plan, and it's a big one, is how we're expected to reprogram the Sentinel with anything like expediency."

"You don't have to, Cyclops," Professor Xavier said, and the X-Men looked at their mentor, who had been silent during the discussion.

"Ms. Cooper will be accompanying the team searching for the Alpha Sentinel," Xavier said.

"Wait a minute," Archangel said, a confused look crossing his features, "I thought the Sentinels had been programmed not to let humans near the city."

"We've worked it out, Mr. Worthington," Cooper said.

Cyclops was about to request further details, particularly about the division of the team for the dual mission to come, but he never got his next question out. Instead, what little privacy they had was breached by the arrival of Henry Peter Gyrich, the man who had been ostensibly in charge of Operation: Wideawake when the Sentinels were stolen.

Gyrich was a bigot. Hated mutants. Hated paranormal humans of all kinds. Hated a lot of things, as far as Cyclops could tell. He was the proverbial snake in the grass, the kind of man the government didn't want to admit it employed. A necessary evil, some would say. As far as Cyclops was concerned, Gyrich was just another egomaniac trying to impress his own agenda on a world spinning out of control.

"Ah, the prodigal mutants return," Gyrich said as he approached.

He didn't even try to hide his sneer. The sun glinted off his mirrored glasses and lit up his red hair like fire. The effect wasn't at all flattering.

"Do you have news, Mr. Gyrich?" Cooper asked. "If not, I would ask that you remove yourself from this discussion. This is my operation here, and, frankly, you're not welcome."

Cyclops was surprised by the undisguised hatred and anger in Cooper's voice and entire manner. Gyrich, however, did not seem taken aback in the least. Apparently, the crisis had stripped bare the lines of tension that had always existed between the two.

"Don't worry, Cooper, this won't take long," Gyrich said with a smirk.

He turned slightly, to address them all. Scott, who considered himself level headed to the point of boredom at times, felt a nearly irrational hatred of Gyrich growing in him. The man's smugness was intolerable.

"Say your piece, Gyrich," he said. "Then why don't you let us mutants get on with the job you *normal* folks can't seem to handle on your own?"

Cooper stared at him, mouth open slightly. Professor Xavier raised one eyebrow. Jean, Gambit, Rogue, and Warren all looked on in stunned silence. All of them were taken aback by his words, and not without reason. Cyclops had always left the attitude to Gambit, or Wolverine, or Bishop, even Warren from time to time. But he was angry now, and a little bitter. He wanted to be with Corsair, making sure his father was all right. Instead, he and the X-Men were once again putting their lives on the line for a society, the majority of whom would have spit on them if they got close enough.

Scott Summers, the quiet one, the stable one, was on the verge of losing his cool. Cooper, Xavier, the other X-Men, were all surprised. But when Cyclops turned to look at Gyrich, he found that the man was not surprised at all. Rather, there was a smile of perverse pleasure on his face. He had riled the leader of the X-Men, and he was happy about it.

Scott felt so stupid he wanted to punch Gyrich, but that would only make matters worse. It was completely unlike him, but he supposed, given the extraordinary crisis at hand, extraordinary reactions would be the order of the day.

"Just because I'm a nice guy, Cyclops," Gyrich said, "I'll get right to the point. The Director of Operation: Wideawake has asked me to pass along this information to you, otherwise I would not have put you even at the bottom of my need-to-know list."

Cooper visibly stiffened. Scott assumed she was irritated that Wideawake's Director had not communicated Gyrich's message directly to her. He himself was annoyed that Cooper would allow such petty concerns as her competition with Gyrich to distract her at such a perilous time.

"In my opinion," Gyrich said, "a full military assault is the only way to end Magneto's terrorist occupation of Manhattan. Sadly, the President does not agree. He has faith in Ms. Cooper's opinion. She has faith in mutants, specifically the X-Men. In any case, he has agreed that your interdiction may proceed."

"That's news?" Cooper asked.

"I'm not finished," Gyrich said, biting off the words with snapping teeth, which finally revealed the extent of his disdain for the woman.

"The President has also ordered the joint armed forces assembled around Manhattan to a full alert. On his word, they are to invade and retake Manhattan island," Gyrich said.

"What?" Professor Xavier asked, astounded. "No simple military assault will be sufficient to destroy the Sentinels, you know as much from your participation in Operation: Wideawake. Not to mention that Magneto has destroyed entire armies before, and will not shrink from doing so again. What you suggest is madness!"

"De hell wit' dat!" Gambit said. "What about de X-Men? De President, he wants us to waltz right into Magneto's home base, and den he gon' to start bombing us all to hell? *Je suis désolé*, but *non. Ça ne me plaît pas.*"

Gyrich glared at Gambit for half a second.

"You're in America, X-Man," Gyrich said with a sneer. "Speak English not French."

"I was born in America, me," Gambit said angrily. "But I'm a Cajun. I speak Cajun, English, French, Creole, but me, maybe I got another language you understand better, eh?"

Cyclops saw that Gambit was extracting a playing card from his right pocket. Explosive energy sparked from his hand to the card and back, and the card began to glow.

"Put it away, Gambit," Cyclops ordered.

Through it all, Professor Xavier said nothing. He would normally have been the one to command Gambit to stand down, to step away from the brewing conflict, but if Gyrich ever knew Xavier's secret, God help them all.

Gambit complied.

"Anytime you want to try me, mutant," Gyrich said with a show of bravado that was not entirely convincing.

"You didn't let me finish, once again," he continued. "The military is holding back for the moment. If you can pull off your mission, there will be no invasion force. But there is a time limit. If you have not defeated Magneto in seven hours, the command will be given."

"Seven hours?" Jean exclaimed. "Why that's out—"

"Seven hours," Gyrich snapped. "And enough of this argument. I don't think you really have time for redundant and useless debate, do you?"

On that, the X-Men were forced to agree.

Gyrich turned to go.

"What happens if the X-Men fail, and the military cannot take Manhattan back?" Professor Xavier asked, as the red-haired man was walking away.

Gyrich turned back, daylight sparking diamonds off his mirrored sunglasses. The smile on his face then was as genuine and uninhibited as any Scott had ever seen on the man.

"It's a simple equation really," Gyrich said. "America does not bargain with terrorists. America will not allow one of its most important cities to fall into terrorist hands. If the military can't pull it off on their own, well, put two and two together, Xavier."

Xavier blanched. Scott felt the blood run from his own face as well.

SALVATION

"By God, you can't be serious," the Professor said. "There are hundreds of thousands of people, perhaps a million, still in that city! No president would take that many lives just to keep the city out of Magneto's hands."

"Even if he wasn't concerned for the people," Archangel added, "the American public would vilify him."

"If they knew what had been done, of course they would," Gyrich agreed. "But if such an atrocity as you describe—which I did not even suggest, by the way—were to take place, well, you can be certain the press would portray it as a terrorist plot that backfired with catastrophic results. It would be seen to."

"Lord help us, you're a monster," Rogue said softly. "You all are. Maybe Magneto has the right idea."

Gyrich had turned to leave once more but was stopped in his tracks by Rogue's words.

"Just what I expected of your kind," he said. "I told the President you'd end up defecting to the other side."

The animosity between Gyrich and the rest of the force gathered on that spot was tangible, powerful. Gyrich looked at his watch.

"Six hours and forty-nine minutes now," he said. "You'd probably better get going."

"When we get back, Gyrich," Cooper said, "you and I are going to have a long chat."

"I highly doubt that," Gyrich answered, then turned and had disappeared into the throng of reporters before Cyclops could even conceive of a retort.

"Okay, Valerie," Scott said, as soon as Gyrich was out of earshot. "How do you want to split the team?"

CHAPTER 2

Howard Chin had leased the three-story building on East Forty-fourth Street for seventeen years. He and his family lived on the second and third floors. The first was Howard's Deli, a storefront delicatessen that had always gotten a lot of business from local customers. There were many companies nearby, and MTV only two blocks away. To get to Grand Central Station or vice versa, commuters had to pass by his storefront window.

Until a couple days earlier, he'd done an excellent business. Made a hell of a living. He'd had no problem putting his daughter, Naomi, through school at the prestigious Marymount up in Westchester. She was going to Fordham Law now, and he was footing that bill too. Gladly. He loved his little deli, his regular customers, waking up at four A.M. to prepare the shop for business. But that life wasn't for everyone. And it sure wasn't for Naomi. She was going to be a lawyer. He'd never been as proud.

Then Magneto and the mutants came, and the city fell apart. It was a catastrophe. Howard had closed the deli when the Sentinels first appeared over the city, but it killed him to do so. The more he thought of it, the more he realized that he couldn't leave. He'd been in the same spot for seventeen years. Magneto promised that life would go on within the new administration. Lucinda Chin had thought her husband more than a little crazy at first. But at six o'clock in the morning, she had finally relented, agreeing to wait and see what developed.

Howard opened the deli ninety minutes late. Fifteen minutes later, the first customer had come in. There hadn't been many. Most of the people still in the city weren't yet brave enough to venture out. But there were a few. And he knew there would be more.

It would be okay. After all, his landlord was a cowardly sort, and probably had already left Manhattan. He expected to renegotiate his lease very soon. The big problem was going to be getting fresh stock in. He had no idea when the conflict would be over and his deliveries would start coming again.

SALVATION

There would be no trucks that day, however. Of that he was certain.

Lucinda was still upstairs doing laundry, he thought, when the bell above the door jingled. Howard looked up and was pleased to see a whole group this time. A woman and four men. He smiled at them, but they didn't smile back.

"What the hell do you think you're doing," the small Latino in the front asked.

"Pardon me?" Howard responded, raising an eyebrow. These people made him nervous.

"He asked what you thought you were doing?" an overweight black man snapped, coming quickly across the deli and crowding Howard where he stood organizing the salad bar.

"Get out of my shop," Howard answered. "I don't know what you want, but if you're not a paying customer, you can go now."

"Are you just stupid, or haven't you seen the news, looked outside your own door?" the woman, who might have been barely out of her teens, asked incredulously.

"Enough of that," said a guy in the back. This one was clean cut, an All-American kind of look, though he wore a gray duster coat like something out of postmodernist cowboy films, which Howard loved. He wished he had a jacket like that.

But now was not the time. Now, he only wanted these people out of his store.

"If you're going to rob me, I'm quite outnumbered," Howard said. "You might as well go on with your business."

"We're not here to rob you, sir," said the All-American. "These people want to know why you're cooperating with Magneto."

Howard didn't get it.

"Cooperating?" he asked, shaking his head. "Who's cooperating? I've never seen Magneto. Don't know as I've ever seen a mutant, really, except for that Blob guy years ago at a carnival, before I'd ever even heard of mutants. I'm just running my business. I'm not going to let this . . . occupation send me running scared."

"That's admirable Mr. . . . . ?" the woman began.

"Chin," he said.

"Mr. Chin. I'm Gabi Frigerio."

She introduced the others. The man who had yet to speak was her brother, Michael, the biggest and most powerful looking of the bunch. The Latino was called Miguelito, and the heavy fellow Lamarre.

"We have moved underground, sir," Gabi continued. "None of us was willing to leave the city, either, but we're also not willing to live as an oppressed people. Don't you understand what it means, what Magneto has done?"

Howard still didn't get it.

"He's declared himself emperor, buddy," Michael said, finally speaking up. "That means whatever he says goes. No voting."

"I never voted anyway," Howard said with a shrug. "I mean, how bad can it be? I was never rich, never expected to be. As long as I have my deli, and life goes on, what's the difference?"

"You'll see the difference when the muties come in and roust you and there isn't a freakin' thing you can do about it. They can do anything they want and you can't even look 'em in the eye," Lamarre said.

"Hey, Lamarre, watch it," the all-American said, glaring at Lamarre ominously.

"You might as well be a serf, or a slave," Gabi said. "In World War II, they shot French people who collaborated with the German army."

"So you're going to shoot me?" Howard asked, having no trouble believing he might be shot, but astonished at the reason behind it.

"No," Miguelito said after a moment. "We don't work that way, Mr. Chin. That's what the mutants might do, for a kick. But not us."

"Last night, Magneto's Acolytes and other mutants were responsible for at least three dozen murders in this city," Michael said.

"I didn't hear that," Howard said, raising an eyebrow.

SALVATION

"The MTV offices have been set up as some kind of guerilla outpost. A lot of reporters are working from there, from different papers and networks. They expect to be brought down at any time, but for now, they're dealing the news straight from the top of the deck," Gabi explained.

"Wow," Howard said, for he could think of no other response. "A lot of those guys are my customers. I should probably bring them some coffee, bagels, or something."

"You just don't get it!" Lamarre snapped at him again. "This is a war, man!"

"Not for me," Howard said, insulted that the man thought he was too stupid to understand them. "I'm forty-seven years old, friend. This shop is all I've got. If the army can't stop Magneto, then I expect I'll be paying my taxes to him next year."

"Don't worry, Mr. Chin," Drake said. "Magneto's going down. But it won't be the army who takes him out of the game."

"Who, then?" Howard asked. "I'm happy to help you people any way I can if I can be sure Magneto's people won't be sticking around. If they do, eventually they'll get around to destroying you and me and this deli, once they know I've been helping you. How can you be sure he'll be gone? Who's strong enough to beat him, and those huge robots, and all the other mutants he's got gathered up?"

"The X-Men," Drake said. "The X-Men will take him down."

"The X-Men have been captured," Howard said, exasperated. "They've already lost."

"Four X-Men were captured," Drake said. "There's plenty more where that came from."

Howard Chin watched in awe as Drake's entire body turned to ice. Only that gray duster didn't freeze.

Howard shivered, staring at Drake. He knew who the man was now, of course. Everyone had read about the X-Men. Drake had to be Iceman. Suddenly Howard had begun to believe everything would be all right after all.

"Who wants coffee?" he offered.

* * *

"So, Caroline, what exactly is your mutant power, anyway?" Kevin O'Leary asked.

"Um, well, see, it's nothing special really," the attractive girl with the gun in her hand answered. "I'm not, like, an Alpha or anything."

"Alpha?"

"Yeah, that's what the Acolytes call a really powerful mutant," Caroline said.

"So what do you do?" Kevin asked again.

"If I concentrate, okay, my skin gives off these chemicals that are like a, whadayacall, a sedative. I make people sleepy, but, see, I haven't quite been able to actually force anyone to go to sleep. Not yet, anyway," she answered, not meeting his eyes, reddening slightly at her embarrassment over having such relatively ineffective mutant abilities.

"Hey," Kevin said warmly, his charisma working overtime, "I think that's a cool power. You could probably be a great hypnotist, take Vegas by storm. You could make a bundle helping insomniacs too."

"Yeah," Caroline said, offering a shy smile. "I guess. But it doesn't do much good in a fight."

"Are you kidding me?" Kevin said incredulously. "I can't believe Magneto doesn't have you at his side all the time. Come on! Anybody wants to attack, you can slow them down enough so they don't have a chance. I'd say that's pretty useful."

"You think so?" Caroline asked hopefully.

Kevin kept piling it on. As Trish Tilby watched, she began to feel bad for the girl, perhaps seventeen or eighteen and none too bright, who'd been assigned to guard them. Magneto obviously thought of them as low risk, and with good reason. They were there by choice, covering the takeover of Manhattan, and if he wanted to keep them there, they wouldn't be able to run far.

On the other hand, Magneto would certainly not want her speaking with or, God forbid, helping the X-Men to escape.

SALVATION

A possibility that he must suspect, given that Dr. Henry Mc-Coy, the Beast, was her ex-boyfriend. Trish and Hank were still friendly, and she respected him immensely, still cared for him a lot. She wouldn't see him imprisoned if there was anything she could do about it.

That's what they were about to find out.

"Speaking of sleepy," she said, startling Caroline slightly, "I'm going to try getting some rest. It's going to be a long night, more than likely, with meetings and all."

"We'll try to be quiet," Kevin responded, and smiled at Caroline again. He patted her hand lightly, as if sharing a joke, and she beamed. Trish felt guilty, taking advantage of the poor girl like that. Kevin was charming and handsome and the more he worked on the girl, the more Trish had to wonder how often he'd ambushed a woman with the same tactics in real life, and then blown her off. She wasn't sure she wanted to know.

She lay down, listening to Kevin whispering to the girl. It was more intimate, and he would have had to move closer to her. It had been obvious since the moment Caroline pulled guard duty that she was attracted to Kevin. Now they just had to see if they could take advantage of the fact.

"Really?" Caroline hissed in a stage whisper. "That's awful. I'd hate that."

Kevin whispered some more.

"I don't know," Caroline answered. "I could get in big trouble."

More whispering. This time, Trish caught a few words that sounded like "if it was you." After a few moments, Caroline stood up and walked over to the spot where Trish lay on a bunch of throw pillows from office sofas.

"Trish?" Caroline asked. "You asleep?"

"Hmm?" Trish answered, feigning the classic half-asleep disorientation.

"Is that Beast guy really your boyfriend?" she asked.

Trish opened her eyes wide, stretched her neck, then sighed deeply.

"Yeah," she lied. "We haven't seen each other in a while,

but he is my boyfriend. Why do you ask? Are you surprised?''

"You love him, huh?'' Caroline persisted, not answering Trish's question.

Trish allowed her concern for Hank, the real pain that was there, to spread across her face.

"Yeah, I do,'' she said, and this time she wasn't lying. She might not be in love with Hank McCoy anymore, but she definitely still loved him.

Caroline looked deep in thought. Though she knew it was uncharitable, Trish couldn't help thinking that anytime she seemed to concentrate, the girl looked as though she were in pain.

"Okay, look,'' Caroline finally said. "I feel bad for you, okay? I think I can understand how bad you feel, how much it sucks. There's a major risk involved here, but if you promise you won't try anything, won't do anything crazy, I'll see what I can do to get you in to see the blue guy.''

"See Hank?'' Trish asked, all excited and hopeful. "Oh, Caroline, my God, do you think you could do that?''

Caroline smiled, reaching back and taking Kevin's hand in her own.

"Yeah,'' she answered. "I'm pretty sure we can pull it off. Just don't say nothin' to anyone. Else we're all in trouble.''

"You're the best, lady,'' Kevin said, and kissed Caroline on the head.

"Hey, a girl's got to be able to be with her man,'' Caroline said, shrugging off the compliment though it was clear she reveled in it. "And it's not like you guys are really the enemy, right? I mean, in a way, you're working with Magneto, same as any of us. Working for a better world.''

"Absolutely,'' Trish agreed, but she felt awful, not only that they were manipulating an innocent girl, but that the same girl actually thought Trish and Kevin could ever be on Magneto's side.

"So, what do we have to do?'' Trish asked, hoping she didn't seem too pushy, wary of the possiblity that Caroline might get skittish and back off.

"Can I trust you here for a couple of minutes by your-selves?" she asked.

"Please!" Kevin protested. "Even if we wanted to leave, where would we go?"

Caroline giggled. "I guess you're right," she said.

She disappeared through the door, gun holstered at her back. A few minutes later, she returned with a huge grin on her face.

"The guards were both exhausted. I didn't force them to sleep, can't do that yet, like I said. But it didn't take much to nudge them toward it. Now, let's hope I can keep them asleep while you talk to your Beast-man," Caroline said excitedly. "Ooh, it's so romantic."

"Kev, you'll have to stay here," she added with regret. "I don't think I can cover for all of us. Just don't go anywhere, okay? They might shoot me or something."

"I'm not going anywhere," he reassured her. And funny thing was, at the moment, Trish believed him. She wondered if Kevin might not actually be taking a liking to the free-spirited mutant girl.

"All right, then," Caroline said. "Let's go."

Caroline led Trish to the stairwell. Since she was supposed to be guarding Trish anyway, nobody looked twice at them. Once at the stairs, she waited to see that nobody was looking, and they started down.

"I took the elevator, but I didn't think we should risk that with you," the girl explained.

"Good idea," Trish agreed. "Listen, thank you so much for doing this. Hank and I both owe you."

"He was so excited to know you were coming," Caroline said, and Trish's eyes widened.

"You talked to him?" she asked, surprised Hank hadn't blown the story.

"Oh, yeah," Caroline said enthusiastically. "He misses you, too, big time. I had to make sure you were telling the truth. He loves you, Trish. No question. You're pretty lucky too. Up close, that blue fur is kind of sexy."

Trish smiled with pleasure and relief. Her feelings and her

plans were getting way too complicated for her own good. Obviously, he'd been smart enough to go along with the story she'd told Caroline. Maybe some of those feelings were for real, for both of them, but she'd hurt Hank McCoy, and Trish didn't figure he'd forgotten that just yet.

Caroline had said something while Trish was musing on the subject of human-mutant relations, hers in particular.

"I'm sorry?"

"I said it must tick you off when other women flirt with him," Caroline repeated.

"You get used to it," Trish said with a shrug, and they continued down the stairs, Caroline babbling on about this boyfriend or that and how badly they had treated her.

Suddenly, it didn't seem quite so harmless the way Trish and Kevin had been taking advantage of the girl. She hoped she could repay Caroline somehow, or at the very least that she could avoid getting the girl in too much trouble. Sure, she was one of Magneto's mutant fascists, but Trish figured Caroline wouldn't have known ideology from physiology. In fact, the more she talked about her boyfriends, it seemed that the girl felt the two were one and the same.

The basement was a long, long way down. Like anyone whose career placed her in the public eye, the pressures of celebrity forced Trish to keep herself in shape. Despite that, and the fact that they were going downstairs, her legs were tired in no time. She had no faith in her ability to make the climb back up with any haste if the need arose.

Finally, they reached an anonymous steel door crossed with a long red bar. Printed on the bar was a warning that an alarm would sound if the door was opened. It was for emergency use only. Apparently, it had been disconnected since Magneto had taken over, because Caroline pushed it open without a glance, and the expected wail of alarm bells did not come.

They traveled more corridors than Trish thought ought to be in a basement, even for a building the size of the Empire State. Finally, Caroline hugged the cement wall as they neared a turn in the hall, and Trish followed suit. For a moment, she felt foolish. It was like she was seven years old again, playing army with her brother and his friends.

Their version of army had been different, though. The Cold War was still on, but they weren't fighting the Soviets, they were fighting a pack of werewolves. They took turns being the werewolves because, even though the army always won, the werewolves were cooler. Only, Trish never got a turn to play werewolf. She was just a girl, and girls weren't strong and mean and nasty enough, or so her brother Billy always said.

To hell with him, she thought now. If Billy had been there, with Magneto's band of super-human terrorists lurking about, he'd have lost control of his bladder the same way he did in the fifth-grade spelling bee. Trish smiled at the memory. Telling that story—or threatening to—had been her favorite weapon when they were kids.

Still, she had to wonder where her brother was now. In a way, she wished he were there. She had always felt better facing the werewolves when the two of them were soldiers together. And though he'd never admitted it, she'd known he felt the same way.

Caroline peered around the corner carefully, her brow furrowed as if she were concentrating. It occurred to Trish that she very probably *was* concentrating, attempting to make sure that the guard she'd turned her forced-narcolepsy mutant power on had stayed under her spell. A moment later, she stepped out into the open, motioning for Trish to stay put. She took several steps down the hall, out of Trish's sight.

In that moment, Trish became afraid. Afraid it had all been a setup, that Magneto was testing her loyalty. Afraid that Caroline would be captured, that they would all be executed—for the Acolytes were notoriously fond of executions. Afraid that she had gotten herself into something she had no hope of extricating herself from, and was proceeding to get in deeper and deeper as the moments ticked past. And, finally, afraid that she would be able to do nothing for the X-Men. That Hank would soon be dead.

No matter what had passed between them, the idea that

Hank might die filled her with a terrible dread unlike anything she had ever experienced. He was the most unique individual she had ever encountered, a fact that had little or nothing to do with his status as a mutant. His intelligence, his humor, his gallantry—she treasured them all, as friend or lover.

Caroline whistled, low and short, and Trish responded by popping out into the hallway. A bald, stocky man in leather sat on a chair, his head back against the wall and his mouth open in a silent snore. Beyond him, Caroline held open another steel door, and beckoned rapidly with her left hand. Trish rushed down the hallway, and turned into the room where the X-Men were being held captive.

She didn't know Bishop well, though she certainly knew who he was. It was her business to know such things. She had known Storm and Wolverine for years, by reputation and personally. Then there was Hank. As Trish looked at his face, at the concern etched there, she worried that he might think her a traitor now. He was captive, she was free, within limits, to do as she pleased. That meant reporting the story as accurately as Magneto would allow. She feared Hank would brand her a collaborator. So, for a moment, she could think of nothing to say except . . .

"Hank."

"Trish," he said, an amused acknowledgement that begged her to continue, to lead the conversation. This was, after all, her show. Caroline was standing by, expecting to witness the drama of lovers reunited, of a woman weeping for her doomed man.

"Oh, God, Hank!" Trish said in a grateful rush, then hurried to where he hung suspended from the techno setup on the wall.

Even as she moved to him, embraced his blue, furry form— though he was unable to return the embrace—Trish was marveling at the technology and wondering how the hell she might be able to break the X-Men out of their restraints. She knew one thing, it wasn't going to happen right then. She held out hope that Hank might be able to direct her.

"I missed you, darling," he said, and she couldn't help but

notice the trace of irony in his voice. He *had* missed her. Just as, in her way, she had missed him. But she didn't want to mistake a crisis for a reunion.

"Caroline, could Hank and I just have one final moment to ourselves?" she said, trying not to be too dramatic, though the girl probably expected something out of a soap opera. "It might be our last chance."

"What about them?" Caroline asked, pointing to the other three X-Men with a quizzical look.

"It isn't as if we can go anywhere," Bishop said angrily, and though Trish winced at the thought that he might alienate Caroline, she was glad his anger was unchecked. It was good for realism.

"We will respect the Beast's right to privacy as much as we are able, though we cannot leave the room," Storm said, her voice confident and reassuring as always.

"Besides," Wolverine growled cynically, "we're like family."

After a moment of uncertainty, Caroline turned and left. Trish thought the girl looked a little disappointed that she was going to miss what she obviously considered the best part. Tough.

"You're placing yourself in tremendous peril, just being here," Hank said when Caroline had gone.

"So what if they catch me?" Trish asked. "They put me down here with you. I might as well be restrained, for the amount of freedom Kevin and I are allowed."

"We appreciate the effort, Ms. Tilby," Storm said, "but the Beast is right. You are a single, human woman. Despite your formidable will, you are weaponless in a city filled with powerful mutants who range from legitimately evil to sadly misled, all at Magneto's command. With all due respect, what do you hope to accomplish?"

Trish knew that Storm was right. It pissed her off.

"Let me get this straight," she said, her voice rising just a touch, not enough to alert Caroline that anything but a sweet reunion was happening inside that room. "You think I'm just going to keep doing my job while the four of you rot down here, waiting for Magneto to decide on a whim to execute you? I don't think so."

Trish glared at Storm, then at the others. Hank was last. He said nothing.

"Ms. Tilby," Bishop began, "while your intentions are honorable, putting yourself in unnecessary jeopardy would be—"

"Unnecessary?" she snapped. "The only way it would be unnecessary would be if you all had figured out a way to escape without my help. I assume you haven't, given that you're still *here*. Now, if you can honestly say that each of you would not do the same in my position, I'll go back to my little cage and not bother you again. But if you're just treating me like I'm useless because I'm human, you're just as bigoted as Graydon Creed and the rest of them. As anyone who ever thought someone couldn't do a job because of their race or gender."

Storm raised an eyebrow and lifted her chin slightly, a motion that gave her an incredibly haughty appearance. Bishop appeared to consider her words. Hank's expression had not changed.

"She's right, Ororo," Wolverine said quietly. "Any one o' us would do the same."

The Beast began to smile.

"What the hell is so funny, Hank?" Trish demanded.

"Not a thing, my dear," he answered, still smiling warmly. "It just occurred to me how elated I am that you are on our side in this conflict. I would loathe having you as an opponent."

Despite herself, Trish had to smile at that. She detailed everything she had gleaned about Magneto's operation and plans from her observations. Sadly, she feared very little of it was helpful, but she was as thorough as possible.

"Do you imagine you might arrange to visit us again?" he asked her.

"Might be tough, but probably," she answered.

"Excellent," Hank said. "Whatever else you discover between now and then will doubtless prove invaluable. If you can contrive a strategy for our emancipation, pass it on then.''

"But . . ." Trish began, and then kept silent. She didn't know what she could say. At the moment, she didn't know how she might be able to free the X-Men. All she did know was that she would not stop trying.

"Otherwise," Hank continued, favoring her with a look of crushing benevolence, "we will simply incorporate you into our deliberations of potential liberation schemes."

"But . . ." she said again.

"Please, Trish," Hank said, his voice urgent, for they both knew Caroline would not stay in the hall forever. "Be content with the knowledge that you have our trust and faith. We shall all endeavor to do what we are able."

The door opened as Trish was about to protest once more. Caroline hissed that the guard would not sleep much longer. Apparently her control over her powers was as limited as she had feared.

Trish moved to embrace Hank once again. She looked into his eyes, so familiar, so intimate in memory.

"I love you, Hank," Trish said.

"And I you, my dear," he responded.

For a moment, they were transported back in time to the day, months earlier, when they had first exchanged such promises. Vows so easily broken.

Trish turned and rushed from the room, partially feigning the appearance of being overcome with emotion. But only partially. She was fleeing, as well, from the moment itself. She and Hank were through. She knew that. But a part of her wanted to forget, wanted to go back.

If there was one thing Trish Tilby knew, there was ever and only one direction in which time flowed. It wasn't so much forward, it seemed to her, as it was away from the past.

Yet, despite what was in the past, and their current situation, she knew she wanted Hank to be in her life in some fashion for as long as he was willing. They had shared too much to drift away from each other, to sacrifice their friendship on the altar of broken romance.

One way or another, Trish was determined, the X-Men would be free.

Chapter 3

I **I** can almost hear that *Mission: Impossible* theme song," Rogue said, and followed the comment with a laugh as gentle as her lilting Southern accent.

Nobody else laughed. Professor Xavier even gave her something of a dirty look, that little frown he had practiced so often when the Xavier Institute was still teaching academics.

"Just tryin' to lighten the moment," she added.

Then she shut up.

In silence, she, Cyclops, and Jean finished the meal that had been hastily cobbled together from the mess tent in the section of Exchange Place that had been taken over by the military. None of them had eaten for a while, and it was good to have something in her belly. Not to mention sitting down for a few minutes. It was almost time to go, to put their collective heads in the proverbial lion's mouth. As far as Rogue was concerned, another few minutes would be welcome.

But she didn't want to wait too long. If she really started to analyze the situation, to calculate the odds, she might head west rather than east when the team began to move out. Gambit and Archangel had already departed with Val Cooper, trying to track the Alpha Sentinel. It would be just the three of them, then—she and Scott and Jean—against the mutant army Magneto was amassing.

They didn't stand a chance.

But they were going anyway.

That's what it meant to be one of the X-Men.

"So, we're sure the others are being kept in the Empire State Building?" Jean asked. "I've tried a psi-scan, but I'm being blocked."

"I'm getting a bit of static myself, Jean, but I did get through," Professor Xavier said. "Storm, Wolverine, Bishop, and the Beast are all still alive and well and Magneto's captives. You three alone will not be able to win the day. Your teammates must be freed before you truly enter into the battle."

SALVATION

"Though I doubt Magneto's hordes are just going to let us walk in," Cyclops said cynically.

Another long silence.

"Have you all read Norse mythology?" Jean asked, a non-sequitur that caused them all to look at her askance.

"The gods and the giants spend tens of thousands of years fighting one another, neither ever really gaining the upper hand. Then the apocalypse comes, only they call it Ragnarok. It's their final battle, and they pull out all the stops. It's total chaos."

"I always enjoyed the stories, Jean," Professor Xavier said. "But is there a point to this?"

"Just that, in the end, neither side is victorious. They are all destroyed."

"And y'think that's us?" Rogue asked, surprised at her teammate's pessimism.

"I hope it's not," Jean said.

"And on that happy note," Cyclops said, shaking his head, "let's get going. We've got some X-Men to liberate, and a city to save."

"I don't suppose we can get a cab to the Empire State Building?" Jean asked, making her own attempt at levity.

Rogue was relieved to see that she wasn't the only one whose jokes were bombing. She understood, though. There just wasn't much to laugh about.

"Jean?" Professor Xavier asked.

"I know, Professor," Jean answered, tapping her temple. "We'll keep in touch."

* * *

Amelia Voght stood side by side with several of her fellow Acolytes, including Senyaka, Cargil, and the Kleinstock brothers, and looked out over a veritable sea of Alpha- and Beta-level mutants. They had gathered for the first formal explanation of how, exactly, Haven was to be governed. What were the laws, they all wanted to know. Voght wanted to know as well.

Magneto had delegated the duty of presenting his imperial

decrees to Major Skolnick, who would serve as a sort of governor for Haven. The gathered mutants seemed somewhat disappointed that Magneto would not be there, but Voght saw the logic.

Better that he remain apart from the others, above and beyond their reach. He was the emperor, after all. The Acolytes had always afforded him the obedience and respect due an omnipotent ruler. But this was different, Voght thought. For the first time, Magneto actually had an empire to rule. Or, at least, the beginnings of one.

Skolnick called for attention, and a hush fell over the gathered mutants. Voght marveled at the sheer power gathered in that room, and felt something akin to awe beginning to grow within her.

One would have to be completely insane to willingly enter into battle with the forces Magneto had at his beck and call. But Voght had to remind herself that she lived in a world with no shortage of insane people.

* * *

"Is it me," Rogue asked, "or are we completely out of our minds?"

Jean grinned and Scott actually cracked a smile.

"It isn't you," Jean answered.

"Thank you."

They had emerged from the Holland Tunnel to find Manhattan's lower west side almost completely devoid of life. The Sentinels had not moved to stop them because the X-Men were, of course, mutants. Still, passing beneath the gargantuan robot had given Rogue a feeling of terrible dread. They were behind enemy lines, now. Anything could happen.

"Talk about *The Twilight Zone*," Jean said quietly.

"You too?" Scott asked.

"Oh, yeah," she said. "With the sun high in the sky, and nobody around, it's like we've been shunted to some side dimension where we can't see or hear anyone else in the city."

"Ain't you two forgettin' somethin'?" Rogue asked. "I

mean, correct me if I'm wrong, but do we really want t'see anyone else?''

They hugged the buildings, taking advantage of what few shadows the midday sun offered. Not far off, Rogue could smell something good cooking, and her stomach grumbled, reminding her that she hadn't had enough to eat before leaving New Jersey.

"Smell that?" Cyclops said. "Obviously, some people are getting on with their lives."

"Lucky them," Rogue muttered.

At West Broadway, they turned north. Six blocks later, they turned east again. There were, they quickly discovered, far more people out and about than they would ever have imagined. Several people had cheered out loud when they had approached or passed by. Nearly as many had ducked or run into hiding. One old man actually hurled a bottle of whiskey at them. It smashed at Jean's feet, but the three X-Men kept moving right along.

They met with no other resistance, human or mutant. No mutant militia showed up to detain them, though all three admitted that Magneto might very well already know they were in the city.

Rogue took point. When she turned north on Sixth Avenue, Scott and Jean were half a block behind. Almost immediately, she heard raucous, drunken laughter and loud male voices. The sounds came from the shattered plate-glass window of a dive with the words KEITH'S PUB in fractured neon above the door.

Quickly, she stepped to the window. The sun's glare made it almost reflective, so she moved to the huge jagged hole in its center, and peered in. Six leather-clad, body-pierced, tattooed young men menaced the bartender, who was serving them whole bottles from behind the bar. The largest man, whom Rogue took to be the leader, had glowing eyes. Mutants. Already fulfilling Magneto's "dream." Though Magneto's words were seductive, Rogue knew that what she was witnessing was the reality of his new empire. Sadistic mutant tyrants would band together to rule Manhatttan, terrorizing the city's human citizens.

One of the mutants, a large man with a ponytail and a pink scar running down his left cheek, noticed her standing in the broken window.

"Hey, hey, boys!" he crowed. "Check out the girly-girl."

The other five mutants, and the cowed bartender, all looked her way. After a heartbeat's pause, the inebriated fools began to swagger toward her. Most of them looked relatively harmless, but the one she had assumed was the leader had an aura of blue energy around him that began to crackle as he moved toward Rogue. He might have the power to back up his attitude.

"Hello, darlin'," the leader said. "Why don't you come on in here and be friendly instead of standin' out there and starin' at us?"

"Actually, I prefer it out here," Rogue said, purposely baiting them. "A girl's got to have fresh air."

The leader's energy aura brightened, flashing around him and rising toward the bar's ceiling like a raging blaze of fire.

"I don't think you heard me," he said, and the bartender was forgotten as all six mutants moved toward Rogue. "Don't you know who we are?"

Rogue raised an eyebrow. For a moment, she imagined how they must see her. A pretty girl, model tall, model thin, auburn hair with that white streak, green eyes, and a Southern accent. The green boots, jacket, and gloves would seem flashy if you didn't know it was a uniform. Despite the exhausting events of the past couple of days, Rogue knew she looked good. And that was all they saw.

Prey.

"Well?" the leader demanded, raising a hand and sending a crackling tendril of energy reaching toward Rogue's face.

"Oh, darlin'," Rogue said, shaking her head with a small smile. "Don't *y'all* know who *I* am?"

Several of the mutants snickered, but the leader didn't find it funny. His lips curled up in a sneer and he stepped even closer to the broken window. The aura surrounding him melted the jagged glass that it came into contact with.

"See, now, I was going to be nice, but you had to go and

get attitude on me,'' he said. "Now I'm going to have to fry you.''

Out of the corner of her eye, Rogue saw the faces of two mutants go slack with sudden fear, and then understanding.

"Uh, Billy?'' one of them asked, tapping the leader on the shoulder.

"Not now!'' Billy snapped.

"But, Billy,'' the other said. "Check the dude with the visor.''

They were all staring now. Cyclops and Jean Grey stood directly behind Rogue, but she didn't turn to acknowledge them, only continued to stare at Billy. For his part, Billy looked from Cyclops, to Rogue, to Jean, back to Cyclops, and finally, back to Rogue, all in about three seconds.

"Oh, God,'' Billy said. "You guys are . . . I know who you guys are. Oh, man. You guys are . . . you're them, aren't you?''

"Yep,'' Rogue said coldly. "We're them.''

"Oh, man,'' Billy said, as his friends moved, very unsubtly, away from him, away from the broken window, back into the bar.

"I'm sorry,'' he added.

"Don't tell us, sugar,'' Rogue said. "Tell the bartender.''

Billy did as he was told.

"Now,'' Rogue added. "All'a you, take out y'wallets, give whatever cash you have to the bartender, and get your butts out of here.''

"Where should we go?'' one of them asked.

Rogue smiled. "Oh, that one's just screamin' for a tasteless comment.''

"You have two choices,'' Jean said. "You can go home and stay inside until Magneto and his little army are gone, or you can leave the city.''

"If we see you again, no more choices,'' Cyclops added.

For a few seconds, the gang members stood unmoving. Then, one by one, they removed their wallets, laid cash on the bar, and headed for the door. Billy glared at them on the way out, but Rogue gave him an extra hard look, and he turned away. When he had hit the street, he ran faster than any of his buddies.

"We've got to get this city back in order before chaos takes complete control," Jean said, shaking her head in disbelief.

But Rogue wasn't listening. She was staring in the direction the mutant punks had gone. A familiar figure had turned the corner. His back was to the sun, casting his face in shadow, but that nearly seven-foot frame and the helmet that stretched almost shoulder to shoulder were unmistakable.

"Scott, Jean," Rogue said. "We got trouble. Magneto ain't wastin' time before sendin' in the big guns."

Cyclops whipped around, even as Jean whispered their old enemy's name.

"Juggernaut."

"Take him down!" Cyclops ordered, and the three X-Men went into action.

Rogue took to the air, speeding toward the Juggernaut even as several of Cyclops's optic blasts slammed into their enemy's chest. The Juggernaut took a single step backward, and looked up in annoyance and what appeared to be confusion as Rogue slammed into him, driving him to the ground but barely able to do even that.

Still, she'd take it. Most of the time it was all she could do to stand toe to toe with Juggernaut and duke it out. A takedown was a step up. After all, that was part of his power, what made him the Juggernaut. Once he had momentum, nothing could stop the Juggernaut. If he'd been coming at her, there was no way he would have gone down.

The Juggernaut's real name was Cain Marko, and much to Charles Xavier's chagrin, he was the Professor's stepbrother. The two had grown up together, with Cain quickly developing into a bully, partially due to abuse he received at his father's hands.

Thing was, Marko wasn't a mutant. It had been his misfortune to discover an ancient jewel mystically endowed with extraordinary power. That gem turned him into the Juggernaut. His stamina was limitless, his onslaught unstoppable, and his body totally indestructible. He could be hurt, but as long as he wore his helmet, which blocked any psionic attack, he could not be beaten.

Which had never stopped the X-Men.

"Hit him, Jean!" Cyclops called.

As Juggernaut leaped to his feet, he was lifted off the ground by Jean's telekinetic power. This time, when Cyclops let loose with an optic blast, Marko tumbled backward through the air and crashed through a brick wall. Rogue knew she was in line for the follow-through, and she was after him in a flash.

But not fast enough. Juggernaut emerged from the debris with a massive hunk of brick masonry in his hands and tossed it at Cyclops. Distracted, Rogue glanced back to see Scott incinerate most of the huge projectile with a blast from his eyes. The rest was about to hit him when it simply stopped in midair and fell to the ground.

Jean again.

Rogue realized her mistake a moment too late. The Juggernaut's massive fist, two or three times the size of an average man's, slammed into her chest and she felt the world slide out from under her. She crashed through a bakery window and landed on a service counter, demolishing it. She was only glad there had not been anyone inside the bakery.

"Girl," she said to herself, "you've just got to start payin' attention."

She stood, brushed off shattered glass, and headed back out to the street. There was one other way they could beat Juggernaut, but Rogue didn't really relish the idea. She could allow her skin to touch his, a process through which she would temporarily absorb all of his abilities and many of his memories. It wasn't something she liked to do under any circumstance, but it did look as though it might become a necessity.

"What the hell is your problem, X-Men?" the Juggernaut roared, even as he bore down on Jean and Scott, head bowed with anger and determination.

"I think you know the answer to that, Marko," Cyclops retorted, and let loose another full-force optic blast.

But the Juggernaut was in motion. It barely fazed him.

Scott and Jean leaped aside at the last minute, and the fight continued. Rogue was reminded of a bullfight she had once seen on a trip to Mexico. That's exactly what this was, she thought. And the *X* all three of them had emblazoned somewhere on their uniforms was like a red flag for the maddened bull called Cain Marko.

"This city's filled with crazy people!" the Juggernaut cried in frustration. "A man can't even get a few days of R & R without all hell breaking loose, then everybody and their brother wants a piece of ya!"

"What are you complainin' about, sugar?" Rogue asked from the air. "Ain't Magneto and his lapdogs treatin' you right?"

"Good God!" Marko shouted. "Do I look stupid to you?"

Suddenly, the Juggernaut's face was battered with a rapid-fire succession of bricks from the wall he'd crashed through. Jean was telekinetically controlling the bricks, trying to keep Marko off balance and vulnerable. Or as vulnerable as the Juggernaut could be.

"Hey!" Juggernaut protested.

Rogue moved in for another attack. With Marko off balance, she wanted to make an attempt to rip off his helmet so Jean could lay him out with a telepathic assault. If that didn't work, she would have to resort to absorbing the Juggernaut's powers. Instantly, she was reminded that the Juggernaut was much faster than he looked. Marko whipped around and gave Rogue a severe backhand that knocked her into a boarded-up corner newsstand. The place fell apart beneath her like kindling.

"That's it!" the Juggernaut roared. "Now I'm really starting to get mad!"

Rogue shivered. *Now* he's getting mad? Just over a day earlier, she had battled Gladiator of the Imperial Guard, one of the physically strongest beings in the universe. Now she was realizing that physical strength didn't count for much when one was dealing with . . . well, for lack of a better word, magic. They would have been better off if Juggernaut *had* been a mutant. At least then, he . . .

Suddenly, doubt overwhelmed her. The Juggernaut hadn't

attacked them, they had attacked him. Certainly, he was one of the team's oldest enemies, since before Rogue had ever met any of the team's members, but he had merely been walking toward them, then standing still, when they had launched their attack.

The key, though, was that Cain Marko was not a mutant. His response when Magneto's name had been mentioned erased any doubts Rogue might have had. The Juggernaut was not working with or for Magneto at all. But then, why . . .

"Rogue, can we get a little assistance here?" Cyclops called, even as the Juggernaut bore down on him again.

"Wait!" Rogue cried. "Stop! All of you! Marko, please, hold on a minute."

The Juggernaut did not slow down. Did not even pay attention to her pleas. And who could blame him? They had, apparently, pushed him much too far.

A moment before he would have been crushed beneath the Juggernaut's attack, Jean telekinetically removed Cyclops from danger, lifting him clear of Marko's path. Rogue knew she had to force the huge man to catch his breath, to take a moment to reevaluate the situation. A moment later, she knew how to do it.

Even as Cyclops was spirited away, Rogue sped toward the Juggernaut's back. When he attempted to slow his momentum, to turn and attack the X-Men anew, Rogue got up behind him and began to push with all her strength. She wasn't trying to stop the Juggernaut. Just the opposite, in fact.

"What the . . . ?" he began, but then he saw the traffic-signal pole sticking out of the sidewalk right in front of him.

The Juggernaut growled, and ran right over the pole, which snapped off as he passed. Turning, he bent down to pick it up, single-handed, then held it like a baseball bat and set his feet to swing at Rogue.

"Juggernaut . . . Cain, just listen a second," she said quickly. "We thought you were with Magneto in this whole thing. Now I'm getting the idea we were wrong. It was a natural mistake, but we're sorry."

The Juggernaut raised and lowered the pole like a batter

choking up, ready for a pitch. She could see the confusion, the hesitation, in his face.

"We're sorry," she said again.

With a heavy sigh and a shake of his head, the Juggernaut tossed the signal pole to one side. He opened his mouth, as if to say something, then flicked both hands in a dismissive gesture and turned to walk away.

"Forget it," he said, and moved south, heading out of the city.

Rogue turned to look at Cyclops and Jean, who were staring at her, mouths open wide.

"How did you know?" Scott asked.

"We attacked him," she explained. "Marko's not a mutant, remember?"

Cyclops slapped himself on the forehead. Jean looked at Rogue, then turned to gaze thoughtfully at the Juggernaut's retreating form.

"Cain," she called after him. "Cain, wait up a moment, would you?"

Jean started walking after him, and Cyclops and Rogue fell in behind her a moment later.

"What is it now?" Marko growled. "I thought we were done with our little 'chat.' "

"You want to walk away from a fight with the X-Men?" Cyclops pushed. "That's a first, I'd say."

"It ain't you, Summers," the Juggernaut barked. "I got no fear of my little stepbrother's mutie encounter group. You chumps have tried time after time to take me out of the game, and I'm still here, ain't I?"

He looked particularly pleased with himself.

"Then why?" Rogue asked.

"Ah, hell," Cain Marko said, rolling his eyes. "I guess you guys aren't gonna leave me alone, are ya?"

The X-Men were silent.

"Nah, didn't think so. Look, I came into Manhattan a couple nights ago to meet this lady . . . and, yeah, the Juggernaut gets dates now and then. She wants to get together the next night, so I stayed another night in the hotel. Then, just before dawn, the world goes all to hell. It's a good thing I brought my gear. Things didn't work out with my ladyfriend, and I just wanted to go home. But, noooooo!''

"Magneto came after you?" Cyclops asked.

Juggernaut laughed.

"Not in the way you mean, Summers. A couple of his little stormtroopers got up in my face, gave me a hard time about joining 'the cause' when all I wanted to do was go home. Then these two German boneheads start in on me, twins they were—"

"The Kleinstocks," Jean said.

"Whatever," Marko said with a wave of his hand. "Magneto's toy soldiers were all over me."

"But you ain't a mutant," Rogue said.

Marko raised an eyebrow. "No kidding. But the morons wouldn't listen. I had to get a little mean with them. And they're like guard dogs, once they get their teeth in, they don't let go until you take them down. Once they saw I meant to leave, and I told them another dozen times I wasn't a mutant, they gave up. Helped that they could barely stand, and that I explained as how me an' Charley Xavier ain't blood related.''

Uncomfortable silence followed. Rogue looked back and forth between Juggernaut and Cyclops. Finally, the huge man shook his head slightly, his helmet rotating slowly from side to side.

"Well," he said, "not like I actually expected an apology or anything. You guys still want to fight?"

"Hmm?" Cyclops asked, as though just returning to a conversation he'd tuned out. And Rogue thought that maybe he had.

"No," Jean said quickly. "No, we don't."

"Suit yourself," Marko said with a shrug, then turned and began to walk south once more.

"Wait!" Rogue said, and glanced at Cyclops and Jean, whose face was creased in an incredulous frown.

"What?" the Juggernaut asked.

"Stay," she said. "We could use the help."

Once again the other X-Men looked at Rogue with incredulity. Juggernaut only laughed.

"You're kidding," he said. "If I wasn't going to help Magneto, what the hell makes you think I'd help you?"

"You ain't payin' attention, are you?" Rogue asked, hand on hip. "Listen up, Marko, maybe I won't have to explain myself twice."

"Um, Rogue," Jean said tentatively, "I'm not even sure why you'd want to, but if you're trying to endear yourself to the Juggernaut, that may not be the best way to—"

"No, Jean, I'm not tryin' to make friends with Mr. Marko," Rogue snapped. "He's been a pain since the first time the X-Men laid eyes on him."

She rounded on the Juggernaut and started to advance. Wide eyed with surprise, he did not attempt to defend himself. There was no need. Rogue's attack was all verbal.

"Thing is, though, you ain't evil, Cain. You're just one mean sucker," she said harshly. "Try to follow me, here. It's the X-Men versus Magneto, the Sentinels, and however many mutants he's got under his thumb already, not to mention whatever others may be on the way. We're working at less than half our strength, and we're flat-out exhausted to boot.

"If we lose, and it don't look like we got much chance of winnin', there's two ways this thing can go. First, New York City ends up gettin' nuked, 'cause you know the army can't beat Magneto. Maybe you don't care about all the people in the city dyin' like that, but I've got a feelin' you ain't as unfeelin' as you make out.

"Second—and you'll like this—Magneto wins, and the Mutant Empire expands faster and faster until the entire Earth has been remade. You'll be bowin' and scrapin' before Emperor Magnus in no time, bein' as how you were so insistent upon provin' that you weren't one of us."

Cain Marko looked from one face to the next. From Rogue, to Jean, to Scott. Rogue wasn't sure what he was searching for, maybe some confirmation that they all believed what she had said.

SALVATION

"I've got friends here, in the city," he said, almost absently.

"Not for long," Rogue answered.

The Juggernaut took several steps forward, until he was standing, towering, over Cyclops. Marko looked down at the leader of the X-Men, eyes hard inside his mask.

"What about it, Summers?" he asked. "This all for real? Your team gonna get trounced here today?"

"It's a distinct possibility," Cyclops reluctantly agreed.

"I don't like you, Summers," the Juggernaut said.

"The feeling's entirely mutual, Marko."

Juggernaut looked around again, at Rogue, then Jean, then back at Cyclops. He put out his hand.

"Just as long as we understand each other."

CHAPTER 4

It was wrong. All wrong.

Once upon a time, the Worthington family had been Manhattan royalty. Richer than God, they'd been. Yet as a boy Warren had been blissfully unaware of the harsh realities life held for others. Little things like being forced to go to bed without supper—for so minute a transgression as drawing on his father's favorite tie with magic markers—those had been the sum total of his childhood hardships.

Then came the wings. Warren had blossomed early, hitting puberty at the tender age of eleven. At first, his parents had terrified him with their own fears, that the growths on his back might be some form of cancer. Soon enough, it became plain to anyone paying the slightest bit of attention exactly what those growths were.

Mother had always called him her little angel. She'd no way of knowing that term of endearment would one day prove prophetic.

He had to admire his parents' fortitude, though. With an inside track on all the latest research—because after all, knowledge was power and Warren K. Worthington Jr. had enough money to buy whatever power he ever needed—his father had determined that little Warren III was a mutant. He paid all the doctors a fortune in hush money, including the man who'd devised the truss that held Warren's wings flat against his back.

His father, Warren had long since determined, had just wanted it all to go away. If the wings weren't seen, they weren't really there. The Worthington family could go on with their business dynasty as if they were unaware of their son's genetic status. Warren grew up to be a playboy, just as his father had expected. But in the privacy of his own home, in his own room, away from the stigma society placed on mutants, the stigma his own parents, by their silence, had placed on him, he unfurled his beautiful wings and dreamed of flying.

He dreamed of it until one day he couldn't stop himself. And Warren Worthington III, his mother's little angel, flew.

Not long thereafter he was packed off to Xavier's School

for Gifted Youngsters. The next time he told his parents he loved them was the day he wept over their graves.

But while his father had been alive, he had shown his mutant son all the wonders of Manhattan, the curious behavior of the city's idle rich. New York City belonged to the captains of industry, he would always say. The wealthy families that were the power behind every company and politician in the region. Like the Worthingtons.

Warren had never understood the attitude of ownership, but he did value Manhattan for everything it had. When others complained of the homelessness, the crime, the corruption, Warren used his family's money to do what he could in those areas. But in doing so, he constantly reminded anyone who would listen that New York was the greatest city in the world.

But now it was all wrong. He glided between old four- and five-story buildings, biometallic razor wings slicing the air, wounding the sky. Once, he'd been an angel, ivory feathers floating, muscles powering him aloft. His new wings matched his altered nature, violent and incisive. He had begun to gain control over the violence that raged within him, but he could never bring back the natural wings that had been mutilated, then amputated.

Something about Archangel would never be right again. Now his city was twisted as well. It looked the same on the outside, but its soul was being drained away, with every person fleeing in terror.

A rare trace of birdsong lilted through the air above. A nice breeze spared him a moment of the stagnant, superheated air that hung in the city's concrete canyons. The sun shone down, glinting off display windows and forcing him to squint. It should have been a perfect New York City day.

But New York City had all but disappeared. The rude, stressed-out tribe that called Manhattan home had been thinned nearly to nothing to make room for a new tribe, a dangerous tribe. That was the way of the wild, but it didn't sit right with him. This wasn't the wild, after all. More than anywhere else, for better or for worse, Manhattan island was civilization.

Or had been. Now it was wild again. The structure of civilization still stood, but rather than brimming with life, it was filled with the terrified and the terrifying, lurking in doorways and subway stations and narrow alleys.

It was wrong. All wrong.

They had already checked out two Sentinels, the robots that stood guard over the Holland and Lincoln Tunnels, respectively, on the western shore of the island. Cooper had said before that there was no visible marking to identify the Sentinels, but had not mentioned that there *were* markings. She had brought infrared goggles in her gear from Washington for that specific purpose.

It would have been a stroke of true luck if one of those Sentinels had turned out to be the Alpha unit. But they just weren't that lucky. Now, Archangel winged his way above, acting as point man and scout, while Gambit and Cooper navigated abandoned cars, cabs, buses, and trucks on the streets below on a motorcycle they'd come upon just beyond the Manhattan-side mouth of the Holland Tunnel.

Gambit had it hot-wired in seconds, literally. Watching him, Warren had realized for the first time that all the talk of Remy LeBeau having been an international master thief before joining the X-Men had been one hundred percent truth. It made him wonder, not for the first time, how much of Gambit's past was still a total mystery to the X-Men.

On the other hand, nobody fought harder than Remy LeBeau. For all his sarcasm, Warren figured Gambit was a good man to have at his back.

Greenwich Village was beneath him now, and the buildings had gotten even shorter. No skyscrapers down here. Offices, warehouses, retail space, that was the old city. The face of this part of the city changed from day to day, new restaurants and boutiques opening as last month's hot spots closed.

Almost directly south, he could see the twin towers of the World Trade Center jutting up next to Battery Park City. Beyond them, over blocks of buildings of every shape and size, Archangel could see the head of the next Sentinel. Canal Street heading southeast and West Street running south were packed with vehicles, so Gambit guided the Harley down Greenwich Street.

They'd already passed several small groups of humans, even a couple of people who appeared, courageously, to be out on their own. Warren figured they were trying to discover how much the city had actually changed. They barely blinked when Gambit and Cooper drove by, but the few who spotted Archangel in the air definitely reacted. Some ran for cover, others threw whatever was at hand, still others merely pointed in fear or astonishment.

It didn't matter that they had decided to stay in the city despite Magneto's rule, these people were not prepared for it. Many of them would die if Magneto were left in charge. The X-Men were not about to allow that to happen.

"Swing over to Broadway when you have a chance," he said into the comm-link on his left wrist. "From there it's a straight shot down to Battery Park. Looks like that's where Robby the Robot is hanging out."

"Check," Cooper responded.

"Val, there are twenty of these bad boys, and we've only checked out two," Warren said, concerned. "It's going to take a while. Isn't there any other way to do this?"

"Not unless you can carry me on a flying circuit of the whole island, Warren," Cooper responded. "No way would we get an airship or a chopper in here, buzz around Manhattan, without Magneto and his goons taking notice, and action."

Archangel sighed. Cooper was right.

"All right," he answered. "Tell me again where they're all located. We may have to split up if we don't get lucky in the next hour or so."

"We did the Holland Tunnel and the Lincoln Tunnel," she answered. "We thought the next one was the downtown heliport, but you said Battery Park, so that's two. Brooklyn Bridge, Williamsburg Bridge, Midtown Tunnel, UN Building, Queensboro Bridge, Metro Hospital Center, Triborough Bridge."

She stopped, presumably to take a breath and rack her brain.

"There's one in Harlem in the one-forties, one at the Cross Bronx, one at the Henry Hudson, the GW Bridge, then four more along Riverside Park facing Jersey."

She paused.

"Warren?"

"Pray for luck, Val," he said. "We're gonna need it."

On the street, the Harley swung east. They were past the Village now, rapidly approaching the financial district. With one thrust of his wings, Warren also turned east, speeding up to get ahead of them, to do his duty as the point man. But he hadn't been paying enough attention.

"Heads up, Remy," he said. "Activity ahead, by City Hall."

They were coming up on City Hall fast, and the street was filled with people. More people than Warren had seen in one spot since entering Manhattan, maybe more people than he'd imagined had stayed behind. But these folks weren't kowtowing to Magneto. They were fighting for their city.

There were hundreds of them, the true melting pot of New York, crossing every imaginary boundary people put between them, race, gender, religion, age, income. They were New Yorkers first and there to fight. Problem was, they were losing.

On the steps of City Hall, police officers and mutants stood side by side, keeping the citizens out. Warren recognized several of the mutants, including Senyaka, an Acolyte in the colorful uniform all of Magneto's inner circle wore. Even as he looked on, Senyaka lashed out with his psionic whip and began to choke one of the men closing in on the cops. The others began to back off.

"My God," Archangel said, then spoke into the comm again. "Magneto's co-opted City Hall, Val. We've got cops and Acolytes working together. These people don't have a chance."

"Back off, Warren!" Val's panicked voice erupted from the comm-link. "Get out of sight immediately. Don't let them see you!"

"What?" Archangel asked. "What are you—"

"*La petite fille* is right, *mon ami*," Gambit interrupted, the roar of the Harley coming through the link with his heavily accented voice. "Gambit don' like it any better den you, but we can't afford to have Magneto and de Acolytes down on us now. We got a job to do."

Warren ground his teeth together, took one last look at the chaos at City Hall, and turned away, heading for cover at top speed. In an instant he was gone, and he didn't think anyone had seen him.

"Let's get this done," he said into the comm.

Yet he knew that no matter how lucky they were, no matter how quickly they might get the job done, the city would be deeply scarred. The psychological scars on the population were a part of it, but there was no way this thing was going to end without some serious collateral damage.

Gambit had turned the Harley down Church Street, only a block away from the City Hall madness. Archangel swiftly followed, catching up as they passed the spires of Trinity Church. Several blocks farther south, Gambit swung left for a block, then turned south onto Broadway. The green lawn of Battery Park was just ahead.

Archangel held back, not wanting to gain more attention from the Sentinel than was absolutely necessary. Now that he saw it, standing its silent, deadly vigil at the southern tip of the island, he realized how vital that particular spot was.

From Battery Park, ferries ran to and from Ellis Island and the Statue of Liberty. Close by was the terminal for the Staten Island Ferry. Far more important, however, were the Brooklyn Battery Tunnel, the downtown heliport, and Fort Jay, the U.S. Coast Guard station on Governors Island, just a short way across the Upper New York Bay.

It occurred to him then that Magneto was very serious about his plans for Haven. His behavior had been eminently reasonable, and insane at the same time. He truly believed that Haven would be able to function with the rest of the world. If he'd thought the island would have to be completely self-sufficient, he'd have ordered the Sentinels to simply destroy the bridges and tunnels and be done with it.

Somehow, the idea that Magneto believed the world might

come to accept his Mutant Empire was more chilling than the inevitable catastrophe that was guaranteed when he realized he was wrong.

"How about it, Val?" Archangel asked over the comm. "What's the infrared say? This our boy?"

"Negative, Warren," she said. "Let's move on."

As they headed for the Brooklyn Bridge, Warren started praying for luck once more. It was all they had.

* * *

The human resistance was growing. The relatively small group of somewhere between one and two hundred that Bobby Drake had gotten involved with had already hooked up with several others. It was a network of people who refused to kneel before Magneto. Some were bigots. Some had not been bigots before Magneto took over, but were gradually devolving into bigotry. But the majority were just people who didn't want to give up without a fight.

Bobby had tagged along, helping out where he could, for most of the morning. In fact, it had been Gabi, one of the resistance fighters, who had confirmed for him that the X-Men were indeed being held inside the Empire State Building. He'd thought about it for quite some time before he realized that he had only one option.

Iceman was going to have to go in after them.

Of course, some of his new friends had offered to help. Gabi and her brother Michael had nearly forced themselves on him, and it had taken some effort to talk them out of it. After all, if the X-Men were the city's best hope, it was in all their interests to break the rest of the team out. Still, they were new to this kind of thing. He'd been risking his neck for years, gone up against Magneto what seemed like dozens of times, and he was still around to talk about it.

Truth be told, once he'd thought about it, he stopped viewing himself as the X-Men's resident clown. He was, in the end, the last X-Man. That was some incredible billing, and fulfilling the role would be a daunting task. Iceman didn't know if he was capable of it, but he was certain of one thing:

SALVATION

If he couldn't rescue the X-Men, it would only be because he himself had either become a captive, or had died in the effort.

A sobering thought. But Bobby had been having quite a few of those today.

Like most buildings of its size, the Empire State Building had several entrances to the lobby. Magneto's own little Gestapo guarded the lobby as if it were Fort Knox, but Bobby knew that the majority of his experienced Acolytes would be off handling more important and immediate tasks throughout the city. In fact, in making a wide circuit of the building, he did not see a single mutant that he recognized. Iceman had assumed that Voght, or Unuscione, or even the Blob, would have been left in charge of the new recruits. But if there was a seasoned warrior among them, it wasn't anyone he'd ever run across.

The lobby was a death trap. But as far as he could tell, little or no attention was being paid to an additional entrance, a service door that did not go into the lobby itself. He had to assume that it would be guarded on the inside, but there was no sentry posted outside the door. That would be his entry point.

Carefully avoiding the conspicuous sight lines of those mutants guarding the lobby, he made his way to the side of the building as quickly as possible. He hoped that anyone seeing him might mistake him for a New Yorker either brave or stupid enough to have come this close to ground zero.

Once at the door, however, he had to work fast. It was a heavy metal thing, probably foam core, and there were two deadbolts above the lock that was in the knob itself. No time for niceties, though. Icing up his right hand, he concentrated on freezing one side of the door frame and the locks. He didn't ice the knob, however. He needed something to hold on to.

Fully human again, for his ice form did not give him any additional strength, Bobby wrapped a hand around the doorknob and yanked with all his might. With a crack, the brittle frozen metal of the deadbolts snapped and the door swung open in his hand.

There was only one guard. The mutant turned toward him

in speechless surprise, jaw slack and eyes wide. Bobby didn't know what his power was, but he knew the guy might call out an alarm any second. Like a batter going for a home run, Iceman swung his hands through the air. Mid-swing, the ice bat formed in his hands, and a second later, it connected with the guard's skull.

The guy went down hard in a shower of ice shards, totally out. Iceman looked down at him, and couldn't help but feel a little guilty.

"Sorry about that, rookie," he said quietly. "But you bet on the wrong horse."

A moment passed and Bobby heard nothing, no shouts or running footfalls. He was in, that was a start. Now he had to do his best to see that nobody knew he was in. There was nothing he could do about the ice on the floor. He would have to hope that it melted before anyone came by to check on or relieve the guard. There were larger problems.

First, of course, was the guard himself. He was out cold, though Bobby checked to make certain he was not seriously injured. It looked like he'd be out for a while. But that wasn't the problem. Sure, he could be stashed in a stairwell or an air duct, but his absence could not go unnoticed for long, so Iceman would have to work fast. On the other hand, given the likelihood that a number of mutants who'd lined up to follow Magneto were already having second thoughts, the guard's superiors would have to consider the possibility that he had gone AWOL.

Bobby crossed his fingers.

Then there was the door. He brushed the remnants of the shattered lock out onto the sidewalk and closed it. Relief spread through him when the door actually stayed closed. It was perfectly balanced, and didn't hang open at all. If someone tugged on it, the cat would be out of the bag. But other than that, and the ice on the floor, he thought he'd be safe for a little while.

Nearby there was a maintenance closet. Inside, he found a mop and bucket, and a sink. Moving as fast as he could, he put some water in the bucket and left it with the mop leaning against a wall. If the ice melted, nobody would think twice about the water.

He called the service elevator, ready for anything when its doors slid open. There was nobody inside, so he pressed STOP and opened the trapdoor in the ceiling. It took all his strength to shove the guard up through the hole—thank God he'd been working out—but he didn't dare use his powers on the elevator. There'd be no way to cover it up.

With all of that taken care of, though, Bobby still had to deal with the biggest problem of all: finding the X-Men.

He stared at the service elevator for a moment, then smiled. It had given him an idea. He didn't have much time, but without knowing where the X-Men were, he also didn't have a lot of options. Bobby pressed the button to call the elevator again and the door slid open. He scanned the floor numbers. Most of Magneto's operations would likely be clumped together in one section of the building—or at least, that was his logic. At random, he pressed twenty-three, then quickly pulled himself up through the trap door where the guard still lay unconscious.

As the floors ticked by, he looked at the welt that had risen on the guard's forehead, already turning black and blue. The guy might have a concussion, if not something worse. It was regrettable, but at least Bobby figured he didn't have to put the guard on ice. That could cause even more medical problems, not to mention giving him away once somebody noticed the cold water dripping down into the elevator from the melting ice.

Luck was with him. The elevator didn't stop on any other floors. He held open the trapdoor slightly, enough to see through. When the doors slid open on twenty-three, he waited a few moments to see that there was nobody there. Then he hung his head down to look out into the hallway. He saw nothing but offices. Apparently empty offices. The door slid shut even as he swung down into the elevator, and he jabbed at the DOOR OPEN button quickly.

Bobby closed the trapdoor, and moved out onto the twenty-third floor, staying close to the wall. Every nerve was tingling, every muscle taut. He didn't think he had ever been so tense.

Tempted to transform into Iceman, he resisted. If he was spotted, staying flesh and blood would hopefully give him some element of surprise and confusion over his enemies. Unless he ran into someone who knew what Bobby Drake looked like.

Magneto, for instance.

But he didn't want to think about that.

Down the hall, he found the main elevator bank. He called the elevator and ducked into an office across from it. When he heard the *ding* of its arrival, he peeked out just as the doors slid open . . . and quickly ducked back in. There were three people on the elevator, likely mutants he did not recognize.

The fourth try, he got an empty elevator. He scrambled up through the trapdoor, this one much smaller than the one on the service elevator, and lay down on top.

Alone in enemy headquarters, he considered what he was doing to be foolhardy at best, completely nuts more likely, and suicidal at worst. But there really wasn't any other choice. He was an X-Man, and the X-Men took care of their own.

No matter what the risk.

The elevator began to move. Iceman lay still, listening, and hoped for the best.

* * *

On the vid-comm unit Magneto had set up in his makeshift office, the stern face of Exodus, as always, showed little emotional reaction to his master's words. For without question, Magneto was the mysterious mutant's master. Exodus had been in some kind of mutant hibernation before Magneto had reawakened him to become the shepherd of Avalon.

Magneto's right hand, Exodus had been left behind on Avalon to continue that job. He was the being responsible for finding only the most powerful, most desirable mutants for relocation to Avalon, where they would make a contribution to the new society. Exodus was also the ferryman, like Charon on the river Styx, who brought those mutants to the space station, the last haven for mutantkind.

After this new Haven that Magneto was building on Earth, of course.

SALVATION

"You seem surprised," Magneto said, though it was only because he was so familiar with Exodus that he could read such an emotion in the mutant's motionless features.

"Dukes and Allerdyce were specifically excluded from Avalon," Exodus explained. "It is somewhat surprising, yes, that you decided to recruit them for Haven."

"Don't be such a snob, Exodus," Magneto said, half attempting humor, an effort he rarely made but which Exodus's stone-faced manner inspired him to. "Pyro and the Blob might not be what we were looking for on Avalon, but Haven is a harsher environment, the testing ground, I suppose, for the final hierarchy of the Mutant Empire.

"In any case, as you know, all mutants are welcome here. It is a sanctuary. We don't have the space or the supplies to make such a broad-minded offer regarding Avalon."

After a brief silence, Exodus nodded.

"But it goes well?" he asked. "I would remind you, Lord Magneto, that you have but to call and I will be instantly at your side."

"Actually," Magneto said, leaning back in the leather chair he'd moved into his office, "it goes extremely well. Most of the Acolytes have been given different duties. We've a city and, eventually, an empire to run. These kinds of things are vital if we are to succeed. Even those you despise have been dispatched for one purpose or another.

"The authorities that remain have wisely chosen to collaborate with us on the new regime. Even now, mutants and human police officers are beginning to implement the new laws I have put into place."

"There is no resistance by the humans?" Exodus asked, obviously surprised. Magneto thought the change in his expression was refreshing.

"There is always resistance among the humans," he responded. "I imagine there always will be. But it is nothing we cannot handle."

"What of the X-Men?"

"Half of them are my prisoners already," Magneto said. "The others are on the prowl, I'm sure, but there are a handful of them and many hundreds, soon maybe even thousands, of us. What can they do?

"No, Exodus," Magneto said, shaking his head slightly. "I don't think I'll be needing you down here. If I do, of course I shall call for you. But for now, continue operating Avalon in my stead. That is all I ask."

"As you command, my Emperor," Exodus answered, the first time he had called Magneto by that title.

It felt right.

CHAPTER 5

For most of his life, Cain Marko had equated kindness in any form with despicable weakness. As a child, he had felt his father's hand more times than he could count. But the physical abuse wasn't the worst part, not nearly. Far more painful were the harsh words, the hard looks, the utter and complete coldness of his father's heart. Watching his stepmother quiver and his stepbrother Charles escape into his studies, Cain nurtured a terrible hatred for them that grew with each passing day.

They were weak. They deserved what they got. Cain vowed that he would be strong, that he would never shrink in fear from anyone or anything, never show weakness. But around his father, he couldn't help himself.

Cain Marko became cruel. Not merely a bully, but a tyrant of the schoolyard, and even worse at home to his stepbrother, who somehow escaped the brunt of his father's wrath.

By the time he discovered the mystical gemstone that transformed him into the Juggernaut, Cain Marko had already developed an inclination toward crime and a sadistic streak wide as the Grand Canyon. His exploits as the Juggernaut, and his career as a criminal, led him, eventually, to make the acquaintance of the man who would change his life.

Tom Cassidy—called "Black Tom" by Interpol, the X-Men, and anybody else who'd ever run into him—was the first person Cain had ever known who could be both ruthless and kind. His kindness to Cain was an awakening of sorts. He had been wrong, for most of his life, about something he had believed in as gospel. Kindness did not always equal weakness. Friendship was possible, even desirable, if one chose carefully.

Steadily, Cain had changed. He was still a criminal. He was still ruthless when it was necessary to get the job done. He still gave no quarter in battle, particularly with the X-Men. He still hated his stepbrother, Charles Xavier.

But the sadistic side of the Juggernaut began to erode. In those quiet moments when he was honest with himself, Cain realized that part of him was almost completely gone, and he was glad. He might be an international fugitive, wanted in nearly every major nation in the world, but he was motivated by confidence, dignity, and greed, now, not pure hatred.

He was never completely certain the change was for the better, but it sure as hell felt like it.

Now this. Now he was going into battle side by side with the X-Men, the goody-two-shoes Boy Scouts he had always gone out of his way to trounce before. Yet, one of the reasons he had always hated them was because of the holier-than-thou crap they constantly spouted, the way they treated him like he was gum on the bottom of their shoe, the same way Charles had always treated him. He hated the way they made their offers of help seem a weakness on his part rather than on their own, so . . . condescending, that was the word.

It infuriated him.

But today was different. After the short fight they'd had, which he had actually enjoyed, they had been almost respectful toward him. Sure, they'd jumped him without so much as a "heads up," but, given the circumstances, he could understand that kind of overreaction. He didn't really blame them.

So he walked down the middle of the street shoulder to shoulder with the X-Men, ready to take back the city, not because he cared about its people or aspired to be a hero in any way—he sure as hell didn't—but because he was a human being and it was his world too. Magneto could kiss his butt, as far as Cain was concerned.

Truth be told, he thought it was pretty cool. Like something out of an old Western flick. Not to mention that the Grey woman and Rogue were both totally delicious-looking company. At the end of the day, he'd be just as happy to kick the crap out of the X-Men all over again, but for the moment. . . .

And the very best part of all, the thing that had clinched it for him, even beyond his determination not to bow to Magneto, was the fact that Charles Xavier, his hated stepbrother, was the founder and benefactor of the X-Men.

Knowing his precious soldiers were heading into battle side by side with the Juggernaut would really get under his skin. Cain loved that. Even if he and the X-Men got their heads handed to them by the Sentinels, it would be worth it.

Far ahead, he could see the Empire State Building jutting up out of the jagged skyline, dwarfing anything around it. It wouldn't be long now.

"Shouldn't we be, I don't know, a little less conspicuous at this point?" he asked. "I mean, the OK Corral has a kind of glamorous history to it, but the odds there were a little more even, y'know."

"What are you saying, Juggernaut?" Cyclops asked.

"I guess what I want to know is, do you have a plan, or are we just going to waltz in and stomp heads until we end up getting stomped, then it's game over?" the Juggernaut explained.

"Both," Rogue said, and smiled.

"Huh?"

"We don't stand a chance without the other X-Men, Cain," Jean Grey said. "Even with you on our side. Now, if we can't get them out, we're going to have to go it alone. But that's the last resort."

"Has it occurred to you people that, if we don't stand a chance of winning, we don't stand a chance of getting in to free your buddies anyway?" Cain asked.

"Not true," Cyclops said. "We have one chance. We lose."

Cain stared at Scott Summers.

"You mean, like, on purpose?" he asked.

"You just said we didn't have a chance of winning, but that doesn't mean we can't get in. If we're going to lose anyway, let's put that to our advantage," Cyclops said.

Before the Juggernaut could protest, Jean spoke up.

"If they're using inhibitor collars, which is highly likely, considering Magneto's past tactics, that won't work for you because you're not a mutant. And since each collar is calibrated for the individual mutant, I can psionically confuse our captors so that we're given the wrong collars," she said.

"Yeah, but to do that, you have to be conscious," Cain replied.

"There are always risks," Rogue said.

"That's a hell of a risk," he said. "Why take the chance? If we're all captured, there isn't anyone left to come to the rescue."

"You have a better idea," Cyclops said, somewhat sarcastically.

Cain's eyes narrowed inside his helmet. The amiable spirit with which he'd been dealing with the X-Men dissipated. Scott Summers was a good tactician, an excellent field commander, and courageous as they came. Just because the X-Men had always been his enemies did not mean he could not appreciate, or even respect, their strengths. But he was something of an academic snob as well. Summers must have figured just because Cain didn't finish high school that he was stupid. Well, he was wrong.

"In fact," he said coldly. "I think I do."

"Well, I for one would like to hear it," Rogue said. "If we can avoid a head-on confrontation until after the X-Men are free, I'd be happy."

"You guys think too heroically," Cain said, and smiled in amusement at his own words. "This martyr-complex thing has got to stop if you want to see breakfast tomorrow. You've got to start to think like a thief, like a criminal. The rule there is, whatever you steal is only valuable if you're still around to benefit from its theft.

"That's why we need a diversion," he said, looking to Jean because he was slightly irked at Cyclops just then. "If me, Summers, and Rogue start raising hell not far from Magneto's headquarters, the attention will be diverted from the building. You probably wouldn't be able to get in and find the X-Men without being discovered, but I'm sure you can convince a guard or three here and there that they didn't see or hear you at all. Right?"

"It's a fine line, Cain," Jean responded, "but I try not to use wholesale telepathic manipulation on people when it can be helped."

"Maybe you wouldn't understand that . . . ." Cyclops began, but let it go when he received an annoyed glance from Grey, his longtime lady. Juggernaut would have been amused, but they didn't have much time.

"Look," he said, "I understand perfectly that you guys try to tread some fine line. To be honest, I think it's pretty cowardly—when you go into a fight, it should be to win, no matter what—but somehow you seem to win anyway, so who's to argue with success, right? Point is, we've got no time for things like good manners here. You said yourselves that this was it, the big one, that the future of the world rests on whether we can beat Magneto or not. Let's worry about crossing boundaries later, okay?

"Besides, once I've started a fight, there's only one way it ends," Cain vowed. "The other guy goes down, or I do. I'm not playing dead for anybody. I just can't do it."

He watched them, what was left of the X-Men, as each weighed what he had said. Except for Wolverine, he'd always considered them a bunch of liberal wimps with their heads in the clouds. Now, though, with the fire in Rogue's eyes, the resolve on Jean Grey's face, and the tightening of Scott Summers's fists, Cain wasn't so sure.

One thing he was certain of, though, was that their plan sucked. Getting captured, on purpose or otherwise, just didn't sit right with him. If they weren't prepared to go along with his alternate suggestion, well, the Juggernaut would have to come up with a third plan for himself. Cain wondered if Summers would be so used to running the show that he'd ignore his suggestion out of spite. After a moment's consideration, he pushed the thought away. Summers was smarter than that.

It wasn't at all that the Juggernaut was extremely intelligent, or a good strategist, or anything of the sort. It was only as he'd said: in his line of work, you got in, grabbed your objective, and got out, one way or another.

Yeah, they'd have to go with his—

"Company," Jean said quietly, taking several steps toward an eccentric clothing store on the right, hugging close to the building.

The others quickly followed, and so did Juggernaut, though he didn't see anyone. He quickly discovered that he wasn't built for stealth, however. He was just too damn big to be inconspicuous, no matter where he was.

"What am I missing?" Cain asked.

Jean held up a finger to shush him. Rogue went to the shop's door, and with a quick twist of the knob that shattered the locks, they were inside. The Juggernaut was about to follow when Cyclops held up a hand, urging him to stay out on the sidewalk.

"We're not close enough," Summers said. "Let's try to do this fast."

"Do what?" Cain replied, beginning to get frustrated.

Then he heard the voices.

Twenty-five yards ahead was an intersection. Traffic lights continued their mute exercise of authority with no regard to the lack of vehicles they might command. The voices were loud, one particularly deep and booming, magnified all the more by the haunting absence of noise in a city normally so saturated with it.

"This is the life, buddy!" the loudest voice thundered. "Always knew being a cop was easy. Free donuts, your own little kingdom like Kurtz in *Apocalypse Now*. It's a pretty good deal."

"Frankly, Fred, I was hoping for a position with a bit more long-term potential, more responsibility," said another male voice, this one with a strong Australian accent.

Juggernaut recognized them both. Grey must have been psi-scanning their immediate area almost constantly, watching for an attack or even a chance meeting, as this apparently was going to be.

Pyro and the Blob came around the corner as close to side by side as they could get, considering the Blob's extraordinary girth. They weren't alone. At least a dozen other mutants trailed behind them, some familiar to him, most not. Blob and Pyro, though, were easy to recognize. They'd been part of Freedom Force for a while, celebrities, but even before that, they'd made the news. Major troublemakers, hellraisers of the first order.

"Well, well, well," Juggernaut said, "what've we got here?"

As a fighting force, these later-generation Acolytes were untrained. Several seemed to freeze, uncertain how to react. Fully half a dozen spread out in attack formation, those who were armed bringing weapons to bear. Mutant mercenaries. Not criminals, not terrorists, just creeps with powers hiring out to the highest bidder without a moment's consideration of who they were working for, what they were destroying. Juggernaut had no illusions: he was no hero, he was one of the bad guys. But even the guys in the black hats in the cowboy flicks had dignity, honor.

Mercenaries were scum.

There were a pair of mutants in the back—a big bruiser and a stout guy with spiky hair all over his body—who looked like tag-team wrestlers and clearly worked as a team. They looked familiar, but Juggernaut couldn't place them. Those two bothered him. They seemed dangerous, far more so than the mercenaries, because these other two were obviously a little nuts.

Pyro and the Blob both merely smiled and kept walking.

"Do my eyes deceive me, Fred, or is that the Juggernaut?" Pyro asked, even as he waved at the mercenaries to be sure they wouldn't attack . . . yet. "Why, I'd heard as how he'd turned tail and abandoned the cause. Was kind of surprised, actually. Not a good idea to piss Lord Magneto off these days."

Lord Magneto, Juggernaut thought with venomous sarcasm. *What a load of crap.*

"How about it, buddy?" the Blob said, ignoring his partner's amused babble. "You come back to tell us you've changed your mind?"

"As a matter of fact, I have," Cain replied.

He could feel the sigh of relief that went through the group. The Juggernaut's reputation had preceded him after all. Who in their right mind would want a battle, no matter what the odds? As Pyro and the Blob stopped a few feet away from him, Cain studied the rest of them, trying to figure out what their powers were. Far as he could tell, the tag-team boys didn't have any kind of weapon, mechanical or natural, other than strength and, he guessed, agility.

Of the four mutants who were obviously inexperienced, two looked as if they might pose a threat—not to him, of course. One had bony spines lining his body, and the way he stood it seemed likely the teenager could fire the spines from his body or from some natural-flesh projectile housing on the back of his hands. The other was leaking phosphorescent radiation or something from his mouth. The rest of the rookies looked harmless, but you could never judge a mutant just on appearance.

The mercenaries were another story. Three were armed with high-powered automatic rifles, so their mutant gifts were probably more cerebral. Another was nearly feral, with a collar and heavy chain leash held by a seven-foot hulk of a man whose flesh seemed made of granite. Then there was the woman, exquisitely beautiful with her tumble of chestnut-brown hair and a gown of some gossamer material so thin it was nearly impossible for Cain to take his eyes off her, even though he could see nothing of her revealed beneath the dress.

They were dangerous, though obviously those armed with conventional weapons were low-level mutants at best.

"Changed your mind, eh?" Pyro sneered. "S'funny. Harlan Kleinstock told me you insisted you weren't a mutant at all. You had a few choice words for him, is what he said, and none of them were real nice."

"That's true," Juggernaut agreed. "But like I said, I changed my mind."

"So now you want to join up—maybe you realized Magneto's gonna be the only game in town pretty soon," the Blob reasoned aloud.

"You got it," Cain admitted. "Magneto's getting ready to change the world. But you're wrong about one thing: I didn't come back to join up."

The Blob narrowed his eyes in confusion. "But I thought you said you changed your mind?" he asked.

"I did, but not how you're thinking," the Juggernaut said,

a thin smile splitting his face. "See, I wasn't lying when I said I wasn't a mutant. Now, I figure, I've got a lot to lose if Magneto makes every human being a second-class citizen—assuming he'll even be that kind about it."

Pyro held up a hand and the mercenaries started to close in, spreading out a bit to be sure that the Juggernaut couldn't escape. With the rookies along for the ride, they started to circle around behind him. What fools, he thought. They actually imagined he was planning to make a break for it, even after he'd been standing there nearly two minutes already.

"Y'know, you actually are as stupid as you are big," the Blob said, smiling a schoolyard bully smile that was as obvious a threat as if he'd been slamming a fist into his palm.

Juggernaut snorted laughter.

"Oh, that's rich," he said. "I've been called big and stupid by a guy named 'The Blob'! That's one to tell the grandchildren!"

The Blob began to go for him, but stopped when Pyro held up a hand and mumbled a warning.

"We're gonna do this the right way, the way Magneto wants it done," Pyro said. "You have been summoned before the Emperor Magneto, Juggernaut. This is a direct order from an Imperial officer. Will you comply?"

"Yeah, right," Juggernaut said derisively.

"In that case, in the name of Emperor Magneto, you are hereby under arrest," Pyro said, one corner of his mouth rising in a bratty smirk. "Okay, people. He's all yours."

The Blob took a step forward, precisely what the Juggernaut had been waiting for. As Fred Dukes was in midstep, Cain hauled back and hit him with all the strength he could muster, right in the face. There was a crack, like bone breaking, and the Blob cried out in pain and fell onto his butt on the pavement, accompanied by a minor earth tremor.

The rest of them would probably be a cinch. Even if he'd been alone. Which he wasn't.

"The X-Men!" Pyro cried as he saw Cyclops, Rogue, and Jean Grey burst from the clothing store.

It got ugly after that.

SALVATION

Pyro tried to flash-fry the Juggernaut where he stood. Cain reached for him, completely unscathed by the flames, and the little man tried to leap away. But the Juggernaut was faster than most of his enemies imagined, and snagged Pyro by the ankle. He tore the gas tanks from the mutant's back, and tossed them away. Then he held Pyro up in front of him and slapped him once across the face. Pyro hung limp, out cold, and the Juggernaut threw him away as carelessly as he had the gas tanks, not even bothering to watch where the Australian landed.

"Next!" he shouted, thrilled by the fight. It was a real kick to see the X-Men fighting beside him, knowing they weren't going to try to stop him because, for once, he was on the side of the angels.

Bullets sprayed the X-Men, bouncing off Rogue and the psi-shield Jean had thrown up around herself and Cyclops. In seconds, all the rookies were down except the one with the phosphorescence around his lips. He opened his mouth as if to speak, and green chemical fire raged forth, and this time, Juggernaut could feel the heat. This was no ordinary flame, but some mutant combination of normal fire, chemical heat, and intense hatred, a psionic blaze with a formidable mind behind it.

Cain snarled at the rookie, snapping one of the armed mutants up in his hands and using the man for a shield. The guy was lucky, his mutant power was a personal force shield. However, it wasn't a very powerful shield. It was going to keep him alive, but not from getting burned.

The Juggernaut heard a howl and before he could turn, the feral mercenary was on his back tearing at his helmet, trying to get it off. He didn't think the thing knew that his helmet protected him from psychic probes and attacks. No, the savage mutant just wanted to tear at his face and eyes, since the flesh of his arms resisted its claws.

Cyclops quickly took out the two other armed mutants, then fired a shot at the ghostly woman who now floated toward him. As Cain looked on, the woman seemed to become a kind of copper mist, sparkling in the sun and yet unmoved by the slight breeze that stirred the day's heat. It enveloped Cyclops, but the Juggernaut couldn't see anymore because the feral mercenary was still on his back. He swatted at it, reaching back to try and get hold of it, but the thing, or man if it still was a man, was too quick.

Cain saw Rogue, about to be pummeled by the huge mutant who appeared made of stone. He spun around, reaching for the wild thing on his shoulders, and saw Jean Grey, using a telekinetic shield to hold off an attack by the green fire breather. Spun again, and there was Cyclops, on the ground, clutching at his throat as if he could find no air to breathe. The copper mist that had been a beautiful mutant woman hung around him in a cloud. He blasted an optic charge into the metallic ether, but with no result.

Part of the Juggernaut wanted to watch, to savor the end of an enemy's life. But that was the part of him, the cruel, sadistic part, that he had been working at eliminating for years. It wasn't professional, and it didn't feel very good either. Besides, for now, Cyclops was on his side.

The Juggernaut stopped spinning and bent over fast. The feral mutant was momentarily thrown into the air, though it kept its clawed hold on his armored neck. Still, it flew up high enough so that Cain could grab it by its odd coat, his invulnerable skin splintering a number of spines that might have been tipped with poison.

He tossed the thing into the poison mist next to the writhing form of Cyclops. Immediately, the woman solidified. Though he ought to have been near death after having been so long without air, his lungs filled with some awful poison until she had drawn herself out of him to reform, Scott Summers was on his knees in a heartbeat. The feral thing reached for him, and Juggernaut worried that he'd made a mistake, that he'd saved Cyclops from one form of poisoning only to confront him with another by way of the savage mutant's porcupine-like spines.

Cyclops toasted it with a full-force optic blast from about three feet away. The savage creature was thrown across the street and through a department store's plate-glass window. It stirred, alive still, but did not rise.

"Scott, get ready!" Jean shouted.

Juggernaut looked over to where Jean still protected herself against the rookie mutant spitting toxic flame. Suddenly, he realized what she intended. She was going to telepathically force the ghostly poison woman to become solid so that Cyclops could take her down—leaving herself deliberately open to attack.

He moved.

"Now!" Jean said, dropping her telekinetic shield and forcing the ghost woman to solidify.

Cyclops decked the woman with a fist as Juggernaut hurled himself in front of the flames that were about to engulf Jean Grey. He howled in agony, and the thing turned on him, advancing, trying to finish the job.

"Thanks, Cain, I just needed a momentary distraction," Jean said, and suddenly, no more fire came out of the mutant's mouth. Even the phosphorescence that had been omnipresent had now disappeared.

The rookie's eyes went wide.

"What did you do?" he said in horror, then, realizing he had no weapon, turned and ran away.

"What *did* you do?" Cain asked.

"Unlike most mutants who have energy powers, like Scott or Gambit, that guy's fire was not merely psionically controlled but psionically generated. I turned it off. He can't remember how to generate it anymore," Jean said, her voice harsh, and yet somehow sad.

"Pretty nasty for the X-Men," Cain remarked. "I wonder if Charley would approve."

"Probably not," Jean admitted. "But we don't have time for manners, or so I'm told."

"Touché," Cain said.

"Juggernaut!" the Blob boomed, just to the left. "You hurt me!"

"Good!" Cain replied, smiling broadly.

"What's wrong with you, siding with them?" the Blob

asked, advancing dangerously, clutching his broken face. "You're a criminal, you're one of us."

"One of you?" the Juggernaut asked. "Don't insult me, man. You haven't got any class at all. You'll hire yourself out to anyone with a plan and some cash, or just tear up a town for the hell of it, because you can. I don't have the time for those tantrums anymore, and I'm not about to become a mercenary. I'm a career criminal, Blob, in it for the gain, not the pain. If Magneto takes over, my career's over."

"If that's the way you feel," the Blob sneered, then winced at the pain it caused. "But your career is over anyway, right now. I know why they call you the Juggernaut. Story says once you're moving, you can't be stopped. Well, try me, buddy. Nothing moves the Blob."

For a moment, Cain flashed back to the schoolyard of his childhood, to the dozens of similar taunting challenges he'd received from kids, mostly older, who'd heard he was a tough guy, a bully, and wanted to build their own reputations by taking him down. That was when he was filled with rage and hatred, when he passed on the pain his father gave him to any loudmouth or wiseass weakling who crossed his path.

There was joy in it then, and he felt that old joy rising again, the sadistic pleasure he could take in hurting his opponents. But he brushed it away. It didn't make him want to take the Blob down any less, but in his mind, attacking was a dismissive gesture. Not to cause pain, but to eliminate an obstacle. And the Blob was the ultimate obstacle.

The Juggernaut roared as he sprinted the distance between himself and the Blob. Just before they collided, the Blob seemed to lose his arrogant certainty, and he flinched slightly, to one side. Then Juggernaut slammed into him, at an angle, and spun away to the left. His head was ringing from the impact, but he turned to take another crack at the Blob.

Who was staring down at his feet. He'd been moved at least twelve inches, and there was no telling what might have happened, to both of them, if he hadn't flinched at the end. The Blob was still holding his shattered cheek, and after a moment, his eyes rolled back in his head and he once again fell to the pavement.

This time, he did not get up.

"What do you know?" Juggernaut said. "Unconscious. Maybe a concussion from the impact."

As he passed the Blob walking back toward Jean Grey, his mean streak resurfaced, just for a moment, and he turned to glare at the huge mutant's unconscious form.

"Loser," he snarled, and kept walking.

"Oh, God!" Rogue shouted suddenly.

Jean and the Juggernaut turned together and ran to where Rogue stood, staring in horror at a pile of rocks on the pavement in front of her.

"Rogue," Cyclops said in a hush as he approached from the other side. "What did you do?"

"I don't . . ." Rogue began, then took a breath before continuing. "It wasn't one'a my punches. I had just thrown him down. I was purposely tryin' not to hit him hard 'cause I wasn't real sure what he was made of. Then he turns around and rushes me, with all he's got.

"I just stood my ground, Scott," she said. "An' he crashed into me an' jus'—jus' broke! I swear I didn't mean to kill him."

"You didn't kill him, Rogue," Cain said in real sympathy. "There wasn't anything else you could have done. The man was just a fool."

After a moment of silence, Cyclops said: "Well, there's nothing to be done for it now. We've just got to move on and get as close to the Empire State as we can before we run into another group like this."

"You've got to wonder how many there are," Jean said.

"I'm trying not to think about it," Scott replied.

The comment hit a nerve. Cain looked around and realized that the two tag-team wrestlers he'd seen originally were not there. Had not been there, in fact, since just after the fight began.

"We'd better hurry," he said. "I think word is already on the way back to Magneto."

The X-Men looked around. Scott and Rogue didn't seem to notice anything. Maybe they hadn't seen the two stout mutants. But Jean realized it right away. She had probably sensed them earlier.

"Hairbag and Slab," she said.

"Those are their names?" the Juggernaut asked. "No wonder they hang around with the Blob."

"They never did before," Cyclops answered.

"Yeah," Rogue said, looking back once more at the remains of the mutant who had, in effect, killed himself using Rogue as his weapon. "It's a whole new world."

Chapter 6

Xavier and Magneto had been in a philosophical war over the future of the mutant race for decades, a war that had suddenly, explosively, entered reality. Magneto had the Sentinels, the Acolytes, hundreds of recently converted followers, and an entire city at his command.

All Charles Xavier had was hope.

Hope that the President of the United States would act with wisdom and caution. Hope that the world would not be irrevocably turned against mutants by Magneto's actions. Hope that Val Cooper could take the Sentinels out of the fight. Hope that the X-Men's small numbers were enough to achieve victory. And, finally, hope that victory would not come at too high a price.

There was one other thing that Xavier had, one other weapon in the war against Magneto's twisted racist dreams of conquest. Power. Charles Xavier might well have been the most powerful mutant on Earth. His strict moral code governed the use of that power very closely. Yet always there were catastrophes that could be averted, wrongs that could be put right, should he decide to throw off the chains of that code and assert his full power. If it came to that, he believed he might be able to end the conflict himself, by altering the minds and thought patterns of all the combatants.

But that would be the most grievous, the most hideous, misuse of power, no matter how many lives might be saved. Even God gave his creations free will, and Charles Xavier knew that he was not God. Did not aspire to be God. His own power held responsibility enough.

Instead, he used his stature as a respected member of society to do as much damage control as possible. He would not allow himself to imagine Magneto victorious, and therefore he tried to prepare the world for Magneto's downfall, tried to soften ahead of time the inevitable anti-mutant backlash.

Xavier was something of a celebrity, if you judged such things by how often a person made the news. Not like a sports star or a musician, an actor, or even a writer. Rather, he was a celebrity the way politicians and scientists became celebrities. They gained a certain status out of a sense of obligation—not because the majority of people really cared to hear about their actions and achievements, but because they felt they ought to care.

But never before had Charles experienced the kind of media feeding frenzy he had been subjected to in the past twenty-four hours. The sharks were tearing him apart, fighting for a piece, and it was his duty to oblige them, to utilize their need for his own purposes.

CNN, ABC, NBC, CBS, Fox, WNN, E!, MTV, several local stations—and that was just the U.S. media—had all asked him to either be an interview subject or part of a debate. His main opponents in the latter were Senator Robert Kelly, whose own fear of mutants had been horribly detrimental to society, and wealthy independent politico and likely presidential candidate Graydon Creed. Strangely, however, Creed had all but disappeared from the media circus since the previous evening. Xavier suspected there was purpose behind his lack of visibility. The man knew that there would be backlash no matter what the outcome. Creed was likely preparing to take advantage of that backlash.

There were plenty of other names and faces on television—the networks were desperate to fill the tense hours with whatever spin doctors they could locate—but Creed's absence meant that Xavier and Kelly were the most prominent among them. ABC had scored a coup by setting up a debate between the two men. Charles was not looking forward to it, but he could hardly back out of it. The opportunity was too great. Many viewers would ignore his words, but many others would not. There were still rational minds and understanding hearts in America. To believe otherwise was to admit that the struggle had all been for nothing. They'd already lost.

"Shouldn't you be getting some sleep?"

Charles started slightly at the voice, then turned to see Annelise Dwyer, the CNN anchor whom he'd become rather friendly with over the past few days, walking toward him. He turned his wheelchair to face her. Privately, he was surprised that she had been able to approach him without his sensing her first. He must really be tired.

"I'd love to, but these media vultures keep picking at my corpse," he said with a grin.

"Tell me about it," she said, rolling her eyes.

Teasing, flirting, silliness in general, these were things Charles did not normally allow himself to indulge in, leaving them instead to his X-Men, who were more than happy to oblige. Even so, and despite his relationship with Lilandra, he had found himself growing quite fond of Annelise. And now, lack of sleep was making him punchy.

"So," Annelise continued, "I see you have a big date with the enemy."

"It's been one long nightmarish blind date with the enemy since this whole thing started," Xavier responded.

Annelise laughed.

"I didn't mean the media in general, Charles," she said. "I meant my number-one enemy, ABC."

"Ah." Xavier nodded. "Yes, thrown to the wolves again."

There was a silent moment, though he did not find it especially uncomfortable. The two of them merely regarded one another, each alone with their thoughts of the precipitous situation that surrounded them.

"When this is all over," Annelise ventured, "I'd like to put business aside and take you to dinner some night. You game?"

Xavier was taken slightly aback. But only for a moment.

"Without question," he answered. "But let's talk about it again, as you say, when this is all over."

* * *

Throughout the debate, Xavier had been impressed, even stunned, by the self control Senator Kelly maintained. The man was calm, rational, and, despite his feelings about mutants, eminently responsible in the way he presented his arguments. Clearly, this was a man who understood the power of his words, and the potential for panic inherent in the current predicament. Charles was very pleased that Graydon Creed had not chosen to participate in the debate. *His* favorite pastime seemed to be fomenting anarchy.

"In closing," Senator Kelly declared, "I will say only this. Our forefathers stated—and we have been fighting about these words for two hundred years—that all of us were created equal. You may call me a bigot if you wish, but I am not quibbling over such superficial differences as race, creed, or gender. Indeed, all men and women were created equal, even if they have not been treated so.

"They were equal—until the advent of mutants. Mutants are not equal to the rest of humanity. They are greater. I do not say better, but greater. More powerful, and thus inherently more dangerous. For the good of the entire world, all mutants must be registered and monitored. Mutants who prove hostile to authority must be dealt with in the harshest possible manner."

The weight of expectation fell on Charles then. The cameras, and the attention of every person in that makeshift studio, including Senator Kelly, was on him, awaiting a response.

"Senator Kelly is an intelligent man, wisely concerned for the welfare of the American people, and the future his children and grandchildren will inherit," Xavier began, playing to those millions already swayed by Kelly's speech.

"After what we have seen Magneto and his followers do, we should all be concerned," he continued. "We should all be afraid. But, I must say, no more afraid of mutant terrorism than we are of other terrorists. The men who set off a bomb in Oklahoma City, or New York's World Trade Center, are also dangerous people, not because of whatever power or weapons they might have at their disposal, but because of the hatred in their hearts.

"Magneto and his followers have not merely proven hostile to authority, they have violently usurped it. I applaud whatever measures can be taken to end this standoff quickly, and to punish those responsible for it.

"But I will not stand by while the senator, in spite of all his wisdom, suggests that we withdraw the civil rights of all mutants. There are many people proficient with guns, or martial arts, many people with extraordinary financial power or great intellect, who could be considered more than equal to the rest of us. No one has suggested we take away the civil rights of those people, who might use their special abilities in ways that make them dangerous to the general public.

"Every American has the right to a certain amount of privacy, the right to freedom of speech, the right to life, liberty, and the pursuit of happiness. These are not empty words, but the defining concepts of our nation. For them to work, they have to stand true for everyone.

"Yes, I implore you, punish criminals and terrorists, mutant or otherwise, to the full extent of the law. But protect the rights of innocent civilians who only want to live good, decent lives. These are your friends, your family, your neighbors, and you don't even know it because they are terrified of being discovered. If there were some great conspiracy, if mutants were the evil some claim, they would already rule the world. The majority of mutants wish for nothing more than to live in peace.

"Whether that will happen is really up to you."

There was silence for a moment after he'd finished. The commentator thanked Kelly and Xavier, and then signed off from the live broadcast. The moment the cameras were off, Senator Kelly crossed the short distance between the chair where he'd been seated and Xavier's wheelchair.

"Professor," he said, by way of acknowledgment.

"Senator," Xavier answered, and after a pause added, "was there something you wanted?"

"Only . . ." Kelly began, paused, and then began again. "Only to say that I know you're right. But I believe in the old axiom that sometimes the needs of the many outweigh the needs of the few," the senator said.

"Indeed?" Xavier asked, raising an eyebrow. "What you seem to have missed, Senator, is that mutants are part of the many you refer to. Part of the human race. It is you, and people like you, who are pushing them away, forcing them to splinter off, to see themselves as something else entirely. Perhaps that is your goal, but if so, you should ask yourself a question.

"If you succeed in alienating mutants, making them feel as though they are another tribe, warring with so-called 'normal' humans, what happens when enough time passes so that mutants have become 'the many,' and 'normal' humans have become 'the few'? What happens then, Senator?"

"I take your point," Kelly answered.

"I pray that you do," Xavier said.

"No matter what," the senator finished, "I hope that this whole debacle is resolved quickly, and as painlessly as possible."

Professor Xavier held up his hand. Surprise evident in his face, Kelly clasped it. They shook.

"That, at least, is something upon which we can agree," Xavier said.

Once again, his thoughts returned to hope.

• • •

"I'm gettin' a little tired o' this sittin' around crap," Wolverine snarled.

"You're not alone, old friend," Storm said, "but it isn't as if we are free to simply walk out and rejoin the fight. Not yet, at least."

"Not for lack of trying," Bishop said.

The Beast said nothing, his mind still rapidly creating and discarding plans for their escape. They had made several attempts already, all halfhearted at best. Nothing any of them had thus far contrived had had even a chance of success.

Each of them would be a formidable opponent, even without their mutant abilities. Bishop was a battle-hardened soldier, Wolverine a savage fighter without peer. Storm had spent quite a bit of time stripped of her mutant powers, and had become a hand-to-hand combatant of the first order. And the Beast's greatest asset, his intellect, was not a mutation.

Unbound, they might have fought their way to freedom without any genetic gifts at all, but the same technology that had temporarily stolen those gifts also imprisoned them.

Hank thought of Trish once again, and wondered, for the first time, if telling her to stay away had been a mistake.

X-MEN: MUTANT EMPIRE

* * *

The Sentinel at the Brooklyn Bridge had turned out to be a drone. With Archangel flying above them, Gambit raced his stolen Harley up the elevated FDR Drive as fast as he dared, while Cooper held on to his chest with a painful grip. It was taking too much time. They only had to get to the Sentinels, and have Val take a look at them with the infrared scope she had on, but still it was too time consuming.

If the Alpha Sentinel was on the other side of the island, if they had to go all the way around Manhattan before they reached it . . . there just wasn't enough time. Gambit could feel the ticking of their seven-hour time limit, could hear it as clearly as if a clock had been set next to his ear. Time was running out.

They were headed for the Williamsburg Bridge, just south of Houston Street and Alphabet City.

"Gambit, hold up!" Archangel's voice erupted from the commlink they all wore. "Pull over a minute."

"What de hell's de problem now, 'Angel?" Gambit asked. "We got no time for foolin' . . ."

"In the park, to your left," Archangel replied.

Gambit looked, and didn't see anything at first. Then Val tapped his shoulder and pointed to a group of people in the midst of a fight. At least a dozen people, maybe more, were beating on two or three others that he could barely see. Any other time, Gambit would naturally have interfered. But time was of the essence. He didn't understand why Archangel was taking such an interest.

Until he saw that one of the people being attacked had large, leathery bat wings protruding from her back.

The Harley's rear tire screeched and Gambit could smell burning rubber as he swung the bike into a stop. Val jumped off and Gambit laid the Harley down on its side as he ran for the guardrail of the elevated highway.

"Warren?" he said into the comm.

"Got it," Archangel replied.

SALVATION

"Sorry, Val," Gambit said without turning around. "We'll just be a minute."

Without hesitation, without slowing, he put one foot on the guardrail and dived over the edge. Warren grabbed him from behind. Without a word, they flew to where the three mutants were being beaten by the mob. Above the crowd, Archangel simply dropped Gambit.

Somersaulting in the air, Remy LeBeau threw four playing cards into the group, which exploded with a minor charge on impact, clearing a spot for him to land and clearing the mob away from the mutants. A moment later, Archangel landed on the other side of the bloody and beaten mutants, and the mob cleared off even further, then began to close once more.

"Just a couple more muties," one man shouted. "No problem."

Archangel took him down with a flash of silver knives, which flew from his wings and sliced into the big man, immediately and temporarily paralyzing him. The musclehead went down like a sinking stone.

"What the hell is the matter with you people?" Archangel yelled.

"You!" a woman screamed back. "You're what's wrong. All of you muties playing stormtrooper for Magneto. We caught these three on their own, figured it was time for some payback, a little vengeance for the Big Apple!"

Gambit looked back at the trio of mutants, the winged one and two others whose mutant powers or enhancements were not immediately visible.

"I was born and raised in New York," one of them said, his accent proving his claim. "We was just tryin' to leave, 'cause we didn't want no part of what Magneto's doin' here!"

"Yeah, right!" a slim Latino man cried, and tossed a hammer he'd been waving right at the mutant who had spoken.

Gambit telescoped out his bo-stick and knocked the hammer from the air, then stepped forward and whacked the Latino man on the shoulder. He hit a nerve cluster, and the man grunted in pain and fell to his knees.

"We're not afraid of you!" another man shouted.

"You idiots!" Gambit hissed. "Don' you even pay attention? You may not be afraid of us, but de t'ree mutants you attackin', dey very afraid of you, *vous comprenez*? Don' you t'ink you should maybe make sure you fightin' the enemy before you waste your time beatin' on innocent people?"

"They're muties, they're not innocent!" the same man cried.

"That's their curse," Archangel said. "They're mutants. Your curse is that you're a bigot. Unfortunately for them, they can't change what they are. The question is, can you?"

The man started to bluster something else, when a teenaged boy spoke up.

"I'm no bigot, mister," he said. "We live here. Magneto and the rest, they're trying to take our homes away."

"But these people were trying to leave, they don't want to live under Magneto any more than you do," Archangel said.

The boy was quiet then, they all were, except the bigot in the back, who grumbled under his breath but dared not say anything. The mood of the group had changed.

"Me an' Archangel, we mutants too," Gambit said. "But we come 'ere, to Manhattan, jus' to try an stop Magneto. We puttin' our lives on de line for a city dat ain't even home to us. You goin' to stomp us a little bit, too, *mes amis*?"

Even the bigot was quiet, then.

The three injured mutants said nothing as they got up and continued on their way out of the city. The Sentinels would not stop them. Gambit only hoped they did not run into any other overzealous citizens.

After they were out of sight, Gambit turned to the mob again. Nobody would look at him. When he wasn't paying attention, the bigot had slipped away, and Remy couldn't help but think he had instigated the beating. He wished he could think of something more to say, but he was disgusted, and they had no time for preaching.

Warren lifted him. As they flew off, he thought he heard the teenaged boy say something that might have been, "Thank you," and might have been something else entirely, something vile.

SALVATION

Gambit wished he could have been sure, or that he had faith enough in humanity to merely assume the best.

But he couldn't. Not today.

* * *

Lieutenant Jack Mariotte was a career soldier. The Army had put him through college, and by the time he'd finished paying them back with his service, he realized he had forgotten how to be anything else. He was old enough to know he'd never be a general, but young enough to believe if enough conflicts presented themselves, he might retire as a colonel, which meant a sweet pension and all the respect that came with the rank.

But he'd never counted on fighting Sentinels.

His squad stood ready at a battery of plasma cannons on the Jersey side of the Hudson, slightly north of the Holland Tunnel but well within range of the Sentinel who towered in silent menace over the river far below. Lieutenant Mariotte had stared at that Sentinel through part of the night, into the dawn, and throughout the morning and early afternoon. He was intimate with it now, knew every contour of its cold and sinister form.

Jack Mariotte was a brave man. He'd always prided himself on that. The Mariottes had always been a courageous family. All the way back to his grandfather, who'd been with the French underground during German occupation. Jack was brave, all right.

But the Sentinels scared the hell out of him. It was only natural, then, that he wanted very badly to destroy them.

One of the reasons the squad was so isolated was that the plasma cannons were a new technology. The media had long since lost any nationality, and coverage shown in one country was shown around the world, if it was important enough. Colonel Tomko had orders to attempt to keep the new tech off camera, to avoid letting any potential foreign enemies get a good look at it. Jack Mariotte thought that was foolishness. Espionage was alive and well—especially in the area of technology. Anyone who wanted to build a plasma cannon could get hold of the plans if they knew who to pay.

But those were his orders.

Coincidentally, their location also meant that Lieutenant Mariotte and his squad were the first, and possibly the only, people to get a good look at the boatload of mutants that was, at that moment, sailing across the Hudson River toward Manhattan.

"Look at that," Ray Keane said. "I'm tellin' ya, guys, that just ain't right."

"You ain't kidding," Bernie Tarver agreed. "We just sit here and do nothing while the muties get constant reinforcements? Why, all the people on that boat are traitors to their country. They're declaring war on us just by being there."

"We ought to blow those mutie traitors out of the water," Keane shot back. "Jesus, I can't stand just sitting here."

Lieutenant Mariotte heard all of this. He did not chastise his men, however, but rather remained silent. In fact, he agreed with them completely, but could never say so. It irked him to no end that they had to sit there, under the threatening glare of the Sentinels, and do nothing as Magneto continued to build his army.

"Traitors!" Tarver screamed across the water to the mutants on the boat, which was, even now, passing less than eighty yards away from them.

"Tarver!" Jack snapped. "Belay that crap!"

"But, Loot, those guys—" Tarver began.

"I gave you an order, Corporal!"

"Yes, sir!" Corporal Tarver replied, and offered a stiff salute.

It might have been over then, but Tarver's cry had not been overlooked by the mutants on the boat, who began taunting them immediately.

"What's wrong, soldier boys?" called one of the mutants, a woman whose hair and skin glowed with a weird blue light. "You flatscans worried that you'll be out of a job once the Mutant Empire starts to spread?"

"Nobody respond!" Jack ordered, and his men complied with obvious reluctance. He didn't blame them. In fact, he figured none of them wanted to scream back at the traitors more than he did.

"No answer, kids?" the woman screamed. "Well, I'm through being ignored!"

A flash of blue light arced across the surface of the water and fried Corporal Bernie Tarver where he stood. The entire squad shielded their eyes from the flash, and when they looked up, Bernie was a memory. The only thing left was a black scar on the shore of the Hudson.

"Mutie freaks!" Keane shouted as he cranked the plasma cannon around to sight on the boat.

"Take cover!" Lieutenant Mariotte ordered. "Do not return fire! Sergeant Keane, do you hear me? I said do not return—"

But Keane didn't hear Jack Mariotte's order. His own screams were too loud. The lieutenant could only watch as a massive plasma burst lanced out toward the boat, and the vessel exploded in a shower of wood, metal and flesh.

"Jesus," the lieutenant whispered.

"Lieutenant!" a green private named Carlos Mattei shouted, and pointed south, across the river.

Before he turned his head, Lieutenant Mariotte felt the nausea rising in his stomach. He knew exactly what Mattei was looking at. The only thing he could be looking at.

Across the river, just to the south, the massive robot head of the Sentinel had turned in their direction. Its red eyes glowed, even though the sun was shining above. It seemed unnatural, impossible somehow, and all the more frightening because of that.

The Sentinel's upper body turned. It lifted an arm, palm up, aiming its weapons systems directly at them. Whether or not it planned to fire was a question that never even occurred to Lieutenant Jack Mariotte. Armageddon was riding down on them hard, and they'd no time to leap from its path, no way to avoid being trampled. Save one. Fight back.

"All stations fire," Jack Mariotte cried, then lowered his voice to a whisper. "And may God have mercy on us all."

CHAPTER 7

The foundation of Haven was going extremely well. There were dozens of Alpha-level mutants, and more than a hundred Betas, who had already joined the empire's ranks. However, Magneto was even more pleased by the number of nonpowered—and therefore most likely noncombatant—mutants who had either emerged from lives of ridicule in New York, or traveled some distance to the welcoming arms of a real home.

Some had intellects accelerated by the mutant x-factor in their genetic codes. Others had minor abilities, enhanced senses, light psi talents. And quite a few of those were also monstrous or bestial in appearance. These misfits and outcasts were the real reason Magneto had created Haven. They needed sanctuary quite badly indeed.

He had gathered these noncombatants so that he might address them, explain that Haven was for them. While some were nervous and flip, most were honored to be in his presence. Several could not contain their need to speak of their pasts, their pitiful existences before Magneto became their savior, and he allowed them the opportunity.

One by one, more than a dozen mutants testified, like sinners at a tent revival, about their suffering, and about their undying gratitude that they had finally found a home.

"Thank you, Emperor Magneto," said a large man whose enhanced senses of smell, taste, and hearing were not enough to compensate for the ferociously canine structure of his face. "I have waited my whole life for salvation, and I'd almost given up until a couple of days ago. We owe you a debt that can never be paid."

Magneto was about to respond when Amelia Voght entered, followed by Unuscione, Cargil, Javits, and the Kleinstock Brothers.

"Voght," he said sternly. "What did I say about—"

"It's begun, my lord," Voght snapped, cutting him off. "The military and the Sentinels have begun firing upon one another all around the island."

SALVATION

Magneto stared at her, brow furrowed in anger and amazement.

"I wish you were joking," he said. "They must be out of their minds, to think they might win such a conflict! The arrogant fools!"

"Is it possible, my lord, that the Sentinels attacked first?" Unuscione asked.

Magneto sneered at her.

"Not at all," he said. "They were programmed to attack only on my order, or in retaliation for a mass attack on mutants."

He paused, listened for the sounds of battle, but could hear nothing so far from the action.

"It's war, then," he said finally. "The Sentinels should be sufficient to destroy any opposition, but I need to be in a position from which to monitor the progress of the conflict. I must go."

Without so much as a wave to acknowledge the Acolytes, or the gathered noncombatant mutants, Magneto was suddenly enveloped in a sphere of crackling energy. Eighteen inches from the floor, he floated toward the huge row of windows. At his approach, glass exploded outward in a spray of jagged shards.

Then he was gone.

Gone to war.

* * *

"All right, then," Voght began. "To work."

She looked around the room at the noncombatant mutants gathered within and, for the first time, truly wondered if Magneto had done them a service by bringing them all together. If Haven survived, of course, they had a wonderful new home. But if Haven collapsed, all they had done was uproot themselves, and many of them had revealed their mutant nature for the first time in their lives. They had had enough faith to believe in Magneto, though, and Voght realized she would have to do the same.

If Haven fell, life would become even more difficult for those mutants who had gathered on the island.

Voght shook her head a moment, gathering her thoughts and her plans.

"What's wrong, Amelia, haven't got the stomach for a real fight, now that one's knockin' at our door?" Unuscione said, a sneer slashing her face. "Cowardice rears its ugly head every time, eh?"

Fighting the urge to snap or strike out at Unuscione, Voght instead simply ignored her.

"Cargil," she said, "go down and relieve whoever is guarding the X-Men. I want one of the Acolytes' inner circle there, looking after our prize catch like your life depended on it. Which, of course, it may."

Before Voght had even finished issuing her instructions, Joanna Cargil was out the door and headed for the elevator. Cargil might not have been on her side, as it were, in the personality conflict she had going with Unuscione, but she knew enough not to jeopardize a combat situation because of individual gripes. She was a soldier.

"Javits, how do you feel?" she asked.

The towering, hugely muscled mutant merely shrugged, raising his eyebrows. Enough of an indication that he was ready for battle, despite wounds he had recently received from Wolverine. It made Voght realize just how many of them Wolverine had injured in the past couple of days, including the Kleinstock brothers. Sven and Harlan had been uncharacteristically silent since their battle with Wolverine. A newly arrived mutant who'd used her healing powers on the evangelical circuit before getting the call—not from God but from Magneto—had healed them both. It hadn't improved their dispositions any.

No question, Wolverine was a dangerous man. Voght was glad he was already their prisoner. Things would go a lot more smoothly with him in a basement cell.

"Okay," she said. "The rookies will be gathering in the lobby and on the street even as we speak. Unuscione, you and Javits head down there and get them moving. I want to touch base with Skolnick at City Hall. Then I'll join you.''

"What about us?'' Harlan Kleinstock asked. "What are we supposed to do?''

"You two are going to see that the noncombatants get down to street level and on their way as quickly as possible. We want them back in their new homes and out of the way ASAP. Then you're with me,'' Voght explained.

Which didn't go over well at all.

"You think you're something else, don't you?'' Sven Kleinstock said. "Magneto appoints you field leader and you get to believing that makes you good at it.''

"It doesn't really matter what I think, Sven,'' Voght said sharply. "And it matters even less what you think. Magneto gave me the job, and I'm going to do it. You have a problem with that, why don't you take it up with him? I've got work to do. We all do.''

Harlan Kleinstock started to speak, perhaps, Amelia considered, because Sven was not bright enough to reply on his own. But Unuscione took a step forward, a cruel smile curling her lip into an unattractive scowl.

"You've made your last mistake, Amelia,'' Unuscione said, pleasantly enough for a woman with murder in her eyes.

"Back off, Carmela,'' Voght snapped. "Now is not the time. Haven is in jeopardy.''

"The hell with that,'' Unuscione said coolly. "We've got the Sentinels to protect us, and Lord Magneto watching out for the big robots. If he needs us at all, it won't be right away.''

Voght sighed. She had never despised anyone as fervently as she hated Carmela Unuscione. She wanted very badly to give Unuscione the lesson the woman had been begging for since Amelia was first made field leader. But now was simply not the time.

Yet, that might not be her call. With Cargil already gone to guard the captured X-Men, and Senyaka down at City Hall with Major Skolnick . . . hell, even the Blob, Toad, and Pyro weren't around. But she supposed she should be grateful for that. Given their appreciation for Unuscione's father, Voght assumed they'd come down on the other woman's side in a conflict, despite their supposed fealty to Magneto.

Cargil and Senyaka, while by no means her friends, would have fulfilled their obligations as Magneto's Acolytes, would have put Haven first. Milan was in the nerve center of the new empire, and he was her only real friend in the ranks of the Acolytes. Even Javits, whose life she had saved only days earlier, was not speaking up for her.

"We're not following you anymore, Voght," Harlan Klein-stock said. "Every time you're in charge, we take a beating. Wolverine almost killed me and my brother last time. You can't be trusted."

"That's how it is?" Voght asked.

There was no response from any of them, save for the widening smile on Unuscione's face.

"We're electing a new field leader, Amelia," Unuscione said. "Namely, me. See, you were killed in the line of duty. I had to take over."

Sven Kleinstock and Javits both started slightly at her mention of killing.

"You didn't say anything about killing her, Unuscione," Sven warned. "She may be a pain, but she's still one of us."

"Shut up, Sven," Voght ordered.

"Fine," Sven said with a shrug. "The hell with you. Die if you want to."

"That's not going to happen," Voght said, and took two steps back, giving herself room to maneuver. "You wanted it, Unuscione? Well, now you've got it. Come and get me. It's time you found out what it means to be in pain."

"Back off, boys," Unuscione motioned to the others to give them room. "This is just between the two of us."

With an electric crackle, Unuscione's psionic exoskeleton appeared in a flash of green light. Voght leaped aside as Unuscione attacked, barely escaping the huge fist of psionic energy that devastated the podium behind her. The noncombatants scattered as Voght landed, knocking chairs aside as she turned to face her attacker.

SALVATION

"You have no idea who or what you're dealing with," Voght said.

"Sure I do," Unuscione said. "A dead woman."

She lunged for Voght again, her exoskeleton stretching out even farther this time. Once more, Amelia barely escaped. Quickly, she tried to grab on to the green force shield that surrounded Unuscione's body.

"Oh, come on," Unuscione yelled, retracting her exoskeleton instantly. "You didn't think I'd let you do that to me again, did you?"

Voght smiled grimly.

"No," she said, and teleported.

Even as she appeared back in her bedroom, and grabbed up the taser gun lying on the desk that functioned as her bedside table, she smiled at the picture in her head. In it, Unuscione and her cronies looked around the room in astonishment for three or four seconds as it began to come into their dim brains that she had actually left.

Then she 'ported back into the room in an instant. Without an enemy to attack, Unuscione had let her guard down, had dropped her exoskeleton in confusion. When Voght appeared in front of her, Unuscione was too stunned to react immediately. She barely saw the taser coming.

Voght fired the taser at Unuscione. Its projectiles popped out and snagged themselves on her uniform, and she jerked around in agony as electricity flooded through her.

"Hey, no fair!" one of the Kleinstocks, or perhaps both—Voght wasn't sure—called out. They reminded her of little boys in the schoolyard. Little boys she had always trounced for pulling her hair. They used to shout "no fair" as well.

Children. That's what they were. Sometimes she wondered if that was what they all were, in the end.

Unuscione was still jerking madly, and Voght yanked back the taser's wired projectiles. Unuscione stopped jerking and glared at her, a twitch on her face that hadn't been there before. A side effect, Voght guessed, of being electroshocked.

"You should have killed me, Amelia," Unuscione said. "It's over for you now."

Unuscione lifted her arms to guide her exoskeleton, but it did not appear. Voght saw the confusion on her face. She knew that the taser had momentarily shorted out the other woman's powers, just for a heartbeat, but she wasn't going to be the one to explain.

She was going to be busy.

"What the . . . ?" Unuscione said.

Voght hit her. She felt a couple of the bones in her hand crack as her fist slammed into Unuscione's face, but it didn't hurt at all. It felt kind of good, actually.

Good enough that she hit Unuscione again.

Fifteen seconds or so later, when she had hit Unuscione many more times, the Kleinstock brothers pulled her off. She teleported them away, dropping them onto the metal chairs from near the ceiling of the room. Unuscione was rising from the ground, blood streaming from her nose and mouth. She still had that snarl that so infuriated Voght. Her exoskeleton was weakly shimmering into being.

Voght kicked her in the gut and Unuscione went down hard, the smirking scowl gone from her face.

"You're out of here," she said, and teleported Unuscione away.

Away.

"What the hell have you done with her?" Harlan Kleinstock demanded angrily.

"I've sent her back to Avalon," Voght responded evenly. "The space station has medical facilities, and Exodus has personnel who can deal with her. She is no longer a part of this mission. Magneto will be very disappointed."

Sven Kleinstock started to move forward, but Harlan stopped him.

"What, Sven?" Voght snapped. "You want to try me too? You don't think much of me as leader, but, by God, you follow orders or I'll teleport your numbskull head right off your shoulders. I don't think either of us wants that, now do we?"

No answer.

"Get moving, all of you," Voght commanded. "Magneto

has made a home for all of us. The least you can do is defend it!''

* * *

Magneto rose above the Empire State Building and propelled himself, effortlessly, toward the Hudson River. The pessimist in him had always assumed that the Mutant Empire could not succeed unless the military had tested his power, and the power of the Sentinels, and realized that they could not be overcome by any conventional means.

But at heart, he was an optimist. He had hoped very deeply that such a conflict would not be necessary. Magneto had no desire to see humanity destroyed, to see cities crumble. His goals raised him above such petty sadism.

Unfortunately, it appeared that the American government was not as rational as he had believed. His opinion of human politicians and soldiers was so low already that this attack, forcing him to lower that opinion even further, was nothing short of astonishing for him.

Already he could hear the plasma cannonfire, and see one of his Sentinels ahead, responding to its attackers with cold, calculated, deadly assaults. As Magneto looked on, the Sentinel blasted an army chopper from the air, and he wondered, idly, why there had not been an air force strike on the Sentinels yet. It didn't seem to fit. It was almost as if the military had not been prepared for the attack, though they had initiated it.

No matter. *Let the humans underestimate me*, he thought. *It will be the end of them. The Mutant Empire will only come more quickly.*

A low, familiar voice whispered in his brain: *Magnus, it's time we had a little talk, wouldn't you say?*

Magneto smiled to himself. He had known it was only a matter of time before Charles Xavier would attempt to contact him directly. Now that war had finally come, Xavier could put it off no longer. Which did not necessarily mean Magneto had to acknowledge him.

I don't think there's anything to talk about, Charles, Magneto thought in response, knowing that Xavier, the world's most powerful telepath, would pick it up.

No, Xavier retorted, and as their minds touched, Magneto felt his old friend's essence, familiar and yet hostile. The foundation of their present relationship. *No, I doubted that you would. However, I must insist. You would be well advised to get something solid beneath you now. You have five seconds.*

Magneto sighed, and lowered himself rapidly to the roof of an apartment building below. Just as his feet touched down, he felt a little queasy, and the world about him began to change. It didn't happen in an eyeblink, but unfolded as if the real world were being torn away, leaving a fabulous landscape behind.

His eyes wide open, Magneto could barely perceive the moment when he moved from tangible reality onto the Astral Plane. But the moment the world began to collapse, the moment buildings and sky peeled away to reveal a dark void, he knew Xavier had yanked his consciousness from his body, into the Astral Plane, so that this conversation could take place.

It appeared to be an asteroid field, the huge stones hurling leisurely through space. But it was an odd version of space, with air and gravity, but no sound. Somehow, in the back of his head, Magneto could hear the sounds of the city he'd left. Or, rather, the city his mind had left. His body was still there, lying, or perhaps standing, since the ground beneath him felt so real, on the top of that same apartment building.

But there was no sound on the Astral Plane. Nothing. Dead air, with a trace of the hiss you hear when you pick up a phone and the lines are down. That was it. It was a sensation he had never become completely comfortable with.

He was also uncomfortable because, without reservation, the Astral Plane belonged to Charles Xavier. Other of the world's telepaths might travel through it, but Xavier was, for all intents and purposes, its master and proprietor.

Magnus, Xavier's mental voice said, and Magneto heard it inside his mind, just as all conversations were held in the silence of the Astral Plane.

Glancing around, he saw Xavier standing on an asteroid

just a short way from his own. He did not approach, however. Let the master of the game make the first move, he had always believed. That was the only way to learn.

It's nice to see you standing, Charles, Magneto said pleasantly. *The chair always makes you look so old.*

Xavier ignored the statement, as Magneto had known he would. But it had always fascinated him that Xavier's astral image did not share his physical body's affliction. He had never been sure if that was because Xavier did not truly consider himself crippled, or because the man was embarrassed by his vulnerability.

I did not want to do this, Xavier thought. *You have left me no choice but to become more directly involved. You realize I could end this now, simply make your mind, your every thought, just go away, though we are separated by miles?*

Of course I know that, Charles, Magneto scoffed. *Just as I know that you would never take such a radical course. It isn't in you. That is part of your weakness, and part of the weakness of your great dream of harmony between humans and mutants. You've just never been very realistic about such things. If I were you, I would have taken me out of the game long ago.*

There was a silence on their mental connection. Then, finally, Xavier's voice in his head again.

Food for thought.

Indeed. But you had something you wanted to discuss, I believe. Don't worry, I haven't killed any of your X-Men. At least, not yet, Magneto thought.

And you won't, Xavier replied calmly. *Not in cold blood. In any case, I haven't dragged you here to discuss the X-Men. As I don't imagine my asking you to set them free would do any good, let's move on to the more immediate subject, shall we? The topic, old friend, is war.*

It surely is, and history is written by the victors.

There are no victors in war, only victims.

Are you going somewhere with this, Charles, or shall I get on with the defense of my nascent empire? Magneto thought.

Xavier sighed. *I am the eternal optimist, Magnus. I con-*

tinue to overestimate you, I suppose. In any case, I have something to show you.

The image of Xavier on the Astral Plane lifted its right hand and gestured. The depths and blackness of space, the moon and stars and asteroids, disappeared. The universe dropped away beneath Magneto and Xavier, and was replaced by a scene of human madness. A highway, cars packed in bumper to bumper, moving just slightly faster than grass grows. People walked alongside, or hung from buses and the backs of military transports.

They're evacuating, Magneto observed, and he could not hide the tinge of surprise in his mental voice. Not that he could have hidden anything from Xavier if the telepath was determined to discover it.

They're evacuating, he thought once more. *Why?*

Come, now, you know the answer to that, Xavier thought. *One of your greatest flaws has always been your underestimation of humanity. In this case, that flaw could be fatal, not merely for yourself, but for hundreds of thousands, probably millions, of people, and an entire city. Never mind the outlying areas.*

They wouldn't dare, Magneto thought, aghast.

That's precisely the attitude I'm talking about. It could cost us our world if you're not careful. In truth, it may already be too late.

What are you babbling about?

Only this, Xavier thought, spreading his arms wide once again to indicate the massive evacuation effort "below" them. *Everything within forty miles of the island of Manhattan is being evacuated, even as we speak. Now that your Sentinels have attacked federal troops—*

They started it! Magneto barked.

How mature of you, Xavier thought, with a shake of his head. His eyes slowly closed, then opened again, a reaction to frustration and disappointment that Magneto knew all too well.

Now that this war has begun, did you honestly think that the President of the United States was going to allow you to win, under any circumstances? Xavier asked.

SALVATION

Magneto smiled. This was more familiar, more confident, territory for him. Xavier was underestimating him again.

Allow me? he laughed. *I don't need anyone to allow me to win. Nor do I need any assistance. Haven is established. It exists. It is too late for anyone to stop that. They may send all the soldiers and weapons they have against me, and they will eventually be forced to respect the sovereignty of the island. And then the growing empire. If you mean to imply that the President is considering the use of nuclear weapons, I find that rather amusing, actually. New York City is far too important to be destroyed. Even if they could get the coordinates recalibrated instantly, between myself and the Sentinels, we could repulse any nuclear attack.*

You believe I underestimate you, Xavier observed. *Untrue. What is true, unfortunately, is that you underestimate the pride, will, and arrogance of humanity. Let me tell you, now, the truth. See if you can recognize it as it presents itself to you. The Pentagon does not need to recalibrate its trajectories and coordinates with any great speed. Russia, a nation that hates you above all other living creatures, is more than willing to take the first shot, destroy all of New York City, if that's what it takes. The American missiles can take their sweet time. No matter how powerful you believe yourself to be, neither you nor the Sentinels can turn them all back.*

Xavier moved his astral form closer as he continued: *These people are being evacuated from their homes to prevent them from being incinerated in case the bomb drops. Not only is nuclear attack one of the options the President is considering, but he has the backing of a lot of Americans. You have drawn about you nearly twenty percent of the world's mutant population. You've made yourself the perfect target. If they destroy New York, they kill you and many of the world's mutants as well. A banner day, a lot of humans would say. Especially now, after what you've done.*

You've miscalculated, Magnus, Xavier thought, shaking his head as he seemed to hover above the ground. *You may have cost us all our lives.*

Ah, Charles, Magneto replied, shaking his own head. *You*

consider yourself an optimist. I would call you a pessimist. Perhaps I have underestimated the courage or the insanity of human society. Even so, I am not concerned. You see, I will be the victor here today. And every day after. It seems to me, if you are so concerned about what the humans might do to our mutant brothers, your only logical course would be to pray I am triumphant. It's entirely possible that, for once, I am the lesser of two evils.

Now, if you're through, I have a war to run.

Magneto felt the heaviness of his body, bogging him down as uncomfortably as if he'd taken a swim fully clothed. He opened his eyes, and blinked back the glare of the sun. The sounds of battle returned to him, and he rose once again into the blue sky over Manhattan.

Xavier had certainly been uncharacteristically curt in ending their communication. Not that Magneto minded; he had better things to do than float around in the psionic ether with a man unwilling to make the most of his extraordinary power. Xavier followed the old maxim, "With great power comes great responsibility." Magneto believed it as well, but interpreted it differently. He could never understand why Xavier would not work to make a home for mutantkind by any means necessary. That was Magneto's maxim.

By any means necessary.

His contact with Xavier had disturbed him a bit. It was entirely possible that Charles was right, that he had begun a chain reaction that could not possibly end in anything but tragedy of incredible proportions. Not that Magneto had lost faith in his ability to triumph. But things had now progressed past the point at which he might be able to prevent whatever catastrophe might result from his defeat.

Therefore, defeat was not an option.

Magneto again considered the brief moments he had spent on the Astral Plane with his old friend and longtime enemy. The nature of the Astral Plane is pure psionic energy—in this case, energy manipulated by Charles Xavier. When Magneto had been drawn there in the past, the place had always been sterile and cold. But this time, there had been a pervasive

SALVATION

feeling of despair in that limbo of souls, of minds.

Charles Xavier's despair.

That bothered him. Xavier was the self-described eternal optimist. Yet he did not merely fear the potential outcome, he was tortured by it. Otherwise Magneto would never have been able to feel even a hint of Xavier's true emotion in his astral presence.

Magneto took a cleansing breath, pushing from his mind anything that might distract him from the protection of the sanctuary he had fought so hard to establish. Several blocks away, a Sentinel was under constant attack from a military helicopter with astounding evasive capacity.

With a moment's concentration, Magneto reached out with his power and grabbed hold of the machine. An errant thought, and the copter was hurled to the surface of the Hudson River, where it exploded on impact.

By any means necessary.

CHAPTER 8

The rhythm of the elevator, up and down, the swoosh of opening and closing doors, the drone of people talking . . . all of it had started to get to Bobby. He struggled to keep his eyes open, stifled a yawn, and tried to pay attention to what was happening in the elevator. Another fifteen minutes, that's all he would give it, and then he'd have to think of some other way to find the X-Men.

By now, he figured, Magneto's followers must know that someone had broken into the building. Were probably looking for him even now. And if he was captured, well, that would be it for the X-Men.

The elevator lurched to a stop. Even before the doors slid open, he could hear the shouts on the floor they'd reached.

"Move it, move it, move it!" a woman barked. "They want a war, people, let's give 'em one! Let's go, move out. You'll get assignments when you hit the street!"

"What the hell's happening here?" a man barked from inside the elevator, and then it rose slightly as the man stepped out onto the floor.

"The feds have attacked!" the same woman snapped in response. "The Sentinels are responding, but we've all got to be in position to finish this fight. You want a home in Haven, buddy, you've gotta fight for it!"

"I had guard duty in the basement in half an hour," the man said. "What about that?"

"The Acolytes have the X-geeks covered, man," the woman snapped. "Just do as you're told. I don't have all day to waste explaining myself to every moron who comes along. Just move!"

Bobby heard pounding feet, cursing . . . an exodus of sorts. Then the elevator started to move up again, called to another floor. That was okay. Ten more minutes, and the place would be near empty. He could slip into the elevator and head for the basement. Or, he could use the a/c ducts. Maybe the stairs? What the hell, he'd figure it out. The most important thing was, he knew where the X-Men were being held. And since the enemy was practically evacuating the building, he would have no trouble getting to them.

Of course, the faceless woman had said the Acolytes were guarding the X-Men. That could be a problem. Bobby crossed his fingers and prayed that it would be *Acolyte*, not *Acolytes*. Which was pretty likely. After all, Magneto would need all the help he could find for a war with the United States.

That thought also troubled him. How had it come to war? Was the President really that foolish? Or perhaps it had been Gyrich's doing. That sounded more likely.

Still, Bobby pictured all the places in Manhattan that he treasured, from Central Park, to Fifth Avenue, to the Coffee-A-Go-Go, to the White Horse Tavern in the Village, and Keen's Chophouse on the Lower West Side. Broadway. The Museum of Natural History. It was all in jeopardy.

Iceman was the joker on the team, but as he began to plan his next move, he dwelled too much on what fate might hold for what he considered the greatest city in the world. And there was nothing funny about it. Nothing at all.

* * *

Val Cooper clung tightly to Remy LeBeau. The Harley was flying along the FDR Drive, headed north. With the wind buffeting her face, whipping her hair back and forth like a flag, her hands on Gambit's washboard abdomen, and the motorcycle humming with power beneath them, she should have felt great. The sun shone down on them, and the sky above Manhattan was unusually clear. None of that mattered.

Instead, she was filled with a profound sense of dread. Not nausea, really, but that first sickening stomach lurch that tells you nausea is on the way. It was that feeling, yet sustained.

With the pavement speeding by below her, and nothing holding her on the Harley but her grip on Gambit and the scissor lock her knees had on the seat, she felt extraordinarily vulnerable. But that wasn't the cause of her extreme unease. She'd been on a motorcycle many times before.

No. Val was disturbed because of the distant thump-thump of explosions she could hear. It was war. She knew it was.

Which meant they had very little time in which to prevent armageddon. It had fallen to them, really: herself, Gambit, and Archangel. She only prayed that these two unpredictable men would come through at perhaps the most precipitous moment the United States had ever faced.

"Number six, dead ahead, Val," Archangel's voice crackled on the comm-link.

"We got visual, 'Angel," Gambit replied, before Val could even think of anything to say. "Valerie, can you see from 'ere, or we gon' have to get a bit closer, eh?"

He barely turned to look at her when asking the question, but Val was entranced by the red glow of his eyes. She had been fascinated by those eyes from the very first time she had met Gambit. The eyes were the window to the soul, it was said. A cliché, she knew. But there was a point to it. You could always read the truth in someone's eyes. Except for Gambit's. His eyes were like burning coals in any battle situation. Impossible to read anything in them but danger.

Cooper slid a hand away from its grip on Gambit, reached up, and tapped a button on the side of the infrared goggles she wore. They had the capacity to magnify anything in view, so it had been possible from quite a distance to check Sentinels for the invisible markings that would signify the Alpha unit. This one, however, was turned away from them at an angle.

"We're going to need to get closer," she said finally. "Or at least find another angle on it."

"You jus' tell Gambit where you need to go, Valerie. I take you dere."

Bellevue Hospital and NYU Medical Center blurred past on the left. It struck Val that there were probably a lot of people holed up in hospitals and places of worship around the city. People too stubborn to leave, but too frightened to remain in their own homes. With every concussive blast on the other side of the island, she grew more worried for Manhattan, and its people.

The Sentinel towered above the UN building, just blocks ahead now. There was a huge explosion to the south, and Val shivered as she realized the war was quickly spreading. She wanted to blame someone. Magneto. Gyrich. The President. Somebody. She needed a face to focus her hatred upon, to condemn for starting the war that would surely kill innocents.

But it was too late for blame. She'd seen enough warfare, in the Middle East and Genosha, not to know that. War was the villain now, war was the enemy. It was the ultimate killer, primal rage unleashed without any conscience whatsoever. It had to be stopped.

"Warren," Val said to Archangel over the comm, "we're going in for a closer look. I can't get a decent view from the highway."

"Be careful, Val," Archangel cautioned. "All three of us are vital to the success of this mission. We can't afford any screwups."

"You're the master of understatement, Warren," Val observed. "With the battle started, the clock is ticking."

Gambit steered the Harley down off the FDR, and they hit the side streets of Manhattan. At First Avenue and Forty-ninth Street, several teenagers came running across a small park, shouting at them, trying to get their attention, and, apparently, assistance.

"Great, more trouble." Archangel sighed softly into the comm. "What now?"

"Nothing, Warren, keep moving," Val said.

Gambit started to slow the Harley.

"Gambit, keep going!" she snapped. "Didn't you hear me? The clock is ticking! We don't have time for anything but the mission now. No matter what we see, we've got to keep going!"

The Cajun started to open his mouth, likely with some smart-aleck response. Then he closed it again. Gambit knew she was right, of course. But she took no pleasure from having her way. As they passed the teens, who still cried out for their help, Val could see that it was not a trick of any kind. These kids needed help; someone, or something, was threatening them.

"We be back for you, kids," Gambit called to them, but even if the kids heard and understood him, their faces did not betray any indication that they believed what he had said.

Frankly, Val didn't believe it either. Even if they took the Sentinels out of the game, the fight wasn't over. But as long as the Sentinels were a part of the equation, the answer was always going to be the same. Magneto would win.

"Hang a right here, Remy," Val said, and Gambit nodded once and swung over to the east side of the avenue. "That's going to put us right between the thing's legs."

"An' you t'ink dis is a good idea?" Gambit asked, his sarcasm as cutting as ever.

But he took the turn. They slowed to make the corner, and Val finally saw Archangel out of the corner of her eye. He didn't acknowledge them, and even from the ground, he looked so grim that Val imagined him to be some colorful angel of death. It wasn't a pleasant thought.

"Dere," Gambit said, as they took the turn.

Directly in front of them, the Sentinel straddling the street like a modern Colossus of Rhodes.

To their left, the south wall of the United Nations building exploded outward in a shower of glass and concrete. Gambit opened up the throttle, speeding away from the explosion and toward the massive Sentinel.

"Incoming!" Archangel shouted, and now he was close enough so Val could have heard him without their comm-link.

"A little late on dat one, *mon ami*," Gambit called back.

Val exhaled, and couldn't remember when she'd last taken a breath. Her body was humming with the energy of anticipating the next explosion, or whatever else might come. For it wasn't the Sentinel attacking. The huge construct was itself under attack.

"We getting too close, *petite*," Gambit said, and Val was so absorbed by their situation that she ignored the diminutive, sexist reference.

Gambit braked, the Harley slid sideways, tires streaking pavement, black on black. They stopped, and Val took another breath. For the first time since they had turned the corner, Val ignored everything around her, tapped the button on her goggles, and studied the Sentinel ahead.

SALVATION

Painted on the Sentinel's back with a substance invisible in all but one light spectrum, infrared, was a massive symbol: the Greek letter Omega. The end. A small joke, back when Val Cooper could still find anything funny.

"That's it!" she cried. "That's the Alpha Sentinel!"

"All right!" Archangel cheered. "Now let's take this tin man apart."

Without warning, a barrage of plasma fire and concussive blasts slammed into the Sentinel, which still faced away from them. It turned its massive head, apparently toward the source of the attack, and lifted a hand. Energy lanced from its palm and ought to have flash-fried whatever it had aimed at. But the attack continued.

"It's time, Valerie," Gambit said. "Maybe you should contact Professor Xavier before we go any farther. Dat Sentinel, he won' let you near him if he knows you're human."

Val nodded, then leaned forward to switch channels on the comm-unit.

"Charles?" she asked. "Are you there?"

Yes, Professor Xavier answered, but the voice was in her head, not on the comm. *I've been monitoring your progress, Val. Now that you have need of me, I'm going to stay with you from here on in.*

"Thanks," Val said aloud, knowing he could hear her one way or another. "It's a comfort to know you're with us. Okay, Warren, Remy, let's get inside that robot's head and see if we can't rearrange things a bit."

Gambit opened the throttle and the Harley shot forward.

* * *

"Do you think she'll go for it?" Trish Tilby asked.

Kevin O'Leary shrugged. "Your guess is as good as mine."

After a moment's consideration, Trish went to the window and looked outside again. The madness in the street was growing, with mutants congregating in front of the lobby and then marching off in groups in different directions. Even inside the building, they could hear the muffled, rapid-fire crack of far-away explosions, like fireworks in the distance. Trish wondered idly if the war might not look like a massive fireworks display, once the sun set.

It dawned on her, then, that Manhattan might be gone long before sundown. Someone had to do something. The only people capable of halting the insanity and destruction were captive in the basement of the Empire State Building, many floors below. They had to get down there, no matter what. No matter who was hurt by it.

"Get your gear," she told Kevin, and he nodded grimly.

More often than not, he was an outgoing, generally happy guy. Not today. But, hell, who could blame him?

Kevin packed up his camera bag with everything he might need. Magneto had seen that they lacked nothing by way of equipment. He hefted the bag to his shoulder, picked up the camera, and gave Trish the thumbs-up.

"Let's go," she said.

They headed out of the small office into the larger foyer area of the firm that had used the space before Magneto took over. Caroline was there, waiting for them.

"What the hell are you doing?" Caroline asked, in a hushed voice, talking more to Kevin than to Trish.

"We're here to cover Magneto's new world order, Caroline," Trish said simply. "This is the biggest part of the story so far. We've got to do our job."

"Yeah, but . . ." she sputtered, then moved to block their access to the door. "Look, you guys, I've put my butt on the line for you already. I really like you, and I know you're not, like, the enemy or anything. But you aren't supposed to go out and tape—heck, you're not supposed to go out at all— without Magneto's say-so."

Kevin approached Caroline and put a hand on her cheek. Trish winced at the way the girl almost seemed to lean into that hand, looking for something to lean on, someone to care. She hoped Kevin really did care, that it wasn't all just a game, a way to get out. Caroline was a sweet kid, though obviously misled. Or, at the very least, misinformed. She didn't deserve heartbreak.

But then, Trish thought, who did?

"Caroline, let's get down to it, huh?" Kevin said.

Not at all the way Trish thought he'd handle it.

"I like you," he said. "I really do. If the world wasn't upside down, I'd love to go out to a movie, maybe have one too many drinks at the Slaughtered Lamb. Hell, I'd like to buy you some roses and rollerblade through Central Park, if you'd like to know the truth of it."

Kevin shook his head just a bit, and his sigh told Trish what she'd wanted to know all along. He wasn't just playing. He really did care for the girl. But with that settled, she still had to wonder if they were using her unfairly.

Hell, she thought. *It's war, right?*

"Kevin," Caroline said. "I—"

"No, let me finish," he interrupted. "I'd like to do all those things. But I can't. We can't. And you know why we can't, don't you?"

Their eyes met, locked, and suddenly Trish felt very much like an intruder. She wanted to crawl under the rug, to flee into the back office. But she didn't dare. Too much rested on the next few moments.

After an excruciating pause, Caroline nodded.

"Good," Kevin said. "If you didn't get it, I don't know how I could have explained it to you. This isn't utopia, sweetheart, and it isn't hell either. One thing for certain, though, it isn't anything like the land of the free that Magneto promised."

"You're not really going out to cover the war, are you?" Caroline asked, looking up at Kevin from beneath long eyelashes.

"You know we're not," Kevin said.

Trish knew that was her cue.

"Caroline," she said, the apology explicit in her voice, "we can do this a lot of ways, but however we do it, it's going to be fast. We can tie you up and leave you here, or we can take you with us. You can try to stop us if you want to, but I think you know the difference between right and wrong, though it's taken you a while to see it."

"You're going to try to free the X-Men?" Caroline asked, though in her face Trish could see that the woman already knew the answer.

"We've no choice," Kevin said. "They're the only hope we've got. Don't you see that nothing good can come of this? Magneto is just going to get himself and a whole lot of other people killed."

"Magneto will kill me," Caroline replied, the terrible words delivered in a drifting, matter-of-fact tone.

"No," Trish interjected quickly. "No, I don't think he would. But the Acolytes would do it in a heartbeat. You've got to come with us."

"You need my help?" Caroline asked.

"We can use all the help we can get," Kevin answered. "But you don't have to help us. Even if you don't, I—I'd still like you to leave here with us, with the X-Men. It isn't safe for you around here, no matter what. Please say you'll come."

Trish was a little taken aback. Kevin usually hid himself behind an impenetrable wall of good humor and sarcasm, a potent mixture. Charm ruled, but it hid raw emotion as well. What she saw now was a Kevin O'Leary stripped bare of all pretension.

Trish could feel the afternoon shadows lengthening in the room around them.

"We've got to move, Caroline," she said. "Everything depends on the X-Men, and the X-Men are depending on us."

Caroline looked at Trish, then back at Kevin. She reached up and grabbed the back of his head, pulled him down, and kissed him long and deep.

"That's for luck," she said when she released him. "Don't play with me, Kevin. I may not be the brightest girl in the world, but I won't be toyed with."

"No games," Kevin promised.

Caroline paused a moment, then nodded. "Giddyup," she said, and gave Kevin a shove out the door.

In the hall, they were challenged immediately.

"Whoa!" cried a burly guard, whom Trish had never seen before.

SALVATION

The man was hideously ugly, and his skin had a gray, life-less color to it. He wore some kind of assault weapon slung across his chest, a good indicator that he had no particular powers behind obvious strength. Definitely not an Alpha mutant, as Caroline had called them.

"Where do you think you're all going?" the man asked.

Trish was going to speak, afraid Caroline would blow the whole thing. But before she could utter a word, the mutant woman stepped right on up to the guard.

"I am Caroline Zarin, Acolyte cadet," she announced. "These people are from the press, not prisoners. I am under direct orders from Lord Magneto to see that they get whatever cooperation they need to correctly document and report upon this incredible event in history. Get out of the way." Caro-line's voice was pregnant with ominous, yet false, authority.

The guard moved. "Sorry," he said. "Just relax. Sheesh."

Caroline pressed the elevator call button and looked at Trish, who raised an eyebrow in appreciation of the woman's performance.

"Brava," she whispered.

When the elevator had arrived, and the doors were closing behind them, she turned to Caroline again.

"No stairs this time?"

"We're in a rush," Caroline answered. "Plus you need to conserve your strength. Lord knows who they've left to guard the X-Men, but you can be sure it's somebody with a bit more brains than Mr. Magoo back there. Whatever your plan is . . ."

She stopped. Looked at Trish. Then Kevin. Then back at Trish.

"You don't have a plan at all, do you?" Caroline gasped.

Trish stood, trying to think of a reply that would make any kind of sense. She failed miserably.

"Sure we have a plan," she finally said. "We're going to break out the X-Men. Whatever it takes to get that accom-plished, that's our plan."

"Jesus," Caroline hissed, and Trish couldn't tell whether the look on the woman's face was one of horror or admiration.

"All right, look," she continued. "I've been working a little on my narcopathy, and—"

"Narcopathy?" Trish asked.

"You know what telepathy is? You know what narcolepsy is? You know what I can do? Figure it out, Trish, we're almost there!" Caroline said, her patience obviously wearing thin.

Trish was appropriately chagrined. Here was a woman she had thought of, until a couple of minutes earlier, as pretty much a dim bulb, making her feel like a moron.

"I think I can get someone to sleep if I concentrate enough," she said. "But I need time, and if there's more than one of them, well . . ."

Ping!

The elevator slid to a stop, the doors began to roll back. Trish braced herself and Caroline squinted with intense concentration. After a moment, Kevin peeked out into the hall, then turned back to them.

"Nothing," he said.

"Real smooth, Mr. Bond," Trish cracked.

Kevin smiled, and the mood lightened for all three of them. What they were doing was insane. As far as Trish was concerned, when you were going over the abyss into bananaland, angst just wasn't acceptable.

As quietly as possible, they moved down the hall toward the L-turn that led to the room where the X-Men were being held. As they approached, Trish had the nearly overwhelming urge to turn tail and run. She had been joking with herself about the mission: impossible they were on, even running the old theme song through her brain. But suddenly it wasn't funny anymore. It was just her and Kevin, and Caroline, two frail humans and a . . . narcopath, whose power worked so slowly that Ted Koppel put people to sleep faster.

Eyes wide with horror at her own thoughts, Trish clamped a hand over her mouth to keep a Woody Woodpecker, maniacal cackle from coming out.

Kevin was first. He paused at the corner and looked around, just barely inching his head forward to get a look at whoever was guarding the captive mutants.

He pulled back fast.

"Good news and bad news," he whispered. "Bad news first: it's Frenzy."

"Who?" Caroline asked in the same tone.

"Joanna Cargil. She was called Frenzy before she joined Magneto's cause," Trish explained, then turned to Kevin. "You did say there was also good news, didn't you?"

"Oh, yeah." He smiled. "We don't have to worry about Caroline's power working. She's already asleep."

Trish wanted to laugh. There just wasn't time.

"More good news," Kevin added, lowering his whisper even more. "She left the door open. Probably wanted to keep an eye on the hallway and the X-Men."

Trish nodded. Hushing Kevin and Caroline, she slipped around the corner and began to move as rapidly and quietly as possible toward the steel door. On the other side of that door, four X-Men were shackled to a wall. A moment later, the others fell into line behind her.

Immediately upon seeing her, Hank and the other X-Men began to make facial motions, to mouth words, to try to warn her off. They couldn't move their arms or legs, but they were doing their best to get her to turn back without actually calling out.

She would have been hurt, would have been angry at them for being so foolish, but they could not have known just how bad things had become in so short a time. Trish knew she was doing the only thing she could do. It was a risk, certainly. But there was so much at stake, it was a risk she had to take.

As Trish passed the slumbering Cargil, Hank's face crinkled like the mug of one of those ugly dogs as he tried to use exaggerated lip movements to warn her off. Trish ignored him. All she had to do was look around for whatever device would bypass the X-Men's bonds, and they'd be home free. Cargil wouldn't last half a second against four X-Men.

She looked back to the prisoners. Each of them was making a strange face at her now, but still none of them would speak for fear of alerting the sleeping Cargil. Storm and Bishop were mouthing words as well, but Trish never claimed to be able to read lips.

Then she saw Wolverine. His face wasn't moving. Only his eyes. First he would stare at Trish, then his eyes would glance past her, behind her, with obvious purpose. He wanted her to turn around.

Frowning in confusion, she turned slowly to see Cargil, wide awake, standing with one hand clutching Kevin's throat, and the other wrapped firmly around Caroline's neck.

* * *

The first sounds of large-weapons fire had stunned them all. *So much for our window*, Cyclops had thought. The clock was no longer ticking on their mission, it had stopped. They were working within that silent moment between the last second ticking away, and the explosion that would end it all. In this case, maybe literally.

Even if they found and defeated Magneto, he had thought as the sound of far-off explosions increased in frequency, it all still depended upon Gambit, Archangel, and Cooper taking the Sentinels out of play.

That had been several minutes ago. The sounds of battle and destruction continued, but Cyclops ignored them now, concentrating only on the goal at hand. He stood in the recessed doorway of a deli on the corner of Sixth Avenue and Thirtieth Street. Across the street, Jean and Rogue hugged the front of a discount music store. The Juggernaut was barely concealed by a massive brown box that would have been a newsstand if its owner hadn't fled in the great Manhattan exodus.

The Juggernaut. It was still difficult for Scott to deal with the fact that they were working with one of their greatest enemies. But he reminded himself of what Cain Marko had said earlier. He was a career criminal, not some menace looking to take over the world. The Juggernaut had just as much of a stake in stopping Magneto as any of them. After all, he wasn't a mutant.

With a rapid gesture, Cyclops signalled for Rogue to take

to the air. He flattened out his hand so she knew to fly close to the tops of buildings.

Now you, Jean, he thought, certain that the psychic rapport they shared would carry the words to her. *Time to cross the street.*

Cyclops smiled. The situation was as tense and dangerous as any he had ever found himself in, but he was not beyond being amused when the idea of crossing the street became ominous. As they neared the Empire State Building, the atmosphere among them, even the air around them, seemed weighted with the expectation of conflict, of consequence, of death.

The smile disappeared from Scott's face.

Jean sprinted across the street. Scott wanted to watch her move, watch her lithe form, wrapped in the snug, practical combat uniform they all wore some version of. But the time for such luxuries was past. He poked his head out from the doorway and glanced around for any sign of attack, any hint of the enemy. Like the laser sighting on many modern weapons, anything Cyclops laid eyes upon was a potential target.

No targets, though. Not this time.

He signaled Juggernaut, and the two of them moved out together, taking it slow and hugging the opposite sides of the street. Cyclops didn't figure they had much chance of sneaking in and breaking out the other X-Men. But it would have been foolish to just charge down the street. It was impossible to predict what they might find when they reached the building. There might be a way in other than the lobby, or they might be able to bluff their way in, using Jean's telepathy as a mask.

No real plan could be instituted until he had seen the building's setup.

Jean moved ahead, with the Juggernaut close behind, and Scott watched them both and monitored his own surroundings. He sped across the street and they all continued up Sixth Avenue. It wouldn't be long now, he thought.

*Scott, we've got—*Jean's telepathic voice filled his head.

"Cyclops, hang back!" Rogue's voice came over the comm-link. "It's an—"

—company!

"—ambush!"

"Hell, it's about time," the Juggernaut cried joyously from across the street. "This sneakin' around crap was gettin' real old real fast!"

Hairbag and Slab came around the corner of Thirty-first Street. They weren't alone. Cowards they might have been, and none too bright. But in some ways, they were far from stupid. At least a dozen other people backed them up, male and female. Mutants, obviously. Most of them looked relatively normal, but there were two figures so gone over into the feral stage common to many mutants that they could no longer stand upright. A strikingly tall woman with tentacles growing out of her face and a dark-skinned man with a massive, scorpionlike tail in back were other standouts.

Then there was the big guy. Forty feet high if he was an inch.

"They call me Humongous!" he bellowed, shattering every window for half a block. "Surrender now, or I'm going to have to crush you."

CHAPTER 9

"Boy, are you flatscans dumb," Cargil sneered, then tossed Kevin and Caroline to the floor in a tumble of limbs. "You didn't think I'd hear the ding of the elevator arriving on this floor?"

"You weren't asleep?" Trish asked, still confused.

"Are you dense?" Cargil snapped. "I heard the elevator. I pretended to be sleeping."

She spun on Caroline, who lay on the floor, eyes slitted in concentration as she stared at Cargil.

"You stop that, girl," Cargil snapped. "I know you're that little sleep-witch, but if you don't quit playing sandman with me, I'm going to have to kill you just to stay awake."

Caroline looked at Trish, then at Kevin. Her eyes opened, her face relaxed, and she began to rise to her feet. She had not abandoned them, at least not as far as Trish could tell. But she wasn't going to throw her life away either.

"Sorry, Kevin," Caroline said. "I did my best."

"We'll be okay, hon," Kevin answered. "Don't worry."

"I wouldn't be so quick to make any promises, flatscan," Cargil said. "I'm just trying to figure out what to do with the three of you."

"Let them go, Joanna," the Beast said. "They've done nothing, really. It's not as if they have a chance of defeating you. Just let them leave."

"No, I'm sorry," Cargil said. "I'll have to think of something just a little better than that."

"I have an idea," Kevin said happily. "Why don't you bleed!"

He leaped at Cargil and landed a solid kick to her face. Then he fell on his butt.

Cargil had barely flinched. Trish knew the woman had scarcely felt Kevin's attack, and a more even-tempered person might have simply ignored it. Or laughed. Nobody had ever accused Joanna Cargil of being even tempered.

"Well, I guess that decides that," she growled. "I'm just going to have to kill you."

"Don't do it, Frenzy!" Storm spoke up, and Cargil turned

to stare at her. It occurred to Trish that the women were polar opposites, Cargil a twisted mirror image of the nobility and purity of Storm's African features. But Cargil *was* twisted, by hate and rage and lust for murder and power. She was Hyde to Storm's Jekyll.

"Back off, Cargil, or I'll spill your guts all over the floor as soon as we're down from here!" Wolverine warned.

Bishop remained silent, his eyes revealing him to have been a witness to far too many hopeless conflicts.

Kevin hopped to his feet and into a kickboxing stance. Trish knew he'd done a little kickboxing, but wasn't sure how good he was. One thing she was certain of, though. Not good enough.

"Go release the X-Men, Trish," Kevin said.

"I'm not leaving you," she said.

"Neither am I," Caroline added, moving closer to him.

With a flurry of blows to the face and body, Kevin did the best he could to slow Cargil down. Caroline frowned again, trying despite Cargil's threats to force the muscular black woman to sleep. They had nothing left to lose, Trish knew. Caroline obviously knew it too.

Kevin threw a haymaker with a lot of power behind it. Cargil blocked it with the side of her hand. She reached in, grabbed him by the throat again, and snapped his neck with a crack so loud it echoed off the tile floor.

"Kevin!" Caroline and Trish screamed in unison.

"Cargil, no!" Storm shouted, and all four X-Men pulled at their restraints.

"And as for you!" Cargil shouted, turning on Caroline. "First you sell out the emperor to a weakling flatscan genetrash loser, then you actually try to use your teeny tiny power on *me*?"

"Oh, my God . . ." Trish said, in a small voice choked with tears and heartache. She and Kevin hadn't been the best of friends, but friends they had been. He had been there because of her, and she felt more than a bit responsible for his death.

She lifted the chair Cargil had been sitting on. Cargil shoved Caroline hard against the wall. Trish shattered the wooden chair on Cargil's head. The Acolyte's head swung around as if she were some kind of mechanical thing.

"Don't worry," she hissed, glaring at Trish. "You're next."

"No!" Trish shouted. "Please, don't—"

Caroline's spine shattered under Joanna Cargil's blows. The life went out of her eyes. Trish couldn't help but think of the ancient TV in her parents' home, and the way the old picture tube seemed to fade away before winking out for good.

The X-Men shouted, screamed for Cargil's attention, trying desperately to distract her. They all cursed her for the cold-blooded murders they had just witnessed. Wolverine and the Beast strained against their bonds. Either of them could easily have ripped the restraints from the wall if their mutant abilities had not been inhibited.

Then Cargil turned toward Trish.

"You're not running," she said. "Why aren't you running, flatscan? I know you're afraid."

Trish said nothing. Her mind was too numb to reply, body too frightened to move.

"Oh, man," someone said softly, just at the end of the hall.

"Well, well, well, a challenge, finally," Cargil said, looking toward the source of the voice.

Iceman.

"Good God, Frenzy, what have you done?" Bobby Drake said.

A lunatic would have laughed, then, grinned and kept on trying to kill. Cargil didn't laugh. She didn't smile. She took a deep breath, shrugged her shoulders with some semblance of regret.

"They pissed me off," she said. "Couldn't be helped."

She wasn't insane. She had killed Kevin and Caroline with full knowledge of her actions, the murders nothing more than petty, immature revenge, committed for lack of a better idea what to do with three unwanted visitors.

Insanity would have made it so much easier to take. Or at least, that's what Trish thought. That she'd done it out of malevolence and immaturity, that was worse. But Iceman had come, to stop Cargil from a third murder. Trish's heart cried out in glee that she was saved, but in the part of her mind where guilt lay waiting, she couldn't shake the idea that it wasn't right. That it was her fault the others were dead, and it wasn't fair that Iceman should have come in time to save her, but too late for them.

"Take her down hard, Drake!" Wolverine growled down the hall.

"Trish!" Bobby yelled. "Move!"

Then there was no more time for regrets. Cargil was reaching for her, hoping, more than likely, to use her as a hostage. Which would be a major handicap for Iceman. Even if he had been the kind of person who would ignore a life in jeopardy, he and Trish knew each other. She and Hank had double-dated with Bobby and several of his girlfriends.

They were friends. She couldn't compromise the fight, she had to get out of the way.

She wasn't fast enough. Cargil snagged her by the hair and started to pull her back.

"No!" Iceman shouted. "No more, you crazy—"

Trish felt cold on the back of her neck, then heard a crackling noise and fell free of Cargil's grip, sprawling to the floor. She scrambled to turn around, to back away. When she looked at Iceman and Cargil, when she understood what had happened, she stopped moving and just stared.

She blinked, then reached around to the back of her head to feel the ragged, ice-flecked edges of the hair that Cargil had clutched. Bobby had frozen Trish's hair on her head, supercooled it to such a low temperature that it had simply shattered in Cargil's grip.

"Trish, you okay?" Bobby asked.

Trish nodded. Iceman turned back to Cargil, who was encased in a block of ice so thick it barely left room to pass by her in the doorway. Only Cargil's head was free, and she was cussing loud and long.

"Shut up," Iceman snapped. "I don't know what happened to you, Joanna. You were never this bloodthirsty before."

"I was never in a war before," Cargil snapped. "You got lucky, Drake. Your problem is, you're not willing to finish it. There will always be a next time, and next time I see you, there won't be any flinching. You're already dead, Iceman. You just don't know it yet.''

"Yeah, I've heard it before," Iceman said.

Trish waited for the characteristic sarcasm, one of the jokes that invariably found its way out of Bobby's mouth. It never came. He took her by the hand, and led her quietly down to where the X-Men were being held.

They looked at one another, all of them: Trish Tilby, Iceman, Storm, Beast, Bishop, and Wolverine. They spoke quietly, gravely, among themselves. They were pleased to know that Bobby was still alive. There was none of the telltale levity that was usually so common, particularly between Iceman and the Beast.

Rather than waste time attempting to figure out how the power-dampening shackles worked, Iceman simply froze the mechanisms, rendering them brittle and useless. All four were then able to free themselves with simple flicks of the wrists and ankles.

As they walked out, Wolverine glared at Cargil, began to walk toward her, but Storm held him back with a hand.

"Not a word," Bishop snarled at her as they left.

Wisely, she remained silent.

Trish whimpered as she stepped past the bodies of her friends.

"God, I'm so sorry," she said quietly, but she wasn't sure if she was apologizing for not having prevented their deaths, or for having remained alive.

A strong hand landed on her shoulder, and then the Beast pulled her close to him. They walked side by side, his blue-furred arm hugging her tightly to him, warm and safe.

"You did what you could," Hank McCoy said. "You did everything you could, Trish."

"I couldn't save them," she said softly.

"No," Wolverine said, the ferocity in his voice startling. "But we can go out and make sure that it ends here, that nobody else dies on some maniac's whim."

"I've got your back, Logan," Bishop said gravely.

"No quarter, X-Men," Storm commanded. "Eliminate any

resistance hard and fast, and don't forget our main objective. Magneto must be defeated."

* * *

The summer day had moved on, the shadows lengthening into that long stretch of waning sunlight called late afternoon. The canyons of the city were already plunged into shadow where the buildings were the tallest. It being summer, night was still a long way off, but those shadows were a warning that it was on the way.

With a nervous glance from side to side, Gabriela Frigerio hurried across the street with her brother Michael and the group she'd come to think of as the inner circle of the resistance: Lamarre, Steve, Joyce, and their de facto leader, Miguelito.

"I don't know about this," Joyce said, her usually radiant face eclipsed with concern. "I mean, how do we know we can trust these people? Isn't it better to stay in the underground, get more organized, before making a move?"

"Yeah," Steve agreed. He was her husband, however, so his support wasn't particularly persuasive.

"That sounds good, lady," Lamarre said, "but it won't work. You don't get it. We've got to make the stand now, before Magneto gets any stronger than he is."

"Lamarre is right," Miguelito said.

He was short enough that they all had to look down to pay attention.

"Magneto is at war now," Miguelito continued. "If the government wins, great, we're all set. But if they lose, it will be over for us, no matter how hard we fight. No, the best time to take a stand is now, when Magneto won't have much time or firepower to dedicate to us.

"We've got hundreds of people waiting for the word, and there are probably thousands of others who will respond if we just set an example for them," Miguelito said.

"Thousands?" Gabi asked

Miguelito smiled, shrugged. "One can hope," he said.

"Hope isn't going to keep us alive," Michael mumbled.

They all looked at him, Gabriela in particular. Just as they had to look down to meet Miguelito's eyes, they had to look up to see Michael's. He was six foot six, at the least, and rarely said a single word.

"Actually, Michael, I disagree," Gabriela said. "I think hope will keep us alive. I think it already has. It's all we're running on, right now. We may not be capable of taking this city back from Magneto on our own, but we can certainly make things more difficult for him. We can make absolutely certain that the human population of this city does not cooperate with him."

"We don't even have to do it for long," Lamarre added. "Much as I hate to rely on any mutie for help, we know the X-Men are going to be moving in on Magneto at any time. As long as we—"

"My God!" Joyce shouted. "Don't any of you hear the bombs falling? Don't you hear the war? We shouldn't be out here at all, we're not ready for this."

For a moment, nobody responded. Steve tried to pull Joyce into a comforting embrace, but she brushed him away. Lamarre started to say something, but Miguelito hushed him.

"Do we hear the war?" he asked rhetorically. "Of course we do. But I'm not willing to let somebody else fight it for me, to let someone destroy my city in order to save it. You want to go back into the subways and take charge of feeding people and giving medical attention, get all that organized, that's okay with me. Nobody is going to think any less of you."

Her eyes widened, and Joyce looked around the group. Finally, she nodded.

"Let's go," she said, pulling Steve after her.

He offered an apologetic glance, but Gabriela thought he seemed more than a little relieved. The man had probably been as frightened as his wife, but she had voiced her fear, risked condemnation and accusations of cowardice. Gabi wondered if that made Joyce any more courageous than her husband. She kind of thought that it did.

With Lamarre and her brother trailing behind, Gabi continued up the sidewalk next to Miguelito. Their weapons were held at the ready, in case they should be set upon by Magneto's forces, or human beings who had used Magneto's conquest as an excuse for vandalism, theft, and chaos.

They walked in silence for several blocks. Halfway down a side street, Miguelito stopped and pointed.

"That's it," he said.

"Who are we meeting here, man?" Lamarre asked.

"What's that, Lamarre, the fortieth time you've asked me that question?" Miguelito responded. "Well, you're about to find out."

It was a bar, a slightly seedy-looking place that was far from being one of the trendy pickup bars that Gabi had frequented before the madness came to New York. This was a place for drinking, not a place for meeting people or socializing.

A glowing window sign advertised Guinness stout, and above the door, a neon tube spelled out the words TOM'S TAP-ROOM.

"Here?" she couldn't stop herself from asking. "Our big powwow is in *here*?"

"Where did you want to do it, Times Square?" Miguelito cracked, then pulled open the door to Tom's Taproom and entered.

They descended half a dozen steps and Gabi blinked several times, eyes struggling to adjust to the darkness of the bar. Dark wood, dim lighting, the eternal odors of old beer and cigarette smoke. The man behind the bar, a stout guy with gray hair but a young face, had one hand on the grip of a shotgun that lay on the oak bar.

"I'm sorry," he said. "We're not open for business."

"Hey, it's us who should be sorry," Miguelito said. "Though you are obviously back there ready to serve drinks to somebody, we're not here to drink. We're here to help."

The stout man's eyes narrowed.

"Miguel?" he asked.

"Yeah, Tom, it's me," Miguelito answered.

Tom smiled and came around the bar. Miguelito went over, allowed the Taproom's owner to look him up and down, and then the two men did the last thing Gabi might have expected.

They hugged.

"God, it's good to see you, kid," Tom said. "Jesus, you grew up fast."

"Nah," Miguelito said. "You just got old, Tommy."

Tom turned toward the murky-looking back room of the bar. Fluorescent light burned, and she was fairly certain there were a couple of pool tables back there.

"Wilson, get on out here," Tom shouted. "You've got visitors."

A man appeared from around a partition that screened much of the back room off from the rest of the bar. He was stocky and dangerous looking, Latino, and Gabi was certain she had seen him somewhere before.

He wasn't alone. One after another, men and women filed out after him. Gabi counted twelve of them in total, and several wore blue uniforms.

"The cops?" Lamarre snarled. "What are you, nuts? You know Magneto's got the cops workin' for him."

"Not all the cops," the man Tom had called Wilson said defensively.

That's when Gabi recognized him. Wilson Ramos, the police commissioner of New York City. She understood Lamarre's anger and confusion. What were they doing there, with the police, with the *commissioner*, for God's sake? They had been told that City Hall, that the entire city government, was now working with Magneto. That meant that . . .

"You set us up?" Michael said softly, startling her.

"No, man, it's not like that at all," Miguelito explained.

"Then what is it like?" Gabi snapped.

Lamarre was already backing toward the door. "This was supposed to be another resistance group, man, not Magneto's pet human soldiers."

"If my little brother hadn't warned me you'd be armed, I'd shoot you just for saying that," Wilson Ramos said. "Now can we get down to business, or what? City Hall is under siege, but the resistance fighters there are unorganized and their numbers are dwindling. They need our help."

"Your little brother?" Gabi asked, astonished.

Miguelito smiled.

SALVATION

"I never used to tell people *mi hermano* was the Apple's top cop," he said. "Not that I was ashamed, but nobody would believe me. Now our differences don't seem like such a big deal anymore."

He turned to Wilson.

"Do they, Willie?"

"Not at all, 'Ito," Ramos said. "But don't call me that, or I'll have to shoot you."

"Seems to me you're just itching to shoot someone," Lamarre said, and Gabi could tell from his tone that he was still greatly suspicious.

"*Oh*, yeah," Wilson responded. "Problem is, the guy I want to shoot can't be killed with bullets. So, if I can't take Magneto out, I can sure as hell take City Hall and sweep out the collaborator trash like Maxine Perkins and Steve Tyree. I'll shoot them if I have to."

Lamarre smiled.

"When do we leave?" he asked.

* * *

Magneto hovered more than one thousand feet above ground, breathing air that was both thinner and more polluted than below. He could see the Empire State Building to the north and the World Trade Center to the south, with the Statue of Liberty beyond it in New York Harbor.

As best he could, he surveyed the war around him, and realized that the military was not closing in at all, not as he had first believed. Indeed, while they were striking out at the Sentinels in a colossal waste of ammunition and losing soldiers to the massive robots' return fire, they were not pressing the battle at all.

Apparently, they were awaiting final orders from the American President. But what Magneto could not determine was exactly what they expected those orders to be.

It was entirely possible that the President was simply being indecisive. But there were two other potential reasons for the military's inaction, both of which concerned Magneto a great deal.

The first, and most bothersome, was that Xavier might be telling the truth. The President might actually be considering thermonuclear attack. They could raze New York City to the ground, and then claim that Magneto himself had set off the nukes to keep the city from returning to American control.

It seemed all too plausible. Even so, and despite the atrocities he had witnessed in his life, Magneto could not bring himself to believe that the leader of the most powerful nation in the world would knowingly murder hundreds of thousands of American citizens merely to save one city from conquest.

The other option was that the President was waiting for something. Perhaps he and Xavier had cooked up a plan. But without the X-Men, what could they hope to accomplish? Even if all of the X-Men were free and in top form, there would be nothing they could do against hundreds of other mutants and a fleet of Sentinels.

With an electric crackle, the gauzy image of the Acolyte Scanner shimmered into existence beside him. It was an odd thing to see, a ghostly female form standing in the middle of the sky without any apparent means of support. But then, Scanner wasn't actually there at all.

"You signaled for me, my Emperor?" Scanner inquired.

"Order all units to await my word before becoming involved in this skirmish," he said. "The war has not actually begun. It is still possible, I believe, to end this conflict without destroying the city. That would be my preference, since we all intend to live here."

Scanner offered a low bow, and flashed out of existence.

Magneto wanted to think that the President was merely having a difficult time committing to a plan. The other two options were far less appealing.

In any case, he had determined to refrain from attacking the military himself unless they directly assaulted him first, or until the President ordered an invasion or a nuclear attack.

If he wanted Haven to still be standing when the conflict was over, Magneto knew he had to make his moves wisely.

CHAPTER 10

LEONARDI
&
AUSTIN

On the steps of City Hall, a swarm of humans wore away at the nerves and resolve of the combined mutant and human force responsible for the building's defense. Police officers loyal to the city government, to the recently promoted mayor, Maxine Perkins, and those simply loyal to the job of keeping the peace, tried to put down the revolt with a minimum of violence. But the patience of policemen, particularly in urban areas, was notoriously thin. And they were well armed.

Side by side with the cops were Acolytes, mutant followers of Magneto, charged with forcing the remaining human populace to afford mutants the respect that was now required.

Heads were cracked open like rotten tomatoes, citizens shot with rubber bullets—and some with the real thing as well. Ivan Skolnick tried desperately not to use his mutant powers, which he still despised. Yet others around him were not so prudish. Senyaka, one of Magneto's Acolytes, lashed his agonizingly painful psionic whip at any human in range. It was a vicious scene.

For a while, it seemed as though the human hordes were like the legendary Hydra: cut off one head and two more would take its place. But after a time, the flow appeared to dwindle.

That was about the time the war started in earnest. Perhaps, Skolnick thought, the attackers realized all was lost, that their efforts meant nothing. Or perhaps they felt there were more important battles to be fought that day. In any case, Skolnick's troops, who were responsible for policing mutant-human relations, were thinning the crowd quite a bit.

"We seem to be winning this part of the war, Major," the usually taciturn Senyaka said at his side. "Since it appears the Emperor may have need of me elsewhere, I assume I can be confident in leaving you to your appointed duties?"

"Absolutely," Skolnick replied.

Senyaka made short contact with someone via comm-link, and was immediately teleported from the defense of City Hall. Skolnick was very happy to see him go. The burning eyes

SALVATION

behind that cowl had disturbed him, most especially with the way they flared whenever Senyaka's psionic whip would wrap around a human limb or throat. As if he was leeching some kind of energy from them.

Skolnick didn't want to have to think about it. Nor did he want to think about Maxine Perkins, and the new police commissioner, the self-righteous Steven Tyree. He tried to turn it off, tried not to see the faces of men, women, and teenagers. The way he viewed it, they were all fighting for that magical place in every heart where a person's hometown will always stay, perfectly preserved from childhood. Despite all its faults, New York inspired as much passion as any small town.

He could not stand those faces, etched with fear and desperation. These people were merely defending their homes, defending the rights that the greatest nation on Earth had given them. Rights that Magneto had taken away. Skolnick was beginning to seriously wonder if he had made a grave error. All his life, Skolnick had wanted to be a soldier. He had become an extraordinary soldier, a credit to his family, a servant of the American ideal.

Now he had betrayed all that. Yes, he was a mutant. Yes, there were hardships to be dealt with because of it. But hardships had been faced by those crusading for gender and race equality, and other "misfits" for centuries.

Had Magneto gone too far?

Bullets chipped brick behind Ivan Skolnick's head, and he ducked, preparing to blast the shooter as quickly as possible. No time for self-recriminations, he thought. This was a war, and he a soldier.

Question was, whose side was he really on? Even he wasn't sure.

* * *

"So much for the element of surprise, eh, Summers?" Cain Marko sneered.

Cyclops knew the Juggernaut's amusement was not feigned. Marko was happy the time for battle had arrived. It was the only thing the man had ever done well.

149

In a way, though he was loath to admit it even to himself, Scott could relate.

"Rogue," he barked, "take down the giant. Marko, you've got Slab. I'm on Hairbag. Jean, reign the others in until we're clear!"

So I'm on crowd control now? Jean's mental voice entered his head, even as Cyclops unleashed an optic blast that knocked Hairbag end over end into the woman with the octopus face.

Scott didn't respond. No need. He knew Jean was just picking on him. And she knew that she had not been relegated to mere crowd control, but given the most work to do. She had to keep a dozen-odd mutants busy all by herself, while the others took down the major players and then came to her assistance. He hated laying all that on her, but they didn't seem to have much other choice.

Not that things ever worked out the way he planned. His skill as a field leader was not even necessarily based on perfect execution of a plan, but on instinctive reaction to complications that might arise.

Like now, for instance.

Hairbag had untangled himself from the tentacles that extended from the forehead and cheeks of the tall woman he had landed on. Cursing her in a voice loud enough to be heard over shouts and cries of pain and anger, Hairbag leaped to his feet much faster than Cyclops might have expected. Rather than rush at him in attack, however, the spiky-haired mutant turned his back on X-Men and Acolyte alike. He bent over slightly, and as if some switch had been thrown, the hair on his back stood up straight and sharp.

That's when Cyclops understood. The "hair" on the stout mutant was not actually hair at all, but a deadly covering of porcupinelike quills. He could guess the rest.

"X-Men!" he shouted. "Eyes on Hairbag!"

Razor-tipped quills erupted from Hairbag's back and flew toward them, as deadly as a hail of arrows. Juggernaut and Rogue wouldn't be harmed, and if she had heard him shout,

SALVATION

Jean could throw up a telekinetic shield. But Cyclops was on his own.

With a quick optic blast, he tore through the blanket of quills flying toward him. In perfect synchronicity, he pulled up into an aerial somersault, deadly quills flashing past him. When he landed on his feet, Hairbag had already lifted his arms to attempt another attack with the quills jutting from the flesh of his shoulders.

"Playing for keeps, now," Cyclops mumbled to himself.

He brought Hairbag down hard with an optic blast to the upper chest that knocked the mutant flat on the pavement.

"You killed him!" octopus-face screamed. "You guys aren't supposed to do that!"

"*No one's* supposed to do that," Cyclops snapped, though he knew that Hairbag was far from dead.

"Your turn!" the woman cried, and her tentacles reached out for him.

No more conversation, Cyclops thought. War required only action. With utmost concentration, he focused his optic beam into a tight, narrow line, and blasted the woman the moment she moved into profile. The blast neatly sliced off two tentacles on the left side of her face, instantly cauterizing the wounds.

Screaming in pain, she looked at Cyclops with agony etched in every line of her face.

"Go away!" he snarled.

She turned and ran.

* * *

"Man," the Juggernaut said in awe, "that was harsh. You guys aren't fooling around this time, are you?"

"The stakes have never been this high, Cain," Jean Grey said beside him. "We're doing what we have to do, that's all. Doesn't mean we enjoy it."

"Yeah? What about Wolverine?" Cain asked.

Jean shot him a nasty glance and turned to face two feral mutants who were ganging up on her. Cain kept moving, unconcerned. Grey was one lady who could definitely take care of herself.

To his left, Rogue was landing blow after blow on the face, head, chest, and back of the forty-foot giant who called himself Humongous. She didn't seem to be faring all that well, and Cain figured he ought to lend a hand. First things first, though. He was working with the X-Men, and he knew firsthand that Scott Summers was an effective field commander. Summers wanted him to take down this big drooling moron called Slab. He could do that.

Like Hairball, Slab had been one of Sinister's Nasty Boys. Cain had heard of them, but never run into them before now. They didn't seem like much. Slab was over seven feet tall, nearly bald, and ugly as a bulldog but without the charm.

The Juggernaut moved, several mutants tried to stop his progress. He laughed. Obviously, they either didn't know who he was, or didn't believe his publicity. Nothing stopped the Juggernaut. He brushed aside the thin black man with the scorpion tail, its stinger striking for his face but hitting only helmet.

Then there was Slab.

"Come on, flatscan," Slab crowed. "Slab's gonna pound your skull."

Cain nearly laughed out loud.

"Man, I thought you looked stupid," he said. "Turns out, you're even dumber than you look! My rep says I ain't the most intelligent guy in the world, but at least I don't refer to myself in the third person."

"Don't make fun of Slab, buddy," Slab warned. "You'll die slower if you do."

"Oh, shut up," Cain said, and hammered Slab in the face with a massive fist that rocked his head back so far, Cain figured he'd given the guy whiplash.

Slab grew. Then he hit back, hard. Cain wasn't in motion, and the blow hurt him, sent him stumbling back several steps.

"Every time you hit Slab, Slab gets stronger, hits back harder," the mutant said. "Slab gets bigger. You can't win."

"That's the game, huh?" Cain replied. "Well, check this out, dog boy."

Cain launched himself at Slab, the Juggernaut steaming down on his enemy. He slammed into the mutant and lifted him off the ground, like a linebacker going for a hard tackle. But instead of knocking Slab down, the Juggernaut kept going. There was a massive financial office building just ahead, its walls constructed of thick granite blocks.

The Juggernaut bent low, and rammed Slab, skull first, into the granite side of the building. The stone gave way, some of it crumbling in chunks to the sidewalk. Cain dropped Slab onto the debris.

"You can't hit me back harder if you're unconscious," he said.

* * *

"Keep hitting me, little bug, and when you get tired I can squash you!" Humongous cried in delight.

Rogue cracked him a good one in the left temple, and this time the forty-foot monstrosity actually yowled with pain and reached for his head. Rogue smiled. *Good*, she thought, *it's about time*.

She was almost incomparably strong, and nearly invulnerable, but in spite of all that, Rogue was having a difficult time with Humongous. On the other hand, at least she was keeping him occupied so he could not help the rest of Magneto's followers.

Humongous was large, but he was also slow and lumbering. If he got hold of her, Rogue suspected the giant might be able to pop her head off as if she were a Pez dispenser. The key, then, was simply not to let him touch her.

Giant hands reached out for her again, and Rogue ducked them, flew in toward his face, and used both fists in a hammer blow that shattered Humongous's nose. The giant screamed in pain and humiliation, as blood began to flow freely over his lips and chin.

When Rogue shot around behind him, into the shadow cast by his massive form, she noticed something unexpected. Humongous had shrunk at least five feet. The massive mutant clutched his face, blood on his hands, and he growled in rage as he spun, trying to find her.

"Hey, ugly," a familiar voice boomed. "Down here!"

Rogue and Humongous looked down together, to see Cain Marko, the Juggernaut, running at the giant mutant. His footfalls echoed in the street. Humongous began to stoop, to attempt to snatch up the Juggernaut, but Rogue dashed through the air and struck him in the side of the head. In the moment that she had distracted him, the Juggernaut slammed into Humongous at ground level.

There was a massive crack, and Humongous cried out in pain. Rogue thought the Juggernaut had broken the giant mutant's leg. Humongous began to fall.

"Uh-uh, sugar, not here," she said absently.

With all her strength, she grabbed Humongous from behind and hauled him off the ground. Rogue flew quickly to the Hudson River and there, more than one hundred feet above the water, let Humongous fall. In no time, she was in the thick of the battle once more.

* * *

Jean lifted the two feral mutants and sent them crashing through the thick glass windows of a trendy Sixth Avenue eatery. Now she faced down half a dozen mutants who gathered around her in a circle of death. A woman whose hands and scalp were on fire. A boy, barely a teenager, who spit long streams of acid that ate the pavement by Jean's feet. The man with the scorpion tail, and others.

Simultaneously, they attacked, intending to murder Jean Grey. But Jean wasn't there, not at all. Her presence was an illusion, telepathically inserted into their minds. Acid burned the scorpion tail, fire scarred a shapeshifter, claws slashed at darkness, and a being of living shadow screamed.

Jean flinched. She hadn't intended them to injure one another. Though it turned the fight to her favor, it gave her a sick feeling in the pit of her stomach. The war between Xavier and Magneto had always been a philosophical one, a Cold

SALVATION

War, with a skirmish here and there. But this was real war, and Jean had quickly discovered that she did not have a taste for it. Not at all.

Several of the mutants had seen her now, and were attempting to close in again. They were more cautious this time, and she wondered if she could take them all down. She didn't need to. An optic blast flashed past her, driving the blazing-skulled woman from her feet. Her head cracked against a fire hydrant, and she lay still. Jean checked psionically to see that she was still alive, and then moved on.

"About time you stopped playing around," she said as Cyclops ran up beside her. "What about the others?"

Before Scott could answer, they heard Cain Marko bellowing.

"I told ya to cut that out!"

They spun in time to see him snag that scorpion tail and whip its owner around several times before slamming him into the side of an abandoned city bus.

"Man, he was drivin' me up a wall with that stinger!" Marko exclaimed.

"Well," Scott said, turning his attention back to Jean, "I guess that about does it for the element of surprise."

"You could say that," Jean agreed with a weak smile.

"Oh, I'll go y'all one better than that," Rogue said as she approached her three comrades.

All three of them turned to look at her. Rogue only pointed in the other direction. The fight had taken them a block and a half farther north, just a stone's throw from the Empire State Building. Jean knew they should be right on top of Magneto's base by now. Rogue shouldn't be surprised if they had met up with more opposition.

That's what she thought. Before she turned to see what Rogue was pointing at.

The street was literally filled with mutants, separating them from their goal: the Empire State Building and the freedom of the rest of the X-Men. Out in front of the pack were several Acolytes they were already familiar with, including Amelia Voght, the Kleinstock brothers, and Senyaka. But Jean could also see other familiar faces, including other members of the Nasty Boys, several Marauders, the Toad, even the Blob and Pyro, who had recovered too fast from their previous skirmish. Magneto obviously had a healer on his staff.

It was a sea of angry, resolute faces, all dedicated to destroying the X-Men in Magneto's name.

"Oh, marvelous," Jean sighed.

"Surrender, X-Men, or be destroyed," Amelia Voght warned. "You have five seconds to decide."

Jean and Scott exchanged a knowing glance. Rogue didn't flinch as she prepared to go on the assault.

"You cannot win against these odds," Voght continued. "Give yourselves up, live in comfort in an empire ruled by Magneto. It's your only choice."

Jean would never have imagined she would see the day, but the Juggernaut spoke for the X-Men, speaking the words that were in all their minds.

"Like hell."

*　*　*

Her hand shook, the barrel of the gun wavering at her side. Gabriela Frigerio had never fired a gun before. They'd had no business giving her one, as far as she was concerned. But give her one they had. And it felt strangely comforting in her hand, though she knew that against the mutant hordes that had overtaken Manhattan, one handgun was little better than a slingshot.

But then, there was always David and Goliath to testify to the efficacy of the slingshot.

They moved together, the upstart resistance fighters led by Miguelito Ramos and the group of police officers and other former city employees led by ex-Police Commissioner Wilson Ramos. An odd group, to say the least, but all dedicated to a single cause: the salvation of New York City. Gabi didn't know what they could do against Magneto. As far as she was concerned, they were powerless. But they might be able to take back City Hall, to become a thorn in Magneto's side. That would have to be enough.

SALVATION

The mob had thinned in front of City Hall. As had its force of defenders. There were fewer than a dozen police officers now, and three or four people who might have been mutants.

"I recognize that one," Wilson Ramos said next to her. "He's one of Magneto's boys; must be powerful too."

"Do you want to hold back a bit?" Miguelito asked.

"Nah," Wilson said after a brief hesitation. "I don't think it's going to get any easier, no matter how long we wait."

"It's now or never," Gabi agreed, and the brothers looked at her oddly.

She wondered if they felt as strongly as she how suddenly real the whole thing had become. Up until that moment, it had seemed more like some college protest. But now the moment had come, the time for actual battle, actual bloodshed.

"My God," she said softly to herself, not bothering to wonder if anyone could hear. "How did we come to this?"

She looked at Michael, at Miguelito and his brother, at Lamarre and all the others, and she wondered how many of them would die in the next few minutes.

"Go!" Wilson Ramos barked into a hand radio.

Several hundred men and women, civilians and police and fire personnel, hustled into the city block around City Hall. On the steps of the venerable building, Magneto's security force and the citizens of Manhattan interrupted their battle to stare around in astonishment at what amounted to the cavalry.

Gabi saw the momentary uncertainty on every face as they attempted to determine whose side the new arrivals were on.

"Attention, Steven Tyree," Ramos boomed into a megaphone. "As police commissioner of New York City, I am placing you under arrest. Every law officer answering to Mr. Tyree is also under arrest, as are Magneto and all of his so-called Acolytes. Throw down your weapons, and wait with your hands up for a duly authorized police officer or civilian deputy to take you into custody!"

The mob was elated. The cops still working for Tyree, whom Magneto had appointed commissioner, far less so. Nobody moved.

"Pileggi, Brereton, Willeford, I see all you guys up there,"

Ramos said. ''Wambaugh, Caruso . . . ah, the hell with it, I'm not here to play Romper Room. Surrender now. You all know the law, and you know you've broken it. Bring out Tyree!''

Another pause.

An Asian man wearing the colors of Magneto's security force stepped forward as if to respond. But when he opened his mouth, rather than speak, the man merely took a deep breath and blew, as if trying to put out a candle.

At first, Gabi thought it was funny. It looked so bizarre. Then a hole appeared in the pay phone in the kiosk on the corner. No explosion, no fire, just a round section of the phone vaporized to nothing. The mutant must have emitted some incredible power from his mouth, a destructive force that eliminated anything in its path until it reached its target:

Wilson Ramos. Who hadn't noticed the phone being perforated, who waited patiently for some response from once faithful officers.

''Down!'' Gabriela cried, and dived on Ramos, dragging him to the pavement a heartbeat before she expected that invisible power to reach him.

The vaporizing funnel bored through the side and engine of a red Chevy Corsica parked behind them, leaving a clean hole they could have looked right through. Gabi saw from Ramos's face that he had made the connection between the mutant and the destruction.

''Now, that's bad breath,'' he said, though she could see his heart wasn't in the humor.

He frowned.

''Why aren't the rest of them attacking?'' he asked aloud. ''Why hasn't that other mutant, the guy in charge, ordered an attack?''

''Maybe they're going to surrender after all?'' she suggested.

''Yeah, right!'' Lamarre said, startling her. She hadn't realized he was so close behind her.

''You have three seconds!'' Ramos called over the megaphone.

Gabi thought she could see the other mutant, the one Wilson Ramos obviously thought was in charge, shake his head and shrug. He lifted his hands, put them together in a kind of clapping motion.

"Take them down," he ordered, and concentrated sound erupted from the slightest tap of his hands together, shooting out toward them.

He missed, but across the street behind them, brick walls began to tumble in on themselves.

"Let's take back our city!" Ramos shouted over the megaphone.

In a wave, the resistance fighters moved toward the steps of City Hall.

* * *

A whirlpool of violence swirled in the street in front of the Empire State Building, with the X-Men at its center. Flashes of energy burned through the massive crowds, Magneto's followers so overcome by their urgent need to defeat the X-Men that they thought nothing of striking down their own comrades just to get at one of Xavier's people. Already, they were fighting among themselves, which offered some little relief for Scott, Jean, Rogue, and the Juggernaut.

There had been a moment, when they were first confronted by such a huge number of enemies, when Rogue wondered if the Juggernaut would bolt. But Marko stood fast with the X-Men, who had been—who, in fact, still were—his enemies. She had to admire that. You didn't generally find career criminals who were also stand-up guys.

Then there was no more time for thought, only action, as Magneto's hordes swarmed in.

Rogue tossed off several attackers, then took to the air, flying to attempt a better view of their circumstances. She ought to have known better. There were a lot of flyers already in the air. Simultaneously, she was buffeted by a bright red, phosphorescent flame, a rainbow-colored laser blast that burned through her costume and singed her flesh, and a hail of tiny darts not much larger than the thorns on a pricker bush.

She let out a cry of pain, surprise, and anger, then glared around at the four flyers closing in on her.

It was easy to tell who was responsible for what. The fire came from a man whose head and neck were intact, but the rest of his body was in flames. The laser from some jerk in a shiny technosuit. The darts flew off a woman with massive insect-type wings, whose body seemed a cross between some kind of bug and plant life.

"They call me Rose," she called. "You'll find it difficult to avoid my thorns."

"Oh, shut up, ya swamp witch!" Rogue said, and as Rose came in for another attack, Rogue grabbed her arm and swung her toward the technojerk.

"What about you?" Rogue asked, turning to the fourth flyer, who had not yet attacked her. "What do you do?"

"I'm Gravity," the man said. "It's self-explanatory."

Gravity pointed at her, and Rogue fell seventy feet to the street, landing hard on top of a guy who seemed to be made of sharpened glass, or crystal. He shattered beneath her momentum, and she hit the pavement. The glass man didn't get up again, and Rogue found that, while she could stand and fight, she could not fly. Though she suspected the effect of Gravity's power would wear off, not being able to fly threw off her battle rhythm considerably.

That moment of confusion cost her. Rogue tried to orient herself in the crowd. Where were Cyclops and Jean? Where was the Juggernaut? She knew they would still be fighting, that despite the odds, they were, all three, people of extraordinary will and endurance. But where—

Rogue cried out in pain as Senyaka's psionic whip lashed around her throat, choking off her air and burning her flesh. She was nearly invulnerable, true, but that merely meant the burning whip would not scar. It still hurt like hell.

Driven by pain and fury, Rogue simply grabbed on to the whip, bent over and pulled, her great strength launching Senyaka deep into the crowd. Without him in proximity, Senyaka's whip quickly dissipated. Before she could even catch her breath, Rogue was set upon by the former Marauder called

SALVATION

Blockbuster, and another musclehead with four arms that she believed was called, unimaginatively, Forearm.

Blockbuster hit her once and her teeth clacked together hard enough that she bit her tongue, but she only moved back a step. Forearm tried to grab her from behind, set her up as a punching bag for Blockbuster, but she turned in time to grab them both. She was about to take them down, about to knock their heads together like something out of the Three Stooges. Then small arms wrapped around her neck and a weight fell on her back, dragging her down.

It was Tusk, or at least a part of him. A large mutant with some kind of armadillo-like shell, and several miniature versions of himself running around. Together, all the aspects of Tusk began beating on Rogue, along with Blockbuster and Forearm. She could take it. Could take them all. But how long could she take it for? That was the question.

Tusk. Forearm. That meant Mutant Liberation Front. Or Dark Riders. Or whatever they were calling themselves these days. Reaper, Dragoness, Tempo, and the others. If they were all there. God, she was finding it so hard to think; she had just enough brainpower to fend off her attackers' blows. Not all of them, though. Some—a lot of them—connected. Hard. And more mutants were joining in.

Faces flashed above her, overpowering her, and Rogue knew her only chance was flight. She willed herself into the air.

Nothing happened. Gravity's power was still affecting her, no telling how long it would last. Through the breaks in the heads and fists moving above her, Rogue saw that the blue had begun to drain from the sky. Late summer afternoon, then. Maybe early evening, dinnertime. A beautiful day.

"Rogue!" she heard a familiar voice snarl. "Get away from her!"

Something wet spilled on Rogue's face, she recognized its coppery smell. Blood. Whose blood?

Mine?

"No!" she cried, brought back into action by the fear that she might actually be bleeding.

With all her strength, she pistoned her legs, kicked out hard, and heard Blockbuster's ribs crack as he went sprawling back. Forearm was trying to hold her, but she swung her legs up again, snagged him by the neck, and whipped him down, across her, onto the pavement. Then there was Tusk, all three of him.

One of them was bleeding. All of them were attacking someone else.

"Kind o' figured you'd fallen asleep down there, Rogue," Wolverine snarled, and slashed at Tusk—the biggest one.

"Just resting," she managed to say, though it was barely funny.

To make sure she could, Rogue flew just off the ground across the few feet to Wolverine, snagged both of the smaller Tusks by their armor-plated necks, and simply threw them.

"No!" Tusk cried, and followed his miniature selves into the crowd.

"Why didn't you stay down, girl?" Senyaka snapped as he moved in toward Rogue and Wolverine.

Then Riptide was there as well, spinning like a miniature twister, tossing sharpened projectiles that sliced Wolverine's flesh and stung Rogue, though they bounced off her body and fell to the street.

"We were coming to free you," Rogue said amiably.

"You were doin' a bang-up job o' it," Wolverine grumbled. "Anyway, Drake beat you to it."

Rogue raised an eyebrow. "Iceman broke into Magneto's headquarters by himself and got you guys out?"

"Him and Trish Tilby," Logan answered.

"Good for him," Rogue said, then launched herself at Riptide even as Wolverine feinted at Senyaka, who dodged right into the spot Logan wanted him.

Rogue squinted, fighting the urge to close her eyes as she flew directly into the tiny storm that was Riptide. He moved so fast, she doubted she would be able to grab hold of him. Instead, she simply slammed into him and kept flying. Riptide went down hard.

Up she flew, then turned around for a better perspective on

SALVATION

the battle, making certain to stay away from enemy flyers.

And there they were. Together again at last.

Cyclops. Jean Grey. The Beast. Iceman. Bishop. Storm. Wolverine. And the wild card in the group, the Juggernaut.

For the moment, these were the X-Men.

Despite the incredible odds against them, standing together, Rogue knew they had a chance. Better than a chance.

Off to the left, Harlan Kleinstock was blasting away at her gathered teammates, her friends. Her family. Rogue scowled and went after him with new confidence.

Chapter 11

The melee at City Hall had gotten ugly. Ivan Skolnick had recognized the police commissioner, Wilson Ramos, immediately. Of course, when the man announced that he was there to arrest all those who were siding with Magneto, it had been almost amusing. To be sure, he had the greater numbers. But he didn't have any mutants on his side. And one or two Alpha mutants, Skolnick had long since realized, made all the difference in the world.

When Funnel had attacked, exhaling a blast of energy that displaced anything in its path into some kind of otherworldly limbo, Skolnick had been forced to attack as well. He was in charge, after all. It wouldn't do for his subordinates to be undermining his command.

But that was one of the many problems with this new world order, too many rebels. The only one anybody obeyed regularly was Magneto, and who knew where the hell he'd gotten off to. No, this was nothing like the hierarchy of command that Skolnick had learned as a military man. Nothing like commanding Special Ops Unit One.

Whom he'd betrayed.

SOU1 was his team. They had faith in him, followed his orders implicitly, the way any crack military squad must do. And he had turned on them. It had been for their own good, he thought, attempting with little success to reassure himself. It was true, though. They were better off as captives of Magneto than as corpses. Taking them down his way had been the best way.

But now, as he hit the rioting crowd with another blast of concentrated sonic energy, Skolnick realized that it had not been the best way. He was frightened, to be sure, of a world where mutants were hated and feared. He expected that one day he would be outed, despite the "don't ask, don't tell" policy the government had adopted, and on that day, he would be forced to leave the military in shame. His family would ignore him. He would become an outcast. He didn't want to live that way, and he could certainly understand how Magneto, and all the other mutants there in Haven, could have come to such a radical decision.

But he was a man first. A military man second. A mutant last. He had not taken the best way out of a tough situation, but the worst. He knew that now. He ought to have gone down with his team, if that was how it had to be. Now even if he turned on Magneto, he would be considered a traitor, court-martialed, dishonorably discharged, and revealed as a mutant. His team would turn their backs on him, without question.

Ivan Skolnick would be alone. He did not want to be alone. And yet, what was he, amid the anarchy of the fight before him, as policemen shot at their brothers-in-blue, as citizens of a city stormed the walls of their own seat of government? What was he, if not alone?

"Skolnick!" Steve Tyree, the man Magneto had appointed police commissioner, shouted at him. "Come on, you idiot. You're the big mutie here, do something!"

Ivan snapped. Rounded on Tyree.

"Mutie?" he cried, marching toward Tyree, who backed off until Skolnick was screaming, spraying spittle into his face, with Tyree against the oaken doors of City Hall.

"Mutie!" he shouted again. "What was that little shared moment of righteousness that you and Magneto had going, Tyree? When he made the speech about bigotry? You were gonna bring the thunder down on the evil bigots with both hands, weren't you? But you're just as bad!"

Skolnick let go of Tyree, wiped his hands on his pants as if he'd gotten something nasty on them. He tried to turn his attention back to the battle, tried to ignore the officious little human, but Tyree pursued him.

"Who do you think you are?" Tyree demanded. "Mutants are a danger to society, not some social group that one is prejudiced against or not. If I live in a world where mutants are in control, I will do what I have to to get by. If that means I can enforce equality, all the better. I have worked for civil rights my whole life, defended the rights of women, stood up for gay marriages. My father was in D.C. when Dr. King made his 'I have a dream' speech, he marched on Montgomery."

"He'd be disgusted if he could see you today," Skolnick said. "Mutants are human beings, you imbecile. With emotions and insecurities, just like everyone else. They need help, not persecution."

Skolnick slammed Tyree's head against the wall, then just let go. He had expended his anger, at Tyree, and at himself. Now he felt only revulsion, and profound regret. He had made a terrible choice. The only questions now were what it would cost him, and if he could repair any of the damage.

Several bullets took chunks of brick out of the wall behind him. Skolnick didn't even duck. If death was justice, he would accept it without complaint. But he hoped to be able to bring about a more effective justice.

"Got you in my sights, Ramos!" Funnel cried, and blew kisses at the police commissioner, the destructive power of his exhalation cutting through half a dozen men and women, ally and enemy alike, on its path toward Ramos. This time it was moving much faster, but Ramos knew what was happening now. He was no fool. He'd get out of the way.

Which did nothing for the people unfortunate enough to have been in Funnel's firing line. The steps of City Hall got bloody very quickly. Cops loyal to Tyree and, as such, to Magneto, fired on those trying to take back the city.

"That's it!" Skolnick shouted. "That's it! No more!"

* * *

In the Oval Office, the President of the United States sat slumped forward, elbows on his desk, face in his hands. He was at a loss. Completely and totally unable, in that moment, to make a solid decision as to how to proceed against Magneto.

Light was slowly leeching from the office, from the world, just as the life was being sucked from his political career. He glanced up through splayed fingers at the seal of his office on the marble floor. No lights were on in the office, and he could barely make out all but the most prominent features of the seal. Appropriate, he thought. It was disappearing with any chance he had of reelection.

SALVATION

If he did nothing, he was screwed. If he sent the troops in, a lot of them would die, and they had almost no chance of winning; in which case, he was screwed. If he nuked Manhattan, well, that one wasn't hard to figure out. He was screwed no matter what tactic he chose.

Somebody knocked "shave and a haircut" on the oaken door of his office, but left off the "two bits."

"Come in, Bob," he said, and pressed a button under his desk that buzzed the door open.

The Director of Operation: Wideawake entered, looking just as haggard as the President felt.

"You want dinner?" the Director asked. "You haven't eaten anything today, and it's past six o'clock."

"Couldn't keep anything down, I don't think," the President replied.

The Director only nodded. He came all the way into the office, shutting the door behind him, and took one of the two large wood-and-leather chairs facing the President's desk.

"So," the Director said.

"So," the President agreed, wholeheartedly.

"Want to hear what the polls have to say?" the Director asked.

"First I want to know how the X-Men are doing, what's happening with Cooper, and if you've been able to keep Gyrich from going over the line."

"My answer to all three is, I don't know."

"Not the answer I was hoping for," the President said, with a calm that didn't fool either of them.

"Magneto has completely jammed our satellite view of Manhattan," the Director explained. "CNN, ABC, and MTV are broadcasting out of the MTV building in Times Square, and Magneto is letting that through. Publicity he wants, observation he doesn't. Reports say there's war, in midtown and downtown at City Hall. The X-Men are involved. That's all we know. No word at all from Cooper."

"I guess no news is good news on that front."

"I'd have to agree," the Director said. "Gyrich, on the other hand, is itching for a resolution."

"He's not alone," the President said. "The whole country wants to know how this thing is going to turn out. Every idiot in the world thinks they know how to solve it. But none of them have to make the decision."

"We can't wait for the X-Men or for Cooper, sir," the Director said.

"Now, just a—"

"No, listen. If Cooper succeeds, all it does is give us an edge. It doesn't win the day, necessarily. The X-Men can't do it alone. There are hundreds of mutants, maybe as many as a thousand, all lined up against what? Eight or ten X-Men? I don't care how good they are, those are not workable odds.

"Then there are the polls. Graydon Creed may be sitting back and taking this all in, but the media knows he's made noises about running against you next election. So they're polling. You're neck and neck, sir, and Creed hasn't even announced. The polls also say why. They like Creed's thinking on the mutant issue, and the Manhattan catastrophe. Between Creed and Senator Kelly, the world is looking for a swift solution, and punishment for Magneto and his followers.

"You can't afford any of this," the Director said. "I'm not saying you nuke the city. Not yet, anyway. But if you don't give the order for full-scale invasion, somebody else may try to give it for you. You need this."

The President shook his head, then swung his chair to gaze out the window at the White House lawn. For a moment, he regretted his rise to political power, considered the gradual change in the decision-making process he had undergone. Once he had done what he wanted to. Now, he was forced to do what he needed to.

"Do it," he said, without turning around. "Full-scale attack, whatever it takes. Get that city back."

"Yes, sir," the Director said. "Should I warn them to be prepared for instant dust-off, in case we have to go with the nukes?"

Still looking out the window, the President shook his head.

"We expect collateral damage and loss of life," he said. "We can't risk giving Magneto warning if it comes to that."

SALVATION

The Director didn't respond. The President heard the other man's shoes click on the tile. The door opened and closed. When he was gone, the President ran his hands through his hair, turned to face his desk, and prayed silently.

* * *

Henry Peter Gyrich had a headache. It wasn't the explosions, the weapons fire, the shouting, the choppers slapping the air above. They made it worse, no doubt about that. But the headache was caused by bureaucracy, pure and simple.

"But, sir," Gyrich pleaded, "Cooper's little plan to fight fire with fire, to use mutants to defeat mutants, was bad enough before conflict erupted in earnest. Things have obviously changed now. We can't just defend ourselves, we've got to go into this thing to the hilt, or we don't have a chance in hell!"

On the tiny vid-comm screen in Gyrich's trailer, the Director of Wideawake shook his head slowly and sighed.

"Gyrich," he said, "if it were up to me, not only would we have gone in full force from the get-go, but my finger would be poised over the panic button, okay? But it's not up to me. The President wants to avoid whatever collateral damage we can. That means giving Cooper more time, giving the X-Men more time. For now, we attack the Sentinels from remote points, but we do not invade. Are you clear on that, Gyrich? At this juncture, we do not invade!"

Gyrich massaged his temples, slowly at first, and then with more vigor. The headache wasn't going away. It was getting worse.

"Gyrich?"

"My head's going to explode."

"Gyrich!" the Director snapped, and he looked up at the man's stern features.

"Yes, sir, we're clear," Gyrich said. "But I don't have to like it."

"No," the Director agreed. "No, you don't."

Gyrich clicked off the vid-comm and pushed back his chair. When he stepped out of the trailer, he noted how the afternoon had moved in, and the temperature had dropped quite a bit. In a way, he was disappointed. As far as he was concerned, hell was supposed to be hot.

In the distance, the shelling and plasma fire continued. Stinger missiles had been brought in, and even now a pair burned toward the face of the Sentinel that overlooked the Hudson River. Without turning its attention from its own attack on the troops massed on the riverbank, the Sentinel burned the Stingers out of the sky.

With an eye on the battle, Gyrich wandered into the no man's land between the military and media camps, prepared to give a statement to the press, just to get them to stop hounding him for fifteen minutes. Halfway there, he passed Cooper's trailer.

Charles Xavier sat in front of the trailer in his wheelchair, eyes closed as if he were resting, or asleep.

"Enjoying the show?" Gyrich asked.

Xavier didn't move.

"Xavier?" Gyrich said, a bit louder, wondering if the man was all right. After all, he had never learned why Xavier was in a wheelchair. What if something was wrong with him?

"Professor Xavier?" he asked again.

The man's eyes snapped open, looking directly at Gyrich. If he had been sleeping, Gyrich had never seen anybody wake up so thoroughly so quickly.

"What can I do for you, Mr. Gyrich?" Xavier asked.

"Sorry to have disturbed you, Xavier," Gyrich said.

"Not at all," Xavier answered. "Just a little meditation to keep alert. After all, none of us really got any sleep last night, did we?"

"No," Gyrich said, "I don't suppose we did."

Though he shrugged it off, Gyrich found something eerie in what Xavier had termed his "meditation." And the comment about sleepless nights had him wondering just what Xavier had been doing all night. Perhaps merely advising Cooper and the President, as he had originally explained. But perhaps something more as well. Gyrich wondered if he would ever know the answer to these questions. Though he was usually confident about such things, for some reason, he doubted he would.

"What was it you had asked?" Xavier inquired.

"Just if you were enjoying the show," Gyrich explained, though the humor seemed to have gone out of the question now.

The two men, allies yet enemies, gazed across Exchange Place toward the scene of the battle. To Gyrich, it seemed less likely with each passing moment that the Sentinels would even be harmed by conventional weapons. He had seen the specs, he knew that was part of the robots' design. But most things the Defense Department built didn't function as well as they were supposed to. He silently cursed them for having hit a bull's-eye with the Sentinels.

Another Stinger shot at the Sentinel's chest was destroyed without any damage.

"No," Xavier said finally, after Gyrich had given up waiting for an answer. "No, I'm not enjoying the show at all."

Gyrich nodded slowly. For several minutes, he stood next to Xavier's wheelchair, and the two men watched the conflict in silence.

* * *

Xavier wanted Gyrich to go away. Val Cooper, Gambit, and Archangel had found the Alpha Sentinel. He had been monitoring their progress when Gyrich interrupted. He was still with Val, his subconscious mind tracking her and maintaining the illusion—for the Sentinel's sake—that she was a mutant. But it was no simple feat to communicate with Gyrich while doing so. He wished he could simply tell the man that Cooper had found the Alpha unit. It would make all their lives easier. But Gyrich would want to know how Xavier had come by such knowledge. That would lead to disaster.

"I am quite drained by all of this, Mr. Gyrich," Xavier said. "What can I do for you?"

Gyrich narrowed his eyes a moment, obviously irked at Xavier's dismissive tone. The Professor was not at all concerned. Gyrich was a dangerous man, but Charles Xavier could be a dangerous man, too, when he wished to be.

"I thought you would want to know," Gyrich said grimly. "The President has ordered a full-scale incursion into Manhattan island. We go in thirty minutes."

"What of the X-Men?" Xavier asked, astonished. "They were to have more time than—"

"Their time ran out when the Sentinels started killing us, Professor," Gyrich replied. "I assumed you would realize that."

Xavier frowned, took a calming breath, then turned back to Gyrich.

"You'd best hope that they succeed despite your foolishness, Mr. Gyrich," Xavier said. "Otherwise, you're going to have a lot of dead soldiers on your hands."

"This is a war, Professor," Gyrich said, without missing a beat. "I'm pleased that the President has started to think of it as one. Perhaps it is time for you to do the same."

Though Gyrich seemed far more composed and more solemn than Xavier might have expected—he would have thought the man would be almost gleeful at this news—his air of superiority, his assumption of greater purpose, was intensely grating.

"It's always been war for me, Mr. Gyrich," Xavier said. "You have no idea."

* * *

When Trish had left the Empire State Building with Beast, Iceman, and the other X-Men Magneto had held captive, she had been stunned to find so little resistance to their escape. When they hit the street, they realized the reason. Every powered mutant among Magneto's followers, and a good number who were not, were out in the street, attacking Cyclops and the others who had come on a belated rescue attempt.

"Thank you," Hank had said, and Trish knew that meant they were about to part ways.

"For what?" Trish said. "All I did was get some people killed."

"Don't think that!" Hank had snapped. "Don't ever think

that! You did what you had to, the only thing you could do. Your friends knew what they were getting themselves into. I'll always be grateful to you for laying it on the line for—for us.''

Their eyes had met then. Trish had known what his hesitation signified. Hank had wanted to say ''for me,'' not ''for us.'' He'd wanted to acknowledge their past, and the small reconciliation that her actions had created. But he hadn't said it. He'd been afraid, she knew, that she hadn't done it for him at all. Afraid that she might mistake his gratitude for something more intimate.

''You're very welcome,'' she had said, and she'd kissed him on the nose the way she had always done in older, better times.

Then he and the others were gone, running to aid their teammates. Trish was on her way as well, heading north on Broadway. In her time with Magneto, she had discovered that her tapes were being delivered to the MTV offices, where they were continuing to broadcast coverage of the occupation of Manhattan.

She reached Times Square and glanced quickly around to orient herself. Just a few years earlier, Times Square had still been one of the more dangerous areas of the city. It had been cleaned up, spit-shined, and marketed to Boomers and GenXers nationwide.

Now it was trashed again.

After a moment, she identified her destination. The Viacom Building, named for MTV's parent company, at 1515 Broadway, the northwest corner of Broadway and Forty-fourth Street. The doors were open, but the escalators were off, so she had to trudge up the long flight of steps to the lobby. At least the elevators were running.

When the elevator slid open, there was a moment of tension as those in the MTV foyer froze, probably wondering if the mutants had finally decided to shut them down. Trish also froze, wondering if they had instituted any security devices she should be aware of.

''Trish?'' a male voice asked.

Among a group clustered around the lobby was Doug Samuels, a camera operator she had worked with before he'd gone on to ABC.

"Oh, Doug, thank God," she said, and rushed to him.

Only when she broke the embrace did she realize that she had been holding on to him for dear life. Then the whole story spilled out of her, with the group surrounding her and Doug growing larger as she spoke. When somebody came out with a camera, though, Trish clammed up.

"What's wrong?" the woman with the camera asked. "We've got to report on all of this. Keep going."

"No," Trish said, shaking her head. "No way. I'm not the subject here, I'm the reporter. I don't care who wants to carry it, but I'm going to be the one reporting the story."

Nobody argued with that. Which was good. Trish would not have been able to handle argument.

When all the cameras were set up, Trish began to speak.

"This is Trish Tilby reporting from hell," she said.

Nobody snickered.

"You've all seen my reports, I assume, but I have no idea what parts of them were censored," Trish continued. "Before I tell you the story, what I've been through, before I talk about Magneto, or the X-Men, or what's really at stake here, I want to tell you about two people.

"Their names were Kevin and Caroline, and they died a little while ago. A man and a woman, a human and a mutant, they gave their lives to see that you, the people of our world, would have an opportunity to decide for yourselves what you want to make of it. They died believing that we, as a race of beings, could separate what Magneto and other mutants have done, from mutantkind in general. That we would do the right thing.

"What saddens me is, I'm not certain if they died in vain. I truthfully don't know if we're all grown up enough, we humans, to judge all beings individually. Or I should say, I know that some of us can and will be fair and logical and rational. Others will not. What I am uncertain about is the numbers. How many of you are the ones Kevin and Caroline died for?

And how many are the kind whose words and beliefs motivate a monster like Magneto?

"I'm trying to have the same faith Kevin and Caroline did. I'm trying so very hard."

* * *

The Harley had been abandoned as they got within half a block of the Alpha Sentinel. Archangel grabbed Gambit and Val Cooper, each by an upraised hand, and flew. Val knew it had to be a strain for Warren. He was powerful, but he had no super-enhanced strength to go along with his other mutant gifts.

Val felt extremely vulnerable, dangling there in the sky with only one man's grip between her and certain death on the street below. Still, it wasn't as if she had any real choice. The Alpha Sentinel had to be reprogrammed and she was the only one who could do it.

As they flew to the height of the Alpha unit's waist, it spoke, its voice a soulless, mechanical drone that seemed, nevertheless, to have a distinctly hostile personality.

"Halt, mutants," it commanded, and Val was relieved that Professor Xavier's psionic presence in her mind had fooled the killing computer.

"You are approaching too close to this unit," it announced. "Please do not approach any further."

Archangel flew higher, and Val felt for a moment as though she was going to slip from his grasp. She was tempted to grab for his hand with her other, but that would throw off his equilibrium, and they might all fall.

"You ready, Gambit?" Archangel asked.

"Gambit was born ready, *mon ami*," the Cajun answered. "Hang on."

Then he dive-bombed the Sentinel, trailing Gambit and Val beneath him. She wanted to scream. She didn't. Perhaps Professor Xavier's psionic presence was calming her, she thought.

"Warning!" the Alpha Sentinel barked. "You are too close to this unit. While this unit is programmed not to attack mutants, this unit is also programmed to defend itself against any attack which is hostile, or which this unit perceives to be hostile.''

"Bombs away!" Archangel shouted as he swooped low above the Sentinel's head and shoulders.

Then he dropped Gambit.

"Allez!" Gambit shouted.

Val couldn't look. As Archangel snagged her other hand, getting a better grip on her, she tried not to think about how close he might have come to dropping her. She tried not to imagine Gambit's calculated fall down to the Sentinel's shoulder.

"Fast, Remy!" Warren shouted. "Move it, man!"

Then Val had to look. Gambit stood on the lip of titanium alloy that separated the Sentinel's shoulder from its neck. With one hand on the upraised seam that surrounded the Alpha unit's head like a crown, Gambit leaned out over open space, many stories above the street.

The Sentinel was reaching for him.

Archangel urged Gambit on. Val was not certain if that urgency was driven by fear for the Cajun's safety—now that the Sentinel was reacting to his presence—or concern that he would not be able to carry Val much longer. She realized rather quickly that she did not want to know.

In the shadow thrown by the robot's massive head, Gambit's eyes glowed red. The Sentinel touched its own shoulder, its hand scrambling with a metal-on-metal scrape that made Val want to scream.

Gambit laid his palm flat on the back of the Sentinel's head, precisely where Val had instructed him to. Instantly, the metal began to glow ever brighter. At the last possible moment, Gambit pulled away and the back of the Sentinel's head exploded.

The Alpha unit reached for him. From within the long duster, Gambit pulled out his bo-stick, which telescoped out in his hands to a length of more than five feet. With one thrust, he threw off the Sentinel's grasp, but that would be his only chance.

He took it. With only two steps to gain momentum, he

leaped up on top of the Sentinel's head, where he would be an easy target for its groping hands. Before it could react, he reached down, grabbed hold of the edge of the hole made by his volatile mutant power, and flipped down inside the Sentinel's head, into the command center whose entrance he had blown wide open.

Once inside, Gambit disappeared from the Sentinel's sensors as if into thin air. As far as it was concerned, he was gone. That left Val and Archangel to deal with.

"Go, Warren, quick, before it gets pissed off enough to swat us out of the sky!" she barked.

With nauseating speed, Archangel swooped low toward the Sentinel's back, then climbed rapidly in a straight line, out of its reach, toward the exposed computerized brain of the robot. A moment later, they were inside and Warren was massaging his strained arm muscles and stretching his fingers. Val let out a long sigh of relief.

Gambit smiled at her.

"Something funny, X-Man?" Val asked, in no mood for humor.

"*Non*, Valerie," he said. "Gambit jus' relieved, de same as you. Look around, *mes amis*, we did it. We're inside."

Then they were all smiling.

"You do your job, Val," Archangel said, "and then it's dinner at Tavern on the Green for everybody, on me!"

Val liked the sound of that. Assuming, of course, that Tavern on the Green was still there. But the smile left her face the moment she turned her attention to the command center of the Alpha Sentinel's brain. If she could reprogram it, something she had vowed to everyone that she could, indeed, do, then the war against Magneto would take an almost surely decisive turn in their favor.

Problem was, she wasn't exactly certain what Magneto had done to them, how he had reprogrammed the Sentinels in the first place. Or if he'd prepared some kind of failsafe that might kill her merely for logging into the command center.

But she was about to find out.

It was the only option. Their only real hope.

CHAPTER 12

"**N**ot another step, Marko, or you will face the wrath of the terrible Toad!" Mortimer Toynbee shrieked, as he leaped into the path of destruction the Juggernaut was tearing through Magneto's forces.

"Hmm, hmm," the Juggernaut said through a smile. "Ya gotta be . . . oh, come on, I . . ."

Then he laughed so hard, he threw back his head and tears rolled down his cheeks inside his mask. Infuriated, the Toad sprang at him and those extraordinarily powerful legs knocked Cain Marko on his butt in the middle of Thirty-third Street. But Cain was still laughing. He tried to get up, and the Toad knocked him down again.

Inside his mystical armor, the Juggernaut felt pain.

"Hey," he said. "That kinda—"

The Toad leaped again, lightning quick, and laid him out in the street with a kick so powerful, it left the Juggernaut gasping for air, even inside his armor.

"I will teach you to laugh at me, you dimwitted . . ." Toynbee began, as he leaped at the Juggernaut for the fourth time, his pistoning feet aimed directly at the neck joint where helmet met armor, the spot where Cain was most vulnerable.

But even those who had seen him move often forgot how fast Cain Marko was, which was understandable given his size. Understandable, but unforgivable.

He snatched the Toad out of the air by his feet, then stood quickly, holding Toynbee upside down. The Juggernaut wasn't laughing anymore.

"You pissed me off, Toynbee," he said. "Yer lucky I don't break both your legs."

"Sure, you're making nice with Xavier's brood now," the Toad said, the mockery quite clear in his voice. "You're a Boy Scout, Marko."

That did it. Cain righted the Toad with one twist, and held the little mutant up so they were face to face, Toynbee's legs ratcheting beneath him, trying to get traction anywhere, even off the Juggernaut's chest. Cain wasn't having any of it.

"You can't win, Marko!" he cried. "Magneto's reign has

SALVATION

come, as I always knew it would. Your kind will be trampled underfoot along with all the other flatscans, and traitors like the X-Men. You're a dead man, Marko. Why don't you lie down like a good boy, so we can bury you?''

Cain was flush with rage, so overwhelmed with fury that he couldn't think straight enough to form any kind of cogent response. He spit his frustration, and gave up trying to speak. Instead, he cracked the Toad across the face with a backhand so massive, and backed by such extraordinary strength, that Toynbee sagged limp in his hands, unconscious from the blow.

''Runt,'' Cain growled, and dropped the Toad at his feet.

He was tempted to step on Toynbee's head, but he was acutely aware of the fight raging around him. That day, he was one of the white hats. It would probably never happen again, but as long as he could, and foolish as it was, he was going to play by Xavier's rules.

''All right,'' he growled. ''Who's next?''

''Try me.'' A bass rumble came from behind him, and a hand, large even by his standards, landed on Cain's shoulder.

The Juggernaut turned to face Javits, one of Magneto's original Acolytes, a powerful mutant even larger than he himself was. The one-eyed Acolyte didn't move.

''There's a difference between brave and stupid,'' Cain said, and slammed a fist into Javits's left cheek.

The Acolyte blinked. That was all.

''Indeed there is,'' Javits said. ''But the difference is lost on you.''

Javits hit him and Cain stumbled backward. He'd heard a crack that he was afraid might be his helmet, and more afraid might be his skull. A second later, he realized it had been one of Javits's fingers breaking. The huge mutant shook his right hand, sucking a breath in between his teeth.

The Juggernaut smiled as he stood, glad the jerk was in pain, and determined to make it continue. He'd been standing still when Javits hit him. When he was moving, it would be a different story. He launched himself toward the Acolyte.

Out of instinct developed over the years because of his size and strength, Javits stood his ground.

"Moron," Cain mumbled under his breath.

He felt ribs snap under his helmet as he slammed headfirst into Javits's chest. The Acolyte cried out and went down, trampled under the Juggernaut's massive boots. He didn't look back to see if Javits was still alive, and despite his attitude about being one of the good guys, he didn't much care.

Half a block away, he saw a group of several dozen people, probably mutants, turning down Fifth Avenue. They might have been moving on to another skirmish, ordered to another location because the Acolytes figured they had the X-Men contained. But the way they were nervously glancing back at the battlefield on Thirty-third Street, Cain didn't think so.

He thought they were running away. It made no sense, but that's how he figured it.

A sudden blast of energy struck him between the shoulder blades, and Cain actually stumbled forward slightly. He turned, ready to fight, but his opponents were not advancing. Not yet.

Three Acolytes faced him: the field leader, Amelia Voght, whom Cain remembered as an old flame of his half-brother's, and a pair of blond bruisers, identical twins down to their Marine buzz-cuts. These were the Kleinstocks, the twerps who had tried to recruit him earlier that day.

"You've caused enough trouble, Juggernaut," Voght said. "Why don't we see if I can teleport that helmet off your head without taking your head with it. Either way, I'm going to win."

"You can try, babe," he snarled. "Either way, I'm gonna—"

Cain faltered. Gears churned in his head, actions and consequences roiled together. He glanced quickly around at the battle that, no matter how long they held out, the X-Men didn't have a chance in hell of winning.

"Ah, screw it," he said.

The Juggernaut turned and ran.

* * *

Ivan Skolnick had had enough. He was loyal to the government, to human society, to the Earth, not because any of those things were perfect—in truth, humanity was little better than a primal beast. But tyranny, like Magneto's new empire, was the ultimate primal beast. Humanity was about choice and evolution, about the collective will of billions of people, not the new order demanded by one individual, no matter how powerful.

Skolnick knew that his own nagging self-doubt and fear had driven him to betray his fundamental faith in humanity, and he now regretted it. He knew, also, that he could never turn back. That he could not expect to be forgiven for actions the American government would consider the most heinous of crimes. There was fear, there, as well, fear of the consequences of his actions.

But all doubt was gone. He knew what he must do.

In the space between breaths, that certainty coalesced into action. As Funnel renewed his attack, as human police officers loyal to Manhattan's conquerors turned their guns on their brothers in blue, Major Ivan Skolnick called up every ounce of concentration he could muster, and turned his mutant powers on his allies.

With a single clap of his hands, Skolnick sent a wave of stunning force toward Funnel, pummeling the other mutant and several police officers. They were driven across the steps, several stumbled and fell, but Funnel stayed up until the force of Skolnick's blast slammed him into a hand railing. Skolnick heard bones break, but he couldn't allow himself to be concerned. It wasn't that difficult. Special Ops had trained him not only to fight, but to kill when necessary and feel remorse only in church.

Funnel wasn't dead, though. He simply wouldn't be getting up for a while.

"Freeze!" two police officers shouted simultaneously.

In the moment it took them to swing their weapons toward Major Skolnick, the moment in which he also swung his empty—but no less deadly—hands toward them, he noted and filed a thought for later amusement. *They actually say "freeze" in real life*, he thought. But then, what else would they say?

The officers fired just as Skolnick snapped his fingers, slap-

ping the bullets back along their trajectories and blowing out
the doors of City Hall.

* * *

Gabi Frigerio hung back as the resistance fighters stormed City
Hall, crying out in triumph over a victory they owed to the
other side. Well, not exactly the other side. Still, it had been
one of Magneto's top people, the former soldier, Major Skolnick, who had been the deciding factor.

The people of Manhattan streamed into City Hall and the
police officers who had remained loyal to Commissioner Ramos began to incarcerate those who had followed Magneto. In
minutes, the building was completely in their control. Maxine Perkins, the woman Magneto had appointed mayor, did
not even argue as she was placed behind bars. Gabi liked to
think it was because the woman had enough sense to be
ashamed of herself.

Major Skolnick stood on the steps, watching the commotion. Gabi thought he looked like a man with nowhere to go.
She could not help but approach him.

"That was a courageous and unbelievably stupid thing you
did," she said. "Why did you?"

For a few moments, Skolnick didn't respond. Then, finally,
he looked up at her as if waking from a daydream.

"It was my only choice," he said cryptically.

"There are always choices," she said. "We just have to
be brave or stupid enough to make them."

Her brother was calling for her from within City Hall. She
looked through the shattered doorway and saw him with Lamarre
and Miguelito, talking to Commissioner Ramos about something. She ignored them, turning her attention back to Major
Skolnick. That he was a mutant did not upset her. That he had
been on Magneto's side did not turn her away. She was fascinated by his actions, and profoundly affected by his despair.

"I guess you're right," he answered, after she'd begun to
think he had forgotten she was there.

For a long time, the day had been growing more dull, less
vibrantly alive. Now, finally, the sky was beginning to darken.

SALVATION

"It's not over, you know," he said suddenly, still watching the sky as if waiting, at any moment, for the judgment of God to thunder down from the heavens.

"What isn't?" she asked.

"The war," he said. "Magneto could take back City Hall in an instant, and he will, the moment it pleases him to do so."

"If he gets the chance," Gabi said offhandedly. "But I don't think the X-Men are going to allow that to happen."

Skolnick sighed. "The X-Men are already his prisoners."

"Wrong," Gabi said happily. "Not only is Iceman around, but the guerrilla news stations that are running out of MTV's offices have reported that the X-Men have escaped and are fighting Magneto's stormtroopers . . . no offense. . . ."

"None taken," he said softly.

"Anyway," she continued, "there's a big battle near the Empire State Building. Of course, with these odds, they don't have much hope."

But even as she said it, she saw Major Skolnick's eyes light up with joyous energy.

"They're free?" he asked.

She nodded. "Yeah. That's what I heard. But with the odds . . ."

Major Skolnick looked at her for the first time, really looked at her. Gabi smiled at him, so infectious was his sudden enthusiasm.

"What's your name, ma'am?" he asked, with perfect military politeness.

"Uh, Gabriela Frigerio," she answered.

"Well, Ms. Frigerio, the odds might be impossible, but we can change the odds, can't we?" he asked, glancing around.

Gabi scanned the rubble on the steps, the ragged doorframe, looked at Commissioner Ramos talking with her comrades inside the building.

"Yeah," she said in realization. "Yeah, we can."

* * *

"You gotta be kidding me," Sven Kleinstock said, and he and his brother began to laugh.

''Shut up and fight, you morons!'' Amelia Voght snapped, and the Kleinstocks responded.

She knew they didn't like her very much. Actually, they didn't like her at all. But they'd seen what she had done to Unuscione, and at least for the duration of the war, they didn't seem like they were going to question her anymore. Magneto had chosen Voght as field leader. She'd done the job, and dealt with the consequences.

She believed in the dream. No question. She had believed in Xavier's dream first, until she came to understand that it was only a dream. That no matter how hard he fought, no matter how clever he might be, or how brilliant, Xavier would never be able to make that dream a reality. It depended on the intelligence, the reason, the goodwill, of humanity. It was a joke.

Magneto's dream, on the other hand, was one that required nothing more than power and the will to use it. Voght understood that, and believed Magneto had the power to make it real. And here it was, right in front of them, the actualization of a dream that had taken years to come to fruition.

The execution had gone smoothly. Haven had been founded with a minumum of trouble. But conquest meant taking land and keeping it, and the latter was far more difficult. They had reached the crisis point now, the time when they had to give everything they had to keep the sanctuary that they had so quickly won. It would not truly be theirs until the challenges had been met and overcome.

But Voght was in it all the way. She pitied Charles Xavier, whom she had loved in a once-upon-a-time past when she had been little more than a naive girl. She pitied the X-Men, who, like their mentor, only wanted the best for the world. But that was their problem. As much as Voght might also pity the humans who weren't ignorant savages, she knew that the choice came down to the same one it always did: them or us.

With those options, Voght knew that she was always going to choose ''us.'' Anything else was foolish. And Xavier the biggest fool of all because he believed there was a third choice.

SALVATION

A belief that, if Voght was correct, was being strongly challenged by Magneto's triumph.

And it would be a triumph, of that she was certain.

The X-Men had no chance. Were there twenty of them, or thirty, or fifty, rather than a mere eight, they would not have defeated Magneto's combined forces. No matter how long the X-Men might hold out, no matter how many mutants they might take out of the fight, it was the eight of them against hundreds of enemies, plus Magneto, and the fleet of Sentinels waiting in the wings if they became necessary.

It was hopeless for them. Voght only wished they would realize it, and surrender. Or run away as the Juggernaut had seemed to. Which was, of course, what the Kleinstocks had been laughing about. Cain Marko, the Juggernaut, one of the most powerful and destructive superhumans in the world, had seen the odds against them and taken off. Voght didn't blame Sven and Harlan for laughing. They saw Marko as a coward, but Voght thought the man was just smart. Against impossible odds, the best bet was simply to retreat.

But not the X-Men. They would never retreat. Voght was saddened to realize that, in all likelihood, this would mean that the Acolytes would be forced to kill Xavier's followers to put a stop to them. A waste that would greatly displease Magneto. But if necessary, Voght would not balk at ordering that execution.

Her train of thought was broken by a plasma blast which cut the street dangerously close to where she stood, and Voght realized how foolish she'd been. She'd cussed out the Kleinstocks for less, and here she was playing walking target for whoever might want to take a shot at her. Well, no more. It was time for the final push. Magneto and the Sentinels would keep the army busy. She had another job.

"Acolytes!" she cried, her upraised arms drawing the attention of Magneto's entire army of followers. "Take them!"

Those who could not hear her words over the din of battle would not fail to understand her meaning.

"You're making a terrible mistake, Voght," Cyclops shouted from behind her.

Foolish of him. Before he could take her out of the fight with an optic blast, Amelia teleported behind him. Cyclops rolled down and away, and was quickly swept up in the tide of battle, which seemed to roil all around Voght like sea currents.

Then she was in the maelstrom again. A blue-furred hand landed on her shoulder, spun her around. It was Hank McCoy, the Beast, and even in the thick of battle, he was attempting to be reasonable. It was obvious that he was hoping for the same from Voght.

"Amelia," he said, using her first name though they had never been anything but enemies, "you never appeared as barbarous, as zealous, as the others are. Do something! You must see that no benefit can come from this. Magneto is leading us all to a war that will tear the world apart, philosophically, and quite possibly, literally."

"Magneto is not going to let that happen, McCoy," she said. "You're wasting your breath. The time for talk—"

Voght launched into a side kick aimed at the Beast's head. She had no great strength, but superior skill, and despite his speed, she caught him on the temple and he stumbled back, more surprised than fazed by her attack.

"—is at an end."

"Apparently," the Beast said, muttering to himself.

Another kick missed completely, and then the Beast grabbed her in a painful, implacable grip, and lifted her from her feet.

"Drop me if you want to keep your hands, McCoy," she snapped. "I'll teleport your arms off your body without a single regret."

In one smooth move, far too fast for Voght to react, the Beast threw her.

"I never intended to hold on, madam," he said, his tone disturbingly genteel.

Voght tumbled through the air, all bearings gone, unable to teleport without any sense of place or destination. She hit someone, or several someones, hard, and went down in a jumble of limbs. The breath knocked out of her, she wheezed in an attempt to get oxygen, and still could not focus as McCoy picked her up again. She didn't have the voice to threaten him again, or the concentration to follow through.

"My chivalry has been sorely tested these last few days," he said whimsically.

The whimsy was what did it. It really pissed her off.

Behind him, she could see the Kleinstocks getting to their feet. The Beast had aimed well, taking the twins down with their own leader. McCoy hesitated, though Voght could not pinpoint exactly why, and in that moment, she knew what to do.

Harlan and Sven were trading fire with Bishop. Each time they buffeted him with their plasma blasts, the future-man would take a step or two back from the brunt of the attack, smile, and return fire. Sven and Harlan were both bleeding. Sven was limping and Harlan was holding one arm to his ribs. Bishop was going to hold his ground until he destroyed them.

Voght couldn't afford to lose. And as much as she hated to admit it, she couldn't afford to lose the Kleinstocks to their own stupidity either. They knew what Bishop could do, had faced his power before. Every time they fired at him, he simply absorbed their power and threw it back at them. While it didn't harm him, it did them severe damage.

The idiots.

"Wolverine," the Beast shouted, "catch!"

Amelia did not want to face off against Wolverine again. She'd gotten lucky the last time they'd clashed. Chances were, he would hold a grudge. Unlike the other X-Men, the diminutive Canadian was just as likely to kill her over it as just try to take her out of play. Killing was more certain, and this was war, after all. But once they started killing, either side, it was going to be a bloodbath.

If only Magneto didn't want the X-Men alive.

The Beast hauled back to toss Voght to Wolverine, who might even use her life to end the conflict. The idea amused her. As if the others would hesitate for a moment before consigning her to execution. Her life meant nothing to them. Less than nothing. But the X-Men didn't know that.

Fortunately, Voght got her voice back.

"Sven!" she shouted.

The Kleinstock brothers looked her way, scoped out the situation, and reacted. War was a function of the lizard brain, the primeval intellect, and required no real intelligence. Voght thanked God for that. The Kleinstocks worked best on instinct, and reacted that way in this situation.

Sven blasted Hank McCoy in the back. The Beast howled in pain and dropped her on the street. The twins began to buffet the Beast and Wolverine with plasma blasts until the two X-Men were driven back into a crowd of less powerful mutants, who nevertheless swarmed over them.

Bishop nailed them. Sven and Harlan went down, hard. They were trying, weakly, to rise, when Bishop moved in for another shot. Here was another X-Man, Voght thought, who might not hesitate to kill if that was the only way to assure victory.

A quick teleport took her behind him. She grabbed Bishop around the waist, teleported twenty stories up, where Rogue, Storm, and several other mutants with the power of flight were struggling with one another. The winds were extraordinary, and Storm was wiping out Magneto's airborne followers.

Voght knew strategy. The moment she appeared with Bishop and began to fall, Storm and Rogue saw her. She teleported back to safety, and watched with interest as Bishop plummeted to the ground with Rogue in pursuit and Storm staving off their other attackers.

Rogue was making a good effort, but Amelia seriously doubted she would catch up to Bishop in time. Which was okay. Of all the X-Men, she knew that Magneto had the least attachment to Bishop. He was an unknown quantity, hostile and dangerous. Magneto wouldn't mind if Bishop died, not at all.

He was expendable.

* * *

A warm July night, and dusk over Manhattan. Two lone stars twinkled above and a pale sliver shadow of moon hung above the city. A time for quiet, for calm, for small children to crawl into bed, for lovers to swing their clasped hands between them as they go off to dinner, or the theater, or window-shopping up Fifth Avenue.

SALVATION

That was how it was supposed to be. Magneto knew it, and in the rare moment when he relaxed his mind, took a tiny respite from the burden of empire, it saddened him greatly. He wanted to bring all of those things, the quiet moments, back to the city. But as his city. As Haven.

Instead, he reached out with his mind, bending the Earth's magnetic field to his will, and tore the George Washington Bridge apart. The matrix of steel beams that forged the upper portions of the bridge broke away. Magneto carried them with him, their weight barely an encumbrance.

Across the Hudson River, American military forces fired again and again upon the Sentinel that stood on the island's shore. Moments earlier, it had been guarding the bridge; now it had nothing to guard. The military had massed on the Jersey side, preparing to cross. Magneto had been astounded at the audacity and foolishness of the move. And at his own foolishness, for not having believed they would invade.

And they were invading. Or at least, attempting to do so. The Sentinels would be a bloody deterrent. Already, soldiers were dying in the attempt, distracting a Sentinel here and there by the bridge and tunnel routes, so their fellows could get across the river.

The center span of the George Washington Bridge collapsed into the Hudson. There would be no invasion via that route. Traditional tanks and those with plasma weapons fired upon the Sentinel still. From gun emplacements on the Jersey shoreline, the shelling continued. Many of the more modern weapons were not made, specifically, of metal, and so were harder for Magneto to latch on to.

Instead, he hovered above the tanks and guns, weapons fire dissipating harmlessly the moment it came into contact with his force field. With his magnetic power, he held the crisscrossed structure of the top of the bridge so that his intention was clear. He was going to drop it, destroying the armored vehicles below.

Silently, he counted to ten, giving the soldiers the opportunity to run. He wasn't certain if his hesitation saved the lives of brilliant men or cowards, and frankly didn't care.

Then he let the massive metalwork fall, crushing the tanks, destroying the guns. Lives probably were lost. Regrettable, he knew. But it was a war. A war that the American military was pressing, unwanted, on the emperor of Haven.

"My lord?" Scanner said, shimmering into view. Distracted by the battle, Magneto had not heard the telltale buzz of her arrival.

"What is it, Scanner?" he asked. "I'm a little busy."

"We . . . I thought you should know that the X-Men are free," she answered.

"Free!" he snapped. Then sighed. "Once more, my good will is flaunted by Xavier's little puppets. No matter, what can four X-Men do?"

"Eight, actually, Emperor," she said, obviously unhappy to be the bearer of bad tidings. "We are fighting them now, in the streets."

Magneto said nothing. So the other X-Men had returned. It was to be expected, he assumed. But he vowed he would not allow it to hurt morale. The X-Men didn't have a chance to win, and he wanted his people to know that he was not going to let it happen.

"One other thing, my lord," Scanner said. "Milan wanted me to pass on to you that one of the Sentinels has reported an attack by mutants, in addition to the human invasion."

"Thank you, Scanner," Magneto said, flying downriver toward the next Sentinel. "That will do."

Scanner flashed out of existence, her disappearance leaving Magneto to blink away bright spots from his eyes. But he could not as easily rid himself of his concern and suspicion. Mutants attacking a Sentinel.

Which mutants?

More to the point, which Sentinel?

Chapter 13

A small flame blazed up in Professor Charles Xavier's gut. It wasn't an ulcer. Another had formed in the back of his head, where all the worst headaches started. Two more, one behind each eye. But in the center of his heart, it was brutally cold, agonizingly painful, without the promise of merciful numbness ever setting in.

The world was collapsing around him. The world he lived in every day, and the one he had envisioned for the future, his future, the future of his friends, colleagues, and students. Falling in a bloody massacre of large-weapons fire and volatile words.

The fire and ice in every inch of his being, in the depths of his soul, were anger and despair. He was a spectator, and it disgusted him. He ought to be in the thick of things, he could most certainly have been of use in the X-Men's battle against Magneto's forces. If he'd had legs. Which he didn't. Instead, he had two choices. He could monitor the fight, help where possible, continue to attempt some kind of spin control; or he could stop Magneto once and for all.

God, it was tempting. Xavier had never felt such grand temptation to perform an act that his conscience told him was so completely wrong, so utterly indecent. It frightened him, that temptation. He pushed it aside, but it didn't go away. It nagged at him, like childhood guilt or romantic infatuation.

He could not bring himself to do it, to take Magneto out of the game. But without that as an active role, he had begun to feel ever more useless.

"Professor," Gyrich said tentatively, though he'd already sensed the man's approach.

Despicable as he found Gyrich, Xavier thought it amusing that the two had found a sort of odd companionship in the disaster that was unfolding. The views they held were radically different, and yet they shared an intense stake in the result of the day's events.

"Mr. Gyrich," he acknowledged.

"I thought you'd want to know, that Tilby woman is broadcasting from the MTV offices, on several networks. Seems the captured X-Men have been freed, and if her story turns out to be true, they're all in there fighting on humanity's side,'' Gyrich said.

Xavier did not need to scan Gyrich's thoughts. He could hear the man's emotions in his voice. And the number one emotion was disappointment. Gyrich did not want the X-Men to be heroes. It didn't fit in with his plan of the way the world should be.

Which was just too bad.

''Thank you,'' Xavier said. ''Frankly, I'm surprised you'd tell me that.''

''Well, don't be,'' Gyrich answered gruffly. ''I may have problems with muties, but you're an academic, you're entitled to your opinion. And, frankly, I tend to agree with you on the outcome to this thing. One way or another, when we bring Magneto down, we could very well have a bloodbath. I don't mind one bit if normal people think the government should carefully regulate mutants. But we don't need another civil war.''

Xavier was disgusted, but with Gyrich, he was becoming used to being disgusted. He wasn't at all sure that was a good thing. Being inured to bigotry might dull the edge of the mission over time, he thought.

''Thank you for the information, Mr. Gyrich,'' he said, in a tone that was clearly meant to dismiss the man.

He was surprised when Gyrich took the hint, and walked away.

Any other day, Xavier might have launched into a tirade against Gyrich and his prejudiced remarks. Not today. It was getting dark, a beautiful night, and Xavier wanted nothing more than to sleep. But he had a duty to his people, and to his dream, and he would never shirk that duty. Already, he was disturbed by how much he was forced to allow others to shoulder what he considered his responsibility.

There was stubble on his chin. He had not slept for two days. He was a man prone to obsession. There was a martial-arts principle which taught that when one dedicated every ounce of energy, every waking moment, to a single goal, little was impossible. Xavier lived his life by that principle, his every breath for the dream.

Moments ago, he had been faltering in his pursuit of that principle, in his faith in the dream.

''Bless you, Trish,'' he whispered to himself, and sent the message out into the darkening Manhattan skies.

She heard his telepathic voice, heard his words, felt his gratitude. Professor Xavier felt her smile. That was their only communication, but it was enough.

If Trish could continue to work her magic over the airwaves, and Xavier did the same with his interviews and debates . . . they might turn the tide. If the X-Men could find a way to defeat Magneto and the Sentinels, Trish Tilby and Charles Xavier himself might be able to make certain the nation didn't destroy itself in the aftermath.

A lot of ifs.

''If you can keep your head, when all around you are losing theirs,'' he said, under his breath once more. But this time, he kept the thought to himself, a bit of whimsy that he would not normally have indulged.

Xavier was getting a little punchy. The lack of sleep was getting to him. He wondered how the X-Men were dealing with it. He would check up on them in a few minutes.

He allowed himself a moment to monitor the progress of Valerie Cooper, Archangel, and Gambit. They seemed to be moving along fine. He would have known if anything significant had gone wrong, because he had kept a telepathic line open to Val throughout their mission. He might not be ''with'' her all the time, but he was still there, listening peripherally.

Then it was time to make another attempt at communicating with his oldest friend, his greatest enemy.

Xavier closed his eyes, and his mind called out the name: *Magnus.*

In the psionic world, the realm of telepathy, the astral plane, Charles Xavier stood. Though in reality he could hardly feel his legs at all, his brain remembered what it felt like to walk, to run. Simply to stand tall and proud. Synapses fired in his mind, for the brain was Xavier's province, and within it, he was capable of anything.

His body was trapped within the steel wheelchair that, despite all the padding he might have installed, would never be truly comfortable. Xavier could not move across a room without that chair.

But in the world of his mind, he stood.

And it was glorious.

Magnus, he called again.

I am here, Charles, though your timing is wretched as ever, Magneto responded.

Their minds linked, and Xavier could see him. Or at least, he could see the mental image that Magneto had of himself. Most people had a mental self-image that was generally better, prettier, stronger, taller—or worse, uglier, weaker, shorter—than they actually were. Magneto was an odd case. His mental self-image was a perfect reflection of the man himself.

But Xavier had no time for pop psychology. There was a war on.

A refreshing change, Magneto thought, his arms spread wide.

Xavier glanced around the Astral Plane, only now becoming conscious of the environment he was psionically creating around them. Unlike the starscape asteroid field he had provided when last he contacted Magneto, this time they stood facing one another in Xavier's own study, back at the Institute in Salem Center.

I'm exhausted, Xavier admitted. *I suppose I thought we could both use a quiet, comfortable space.*

Within the psychic manifestation of his study, Charles Xavier walked across the floor, enjoying the feeling of the hardwood beneath the soles of his shoes, until he stood only a few steps before the mutant conqueror.

Conqueror? Magneto thought, surprising Xavier by picking up the thought. He was more tired than he realized. *Conqueror brings to mind so many negatives, images of tyranny and slaughter. I want none of those things. Only freedom to live, for myself and the rest of my kind. That includes you, Charles.*

X-MEN: MUTANT EMPIRE

You may not want to be a tyrant, Magnus. You may not want to oppress, to slaughter, to destroy. But surely you have realized by now that those things cannot be avoided. You have become what you once most despised, Xavier retorted.

Magneto's face grew cold, all the amused detachment becoming a shattered mask, falling away in pieces.

How dare you? Magneto hissed.

I am the only one who would dare, and the only one who would know enough to tell you what you've done, Xavier thought. *As oppressive as society has become for mutants, we are still captains of our own destiny. What you have begun will only lead to the enslavement of humanity. What next, Magnus, work camps?*

Magneto's gray-blue eyes narrowed with fury. His jaw worked as he clenched his teeth together. Then he punched Charles Xavier in the face, nearly breaking his nose.

That hurt, Xavier thought.

We're on the Astral Plane, Charles, how could that have hurt you?

Perhaps I allowed it to, or maybe I'm too tired to care, too tired to separate conscious from subconscious. But I guess I hit a nerve.

You know you did. That was your intention, Magneto thought. *But don't think it's going to deter me. I may have lost everything to the Nazis, but I myself am not a Nazi. I will not allow my dream to be corrupted that way.*

It isn't up to you, Magnus, Xavier replied. *You can't micromanage the world. Violence begets violence. No matter that you are more high minded than many of those who serve your cause. That isn't going to change them. You've fed their paranoia and hatred so long, and now all you're doing is giving them a license to punish humanity for its transgressions.*

They need a home, a sanctuary, a place where they can find love and confidence and security. I'm giving them that. I'm giving them salvation, Magneto explained, his tone less sure now.

How presumptuous to think you can save them by yourself, Xavier pointed out. *You're no savior, old friend. You aren't*

SALVATION

offering the world salvation. We all need to be saved from your dream, not by it.

There was silence then. Magneto sat in one of the soft leather chairs in Xavier's study. Xavier knew he should sit as well, but he could not bring himself to do so. Though all of it was pretense, it felt like standing, and standing felt wonderful. He wouldn't sit down, not for a moment.

You may be right, Magneto finally admitted. *But even if you are, it is too late to turn back. Hundreds, thousands of mutants have come to take the new life I have offered to them. Most of them are innocents, Charles. Without me, they have nothing but the hellish life they left to come here.*

Xavier nodded.

Perhaps you have become a kind of salvation for some, he admitted. *But at what price, Magnus? That is my question for you today. At what price? What value is a home that has been razed to the ground by hatred, by war? How happily can one live in the shadow of sixty-foot-high murder machines?*

In that moment, Magneto seemed to be listening in despair. To Xavier he seemed older than he had ever been, burdened by the consequences of victory. He felt that he might actually be getting through. Magneto understood what he was saying, there was no doubt about that. But Charles thought Magneto might actually have begun to realize that his dream was flawed.

His old friend, a man whose name was feared in every corner of the globe, looked up at him with a terrible confusion in his eyes. He seemed about to speak. Then Magneto's eyes went wide with surprise, narrowed with fury.

What a fool you must think me, Charles, he cried, leaping to his feet, *to spout this gibberish from the pulpit of your arrogance and expect me to prostrate myself in some foul act of contrition. And what a fool I am to believe your appeal was in earnest, rather than some shoddy attempt to distract me from your true goal.*

Magnus, I don't know what— Xavier began.

The Mutant Empire is not a threat any longer, Charles, it is a reality, Magnus said. *There is nothing that you, or your toy soldiers can do about it. Now, if you'll excuse me, I obviously have somewhere else to be.*

Even as Magneto faded away, ghostlike, from the Astral Plane, Xavier tried to understand what had happened. He had been so close to breaking through to the man, at least partially. He had felt it in the psychic ether, the psionic communication between them. What could have . . . ?

No, he thought.

In his mind, Xavier turned to see that the corner of the study was gone. In its place, a mental window on the command center of the Alpha Sentinel, where Val Cooper, Gambit, and Archangel were hard at work trying to reprogram the monstrous robots. Xavier was so exhausted, that he had not been able to . . . no, in truth, he had not even attempted to hide the telepathic connection he still maintained with Val Cooper. Magneto had seen, and understood.

Dear God, he thought, even as the Astral Plane disappeared around him, and back in his flesh and blood body, back in the wheelchair, he opened his eyes.

"What have I done?" he asked aloud.

* * *

As Valerie Cooper worked, bent over the command-center terminal, furiously trying to get around the failsafes Magneto had implanted in the Alpha Sentinel's programming, Gambit and Archangel could do nothing but wait. It didn't seem to bother Archangel much, but it was driving Gambit crazy.

"How's it going, Val?" Archangel asked.

The woman mumbled something in response.

"I don' know 'bout you, 'Angel," Gambit said, "but most of de time, I need words to understand what somebody is trying to say."

Archangel smiled, and suddenly Val was brought out of her almost trancelike concentration by what Gambit had always thought of as "a change in de weather," a significant alteration of the emotional climate of the room. He believed that people knew when they were being spoken to, or focused upon.

"Sorry," she said sheepishly. "Were you guys talking to me?"

"*Oui*," Gambit said. "Why don' you tell us what's happening. De suspense is starting to get to me. Not to mention dat all dis swaying back and forth as de Sentinel walks . . . *je me sens mal*."

"I don't speak French," Cooper said.

"I feel like t'rowin' up," Gambit explained, with a weak smile.

"I have the opposite problem," Archangel said. "I'm tired and hungry and cranky, and I could do without being inside a giant robot that's being shot at. It's like having a metal barrel over your head and having people throw rocks at it. What's the story? We getting out of here soon?"

"I'm trying," Val answered. "I'm having a problem getting through Magneto's program, though. The override codes are useless if I can't get into the system in the first place."

"Why don' you try another way in?" Gambit asked. "Dere must be a back door or somet'ing, *non?*"

Cooper paused before looking down at the keyboard, then at the monitor in front of her. Finally, she looked back at them.

"I'm sure there is. Magneto had to have a back door built in to reprogram them in the first place," Cooper explained. "I've been doing a lot of thinking about this. We know he was involved with the Hellfire Club for a while. Well, before anyone knew he was a mutant, Sebastian Shaw was building Sentinels for the government. He could have put something in, told Magneto. That's all I can think of."

"But we aren't going to get that information, are we?" Archangel reasoned.

"Well, that back door was probably set up for a single use anyway," she replied.

"So what are our other options?" Gambit asked.

"Only one," Cooper answered. "Gyrich."

"You expect him to help you?" Archangel asked.

"Hey," Gambit broke in, "if he don' help us, his *derrière* is on de fire right along wit' de rest of us."

"That doesn't mean he'll help, though," Val said. "Still,

it may be our best hope. Let me try to get him on the comm-link."

She reached for the comm-unit on her wrist. Before she could speak, something slammed into the Alpha Sentinel, rocking it hard. Val fell to the floor from her seat. Gambit and Archangel stumbled, nearly falling themselves. Another blast struck the Sentinel, and plasma burst through the hole Gambit had blown in the metal hunter's head.

"Cover!" Cooper yelled, and all three of them flattened out on the floor.

Sparks flew in the command center, but Gambit did not think there had been any real damage. Still, it had been a close call.

"Enough of that!" Val said, and slid into her seat once more. "Let me just adjust the frequency of this thing and . . .

"Gyrich!" she barked into the comm-unit. "Come in, Gyrich!"

"Who the hell is this?" an unfamiliar but authoritative voice demanded on the link.

"This is Valerie Cooper," Val snapped. "You know the name?"

"Well, yes, Ms. Cooper, I—"

"Get me Gyrich on the comm," she said.

"Ma'am, I'm sorry, I—" the military man began.

"Now!" she ordered.

"Yes, ma'am," the soldier complied.

They waited.

"Warning!" the Alpha Sentinel said, its voice loud enough to hurt their ears. "Intruders detected. Commencing termination."

* * *

"I can't believe Marko turned coward and ran," Wolverine snarled, and popped a single claw through the lower abdomen of a mutant whose main power seemed to be particularly repulsive body odor, backed up by a small dose of telekinesis.

"Find a doctor," he said gruffly to the mutant, and then turned away.

The man would live, but he was most definitely out of the fight.

"You're showing amazing restraint," Iceman said, watching the mutant clutch his belly and stumble into the midst of the mosh pit that passed for a battleground.

Wolverine grunted something in return. Drake was right. While the others were going a bit farther than usual—not killing, but not holding back nearly as much as they normally would—he was drawing the line. Most of their enemies were relatively decent folks duped into a war they had never asked for by Magneto himself. 'Course, if he ended up ripping open Senyaka's rib cage, or Voght's, well, that was another story. He had plans for that punk Pyro too. If he ever got his hands on the guy.

"You're right about Marko, though," Iceman said. "I mean, I was stunned as anyone to see him fighting with us instead of against us. But then to turn tail and run—it just doesn't make sense."

They spun and danced and cut and bludgeoned their way through half a dozen of Magneto's faithful. Wolverine's healing factor made up quite handily for his lack of sleep. He had no idea how the others were even standing up.

"Getting dark," Drake observed at his side.

"Yeah," Wolverine agreed, "good for us. Bad for them."

"Look around, Logan," Iceman said. "You actually think we've got a shot at winning this thing?"

"More than a shot," Wolverine answered. "We're gonna win because that's the only acceptable outcome. No matter what it takes, we have to win. It wouldn't hurt if we had more help, I'll tell ya, but we'll make do."

But even as he said it, Wolverine recognized that his words were empty. There was the distinct possibility, given the numbers involved, that they would fail. Off to the left, he could see Rogue and the Beast driving through a parade of attackers. Scott and Jean were somewhere up the street, and Storm was above them, dropping miniature tornadoes and hailstorms on the enemy. She might be their greatest asset in a battle this size, he thought. He didn't know where the hell Bishop had gotten to. The last time Wolverine had seen him, the future X-Man had been falling out of the sky, and Rogue had barely saved him from becoming so much Manhattan road pizza.

"Time to die, traitors!" cried a thin man with skin like polished ebony and features so angular, they might be diamond sharp.

He slashed long fingers toward Wolverine, who put his fists up, claws in the air, and blocked the attack. The crystalline man grunted his displeasure, but before he could withdraw his deadly hands, Wolverine whipped his claws to either side, neatly slicing off the end of each digit. The man screamed in pain.

"Traitors!" he cried again, this time making the word a pained curse.

A swarm of other mutants moved in. They'd been backed up to the massive glass display window of a designer clothing store. Thirty of Magneto's followers, and only two of them. Wolverine knew that he couldn't beat them all without killing some of them, or at least he feared that was the case.

"Freeze 'em," Wolverine growled.

Iceman didn't miss a beat. He might have been an X-Man a lot longer than Wolverine, but he never failed to defer to Logan in the field. Wolverine chalked that up to good teamwork. Drake had proven over and over in the past few days something that Wolverine had always known but never voiced. Iceman was a lot better at being an X-Man than anyone ever gave him credit for.

With a muttered, regretful curse that Wolverine's enhanced hearing could not have failed to pick up, Bobby Drake lifted both his hands, and poured on the ice.

"Traitors?" he screamed in fury. "We're traitors? To what? Insanity? All we want is an end to this kind of garbage. All we want is peace! There are humans who hate all mutants because of your actions, your beliefs. You're no better than they are!"

Thirty mutants were frozen in the street. Iceman controlled his powers to an extent Wolverine had never witnessed, leaving, in every case, only the individual's head exposed. Just enough to breathe. As he produced the ice, Bobby slid along, propelling himself with his power, as he would on an ice slide. Wolverine scrambled after him, looking for trouble, watching for an aerial attack.

Bobby continued out into the middle of the street, freezing at least a dozen more mutants. Rogue had to fly the Beast out of the way so Iceman could continue. Half a dozen more of the enemy force were frozen solid. Rogue landed with the Beast just behind Wolverine, and they marched on with him, over the newly made tundra.

"I've never seen anything like it," she said in awe.

"Nor I, dear Rogue," Hank said. "And I've known the boy for many years."

"I just wish he'd thought o' this a while ago," Wolverine grumbled.

Ahead of them, Iceman stumbled.

And fell.

"Bobby!" Rogue called, and went toward him.

"I was afraid of this," the Beast said, mainly to himself, and followed. "He's completely drained himself."

Wolverine was going to follow, but he heard the sounds of battle moving toward him from behind. He turned, and across the ice came the war, Scott and Jean and Bishop trying their best to hold back hordes of mutants, more than Wolverine had even imagined they were facing.

"Wolverine, we've got to regroup, watch each other's backs!" Cyclops shouted over the din. "Otherwise, we're dead!"

Logan snapped his head around to pass the command on to Rogue and the others, but she and Hank were in a battle to keep Iceman's unconscious form from being dragged away.

It looked awfully grim. Wolverine held his claws up in front of him in battle stance, and hung his head a moment. With a deep breath, he prepared to experience the worst life had to offer, and not for the first time. He had seen friends die before, faced death himself many times. He had killed. Whatever it took, that's what Wolverine would do.

Whatever it took.

Then, beyond the mob attacking Rogue and Hank and Bobby, came a familiar, thundering noise that shook the half-block-long field of ice Logan stood upon.

"One side, goons!" a deep voice rumbled. "The cavalry's comin', and you're all in for a world of hurt!"

It was a sight Wolverine never would have imagined he would see, could barely believe even though it was right before his eyes. With nearly twenty other mutants behind him, Cain Marko was tearing a wide swath through the enemy lines.

Incredibly, the Juggernaut had come to the rescue.

Chapter 14

"**H**ow the hell did the thing know where we were?" Val shouted. "There are no sensors in here!"

Massive fingers began to grope around the opening in the back of the Sentinel's head. It had figured out their location, and now it was determined to pull them out of its skull and vaporize them, or stomp them underfoot, or something equally nasty.

Val was not happy.

"How . . . ?" she began to ask again.

"No sensors?" Archangel asked.

"Are you sure 'bout dat?" Gambit added.

"Absolutely!"

"You t'inkin' what Gambit is t'inkin', *mon ami*?" the Cajun asked his teammate.

"Oh, yeah."

"Enough of this cryptic stuff," Val shouted at them. "What? What?"

"Well, if there are no sensors, then somebody told it we were in here," Archangel explained. "Who has contact with the Alpha unit? Who can give it orders?"

"Oh, my God," Val said. "Not now! We haven't done the override yet!"

There was a shrieking of metal and the Sentinel began to widen the hole in the back of its skull, tearing at it as if it were peeling a piece of fruit.

"We in trouble," Gambit said softly. "But Magneto can't be here yet, or he'd come in after us, right? *Dépêchez-vous*, Valerie. Hurry up!"

"Cooper, are you there?" Gyrich's voice came over the comm.

Val, Gambit, and Archangel all looked at one another in horror, as they realized that the success of their mission, and their lives, might depend upon a man who hated them all.

"Gyrich, listen," Val said hurriedly. "The thing knows we're in here, Magneto's on the way. I need a back door. A bypass, before I can even enter the override codes to restart the original program."

SALVATION

Silence. Then Gyrich said, "Let me think."

"Not what we want to hear, Gyrich!" Archangel shouted. "We don't have time for games."

"Nobody's playing," Gyrich said. "I'm trying to remember the code phrase."

"A phrase," Val asked, panicking. "A quote of some kind, a rhyme, what is it?"

"Just give me a second," Gyrich roared in frustration.

He was serious, not toying with them. All the barriers had fallen, all the political differences, philosophical arguments, were cast aside. Everything that meant anything was in jeopardy. Gyrich was a mean-spirited, ignorant fool, but not fool enough that he didn't understand the stakes. Val would like to have been relieved, but they didn't have time for sentiment.

Screeching metal. Val whipped around even as Gambit said, "He comin' in, Valerie," so calmly that she wanted to slap him.

"Oh, God," she said, looking around the command center frantically for some way to stop it.

"Gyrich!" she snapped.

"I'm thinking!" he yelled back.

"No, wait, first tell me, can we disable this thing from in here, shut down its motor controls without cutting off our ability to shut down all the others from in here?" she asked.

"Well, yes, but—"

"Gambit, 'Angel, those panels!" Val barked, and pointed.

Remy and Warren fired everything they had at the motor controls of the Sentinel, leaving its brain and memory intact but stopping it cold. It froze in the street, completely paralyzed. The hand stopped clawing at them, but it blocked their exit. Val figured they could worry about that when the job was done.

"Cooper!" Gyrich shouted, trying to get her attention.

"What?" she asked.

"What I was saying was, you can disable the Sentinel, but you'll be a sitting duck for the army in there. No defenses. Which Sentinel is it?"

"The one by the UN. Tell them to cease fire on us," she said. "And give me the back door code."

"It's Shakespeare," Gyrich said. "I'm trying to remember what the quote is."

"Well, hurry," she said.

They were quiet then, all staring at the monitor, which showed some of her failed attempts at hacking Magneto's program. She would have been able to break it, eventually, she knew. But they didn't have time for eventually.

A clanging broke the silence. A repetitive noise, like the sounding of a large bell.

"What in the name of God is—" she began.

"Somebody's knocking," Archangel said.

"I guess we know who it is too," Gambit added.

There was a terrible shrieking sound as the metal hand of the Sentinel was torn away and flung down onto the street below. Outside the hole in the robot's skull, Magneto hovered in the air, encapsulated in magnetic power.

"You three are trying my patience," he said.

* * *

It was all Bishop could do to keep from screaming. All the horrors that he had witnessed in the not-so-distant future where he had been born and raised, every act of violence or oppression, every broken spirit or cowering soul, were there all around him. But it wasn't supposed to be like this. Not so soon. The Sentinels, and the chaos and the destruction, it was decades early.

He wanted to close his eyes, wanted to pretend it was just another session in the Danger Room. But he knew it was true, all of it. And the only way he could prevent that hellish future from coming to pass that very night, was by fighting as he had never fought before.

So he clenched his teeth to bite off a scream unvoiced, and he pumped round after round of plasma fire into the attacking mutant hordes. It was everything he'd been trained to do in the XSE, the mutant police force of that future time, but even the XSE's worst-case-scenario battle plans never accounted for something like this.

It was getting dark now but the sky was still lit with the memory of sunshine. A bright day had ended in low clouds, which reflected the sickly glow of fires and the streaking, whistling, pastel contrails of overland missiles and other large-weapons fire.

For Bishop, it was as if every nightmare he had ever had, those fever dreams of terror yet to come, had not ended in his waking warm and safe in his bed at the Xavier Institute. A nightmare that might never end.

"No," he said simply, softly, to himself.

Bishop used his elbows, his forehead, his knees, the butt of his plasma rifle, and the hard set of his face to splinter passage through a tight knot of mutants ahead. He left the other X-Men behind, though Cyclops had called for them to regroup. The man was a more-than-capable field leader, but Bishop thought that Cyclops didn't want to understand what was really happening here. Bishop knew war. He knew you never put all your soldiers in one spot, or the war could be over very, very quickly.

A low growl that erupted into a full-throated battle cry came unbidden from his lips as he slammed into, then trampled over, a man whose empty eye sockets swirled with orange mist. He leaped to the trunk, and then the roof, of an Oldsmobile. The thin roof buckled slightly under his weight.

Trembling with the fury and the fear that raged within him, Bishop turned his plasma rifle on the crowd of mutants trying to take advantage of his sudden separation from his comrades.

"Fools!" he shouted. "You're just giving them what they want! All the people who want to see us caged, or dead. You're handing them the very tools they can use to destroy us!"

A narrow-focus beam of electric flame sliced across his face. If anyone else had been the target, it would have sliced their head in half. Bishop absorbed the energy of the attack, held the plasma rifle in one hand, and prepared to cut down the crowd with that devastating blade of fire.

In his own time, he wouldn't have thought twice about it. But this was a different time. It wasn't the XSE. He had learned much since he came to live and fight beside the very legends he had venerated as a boy. Killing was the final option, invoked rarely enough that the gravity of it had finally reached him. Though Wolverine would likely not have hesitated, Bishop had changed. The X-Men had changed him.

He discharged the killing blast into the pavement in front of the Olds.

Then the barrage came, energy blasts of every type arcing toward him. No projectile weapons. They were mutants, after all. How foolish they were. Apparently, none of them were paying attention.

Channeling the attackers' energy into his plasma rifle, Bishop cut a wide swath through Magneto's followers. Nearly two dozen mutants fell under his furious assault, as he stood upon the car and swung the weapon back and forth like a fire hose. Two dozen. And he was fairly certain that all of them would live. Fairly certain.

"Bishop!"

He turned to see Cyclops coming toward him, taking advantage of their enemies' momentary confusion and fear to run a clean path and leap up onto the car.

"I give orders for a reason, friend," Cyclops said sternly. "Get back to your teammates so we can give each other cover."

He wanted to snap at Cyclops. Wanted to say something about "getting results" in a flip way that would let the man know he didn't like to be ordered around. But, though he didn't like it, he was used to it. Hierarchy was valuable, leadership important. Summers wasn't perfect, but he was a good leader. And Bishop? Bishop was a good soldier.

"Bishop?" Cyclops asked, a note of concern in his voice.

"I'm okay," Bishop said, "it's all just a bit too close to my reality."

"Down!" Cyclops shouted, and Bishop responded instantly, no thought given to the rapid change in tone on the battlefield.

SALVATION

A burst of energy shot from Cyclops's visor, and tore up the street and the advancing enemy behind them. Bishop fired his plasma rifle in the opposite direction, defeating the quickly hatched two-pronged attack.

Two-pronged. But they were dealing with mutants, so . . .

Bishop let himself fall backward off the roof of the car, firing straight into the air even before he slammed into the hood of the Olds. A woman, whose body was so distended she resembled nothing so much as a manta ray, had been floating down on top of them, her open mouth lined with rows of razor teeth and her talons reaching for the next kill.

Bishop shot her out of the sky, and rolled off the car to hit pavement. Cyclops took out two more attackers on the ground with his optic blasts, then jumped down to join Bishop in the street.

"Let's move," Cyclops said.

Bishop led the way, breaking bones and banging heads as he went. When they reached the X-Men, Bishop at first thought the team was about to be ambushed. He trained his plasma rifle on three mutants who stood by Jean Grey, ready to shoot them down.

A huge hand landed on the rifle, and pushed its barrel up.

"They're with me," the Juggernaut said. "The odds are bad enough without you firin' on your allies."

Bishop nodded. It disturbed him to have the Juggernaut fighting at his side. There was no question that the man was fighting in earnest, that he was fully aligned with the X-Men for the duration of the battle. But who knew what might happen after? That was what disturbed Bishop. Enemies never made comfortable allies.

But with the team so horribly outmatched, with so little on which to pin their hopes, any help was appreciated, no matter its origins.

Rogue and Wolverine seemed to be handling an enemy attack without help off to one side. The woman Arclight, who'd been among the Marauders they had defeated in the small hours of the morning, was attacking once more. Apparently she was too stubborn or too stupid to quit while she could still walk upright.

Bishop trained his weapon on her.

"Who's that?" Jean Grey asked, and he was startled that she'd come up so close by without his noticing her approach.

He glanced at her in confusion, and she pointed toward a commotion taking place a block or so to the south. Mutants were turning to face some new threat, but the weakest ones had hung back, not wanting to risk battle with the X-Men. A line of humans—humans!—marched down the center of the street. Many of them were police officers, armed with guns and tear gas. Both were fired into the tightly knit group of mutant aggressors, which was broken up quickly enough.

Some wore gas masks, but most did not. It didn't matter, though. The man in front, who Bishop thought looked familiar, lifted his hands, made a small movement with them, and the gas seemed to be lifted from the street, pushed into the sky. Hacking, coughing mutants tried to stumble away, but the same man motioned again and they went down as if rammed by a fast-moving car.

That's when Bishop knew him. Skolnick was his name, a military man who'd defected to become one of Magneto's lap-dogs. Bishop had seen him on the dais with Magneto that very morning. Magneto had crowed about his defection, about what it meant for mutantkind. Obviously, Skolnick had seen the error of his ways. He was fighting the good fight again, and this time, he wasn't alone. Bishop didn't have time to count the cops and human civilians backing Skolnick up, but there were well over one hundred.

He worried for them, that they would be cattle to the slaughter in a battle of mutants. But the X-Men could use all the help they could find.

The odds looked a little brighter. Now if the others could only take care of the Sentinels, he thought. . . .

* * *

"Gyrich!" Val Cooper screamed. "We don't have time to waste! Let's have that code!"

SALVATION

"God, I'm thinking, I'm thinking," he answered over the comm.

"We're dead," Archangel said, mostly to himself, as he and Gambit raced to the hole torn out of the Sentinel's skull.

Magneto floated in a ball of electromagnetic power, just beyond the hole, and a sixty-foot drop waited below. Archangel knew that he alone was no match for Magneto. In the end, none of them were. But up there he wasn't even sure what kind of help Gambit would be, given that he could not fly.

He moved to the attack, but it was a futile gesture. He knew it in his heart, and he saw it in Magneto's eyes, in the face of the greatest enemy Archangel, and the X-Men's mentor, Professor Xavier, had ever had. Magneto could destroy him utterly, with little effort, if murder was his goal. And there was so very little that Warren could do, given that sphere of energy that protected Magneto from attack.

Together, Archangel knew that he and Gambit could buy Valerie mere moments. No more. But it might be . . .

"*Allez-vous-en,* Magneto! Go home, we don' want you here!" Gambit cried madly.

But his manic chatter was a pale shadow of the insanity of his actions. Before Archangel could even register what his teammate was up to, Gambit had telescoped out his bo-staff and was catapulting himself into the air. He flew toward Magneto, sixty feet from the ground. The mutant tyrant only watched in amused and somewhat surprised silence as Gambit slammed into the force shield surrounding him.

Gambit screamed. Archangel imagined it was something like being electrocuted; then he remembered that the Cajun actually had been electroshocked days earlier.

Slowly, he slid down through the field that surrounded Magneto. Magneto only watched. In seconds, Gambit would fall to his death, or Archangel would have to save him, leaving Valerie defenseless, and it would all be for nothing. Warren was at a loss. He had never felt more vulnerable.

Then he saw Gambit's eyes. Despite the pain he was in, despite the danger, he was fighting. Halfway in, halfway out of Magneto's defensive shielding, Gambit still held on to his bo-stick. He charged it with the explosive power that genetic fate had given him, and shoved it toward Magneto's chest.

The stick exploded, throwing Magneto backward through the air.

Gambit fell.

Archangel dived after him, ignoring Magneto for that moment. Gambit was nearly unconscious when Warren snatched him out of the sky, but he could not take the time to put Remy down. As fast as he was able, he turned in midair, and carried Gambit back toward the Sentinel's gaping head, and back toward Magneto.

Magneto had fallen for a moment. Warren had seen it out of the corner of his eye. But he had quickly recovered and was moving toward them again. Magneto's uniform was durable enough to have significantly protected him from the blast. Still, he was shaken, and there was a blackened circle on his abdomen.

Warren did the only thing he could do. He launched a flurry of his wing-knives, biometallic feather blades, at Magneto's newly restructured force shield.

Magneto was no longer amused, but he barely reacted to the attack. Archangel's new wings were, after all, metal. His facing Magneto was almost laughable. Or it seemed so.

Until the wing-knives penetrated the shield and hit Magneto's body armor. Where Gambit had attacked, on that burnt area of Magneto's uniform, the knives passed through, slicing into Magneto's skin.

The look of surprise on Magneto's face was almost comical. He could control any metal, even the iron in human blood, if he concentrated, if he focused on it enough. Surely, Archangel's wings, created by Apocalypse, had some kind of metal alloy as their base. But there was more to them than that, perhaps more flesh or living tissue than Warren had ever imagined. Magneto had miscalculated, a mistake he would not make again.

But once was enough.

Magneto was momentarily paralyzed.

SALVATION

Archangel could not believe his luck.

Then he realized that Magneto did not need to move to use his power, and all that good feeling went away fast.

Val had seconds. Seconds.

* * *

"Gyrich!" Val screamed. "I need that back door code now, or we're dead!"

"I—I—" Gyrich fumbled. "I just . . . *What dreams may come!*" he shouted.

"What?" she cried.

"From *Hamlet*," he said. " 'For in such sleep, *what dreams may come*'!"

Val keyed in the phrase, praying as she never had before that Magneto's tinkering would not have affected the back door Gyrich's people had built into the Alpha Sentinel's control systems.

The word ONLINE blinked on the screen. Then the command prompt.

Val typed one more word.

RESET.

She waited half a dozen eternal seconds, holding her breath.

MUTANT TARGET DESIGNATE? the system, now back to its original programming, prompted.

She typed his name, and Magneto's file scrolled across every screen, as if the Alpha Sentinel had suddenly gone mad. It couldn't move, she had made certain of that. Now she had to make sure Magneto couldn't get back in.

LOCKOUT UNTIL TARGET ACQUISITION? the computer asked.

Oh, yes, Valerie thought, and hit the affirmative command.

Nobody could abort the new mission until it had succeeded. Nobody.

* * *

Rogue was on the ground with the rest of the X-Men, backing their play. Storm was still in the air, though. Crowds played hell with her claustrophobia, Rogue knew. And she was much more effective from the sky. After all, Ororo had already been decisive in the battle, literally sweeping one end of the street clean of enemies with hurricane-force winds. A number of those were injured, still others simply walked away, realizing that Storm could keep them away for as long as she wished.

For the first time, Rogue began to think that they might all have a chance at surviving to see the next day. And, if they were extremely fortunate, the day after that as well.

"Rogue," Cyclops barked. "Get Iceman somewhere safe. We can't fight and protect him at the same time."

"Any ideas, Cyke?" she asked, only half sarcastically.

Cyclops ignored her, so Rogue gathered the unconscious Iceman up into her arms, and flew north.

"Rogue?" he asked weakly, coming around for the first time since his extraordinary effort had evened the odds in the war, at least for a little while.

"Relax, Bobby," she said gently. "You've earned it."

Bobby Drake started to drift off again, comfortable in her arms. Then his eyes snapped awake, as if he had truly realized, for the first time, exactly where he was.

"Whoa," he said. "Where we going?"

"Someplace you can rest," she answered.

"No."

Rogue ignored him.

"No, Rogue, take me back," Bobby demanded.

"Bobby, listen," she began.

"No," he interrupted. "I'm an X-Man, Rogue. As long as I'm alive, I'm not leaving my team in the field. Take me back there. We need all the help we can get."

She thought about it for a moment, then turned back toward the field of battle, which had moved now to just outside the Empire State Building, between Fifth and Sixth Avenues.

"Y'gonna have to explain it to Scott," she said.

"You let me worry about Scott," Iceman responded. "I've been disobeying his orders since I was sixteen years old."

With pained concentration, he began to ice up again. Rogue was concerned for him, as well as impressed, surprised, and proud, all at the same time.

"How we doing?" he asked.

SALVATION

"See for yourself," she suggested.

With Bobby hanging beneath her now, her hands holding him under the arms, Rogue flew a circuit of the battlefield. The only mutants she recognized from above were Arclight, the Blob, and several Acolytes including Amelia Voght, Senyaka, and the Kleinstock brothers.

"God," Bobby said. "The Kleinstocks again? I feel like we've been fighting them for days."

"You have," Rogue said, and smiled to herself.

"Then I wish they'd just stay down," Iceman said grimly. "In fact, why don't you drop me down by them?"

"In a few minutes, if you think you can . . ." She let the comment trail off. Bobby was a big boy. He could take care of himself.

She flew down until she was about twenty feet above Sven and Harlan Kleinstock, then she let Bobby go. He did a forward roll, and when he came out of it, he was forming an ice ramp beneath him as if he were surfing a curl. She watched a moment longer, as he whipped up a huge club or bat made of ice, and as he fell on the unsuspecting Kleinstocks, he nailed a home run off Sven Kleinstock's head. Rogue heard the crack, and when Sven crumpled to the pavement, she knew he wasn't getting up soon. He was out of it.

From above, she scoped out the war again. Since the Juggernaut had arrived with converts, and the huge wave of cops and civilians had shown up, the battle had most definitely turned. It was chess, now. Piece by piece, they would all be taken off the board. Pawns. Knights. Kings. Attrition ruled.

She started to turn back toward where her teammates were fighting hard, joined now by so many others that it was hard to tell who was friend and who was foe. There was a low rumbling noise, and Rogue turned just in time to see the earth erupt in a geyser of pavement, cement, stone, and soil—how deep it had come from she could not have said—a tower built instantaneously, and just as quickly put to use.

Like some monstrous earthen tentacle, the tower whipped and turned and slammed down on top of the Juggernaut and half a dozen other mutants. Rogue could only watch in horror.

X-MEN: MUTANT EMPIRE

When Cain Marko crawled from the massive tumble of debris, he was alone. There was no other movement under the stone and pavement. Nor had Rogue expected there to be.

The fury came upon her sudden as a heart attack, and Rogue scanned the street for the one man she knew might be responsible for such an assault. After a moment, she realized that he would need a line of sight for his power to work properly, and she raised her search up several stories. She saw him a few seconds later, standing atop a four-story office and retail building. She wouldn't have seen him at all in the dark, despite the streetlights and still-burning neon, but the silver metal of his body armor caught the multicolored city lights and threw back a twisted reflection.

Rogue thought of Bobby and the Kleinstock brothers, of the five or six lives just snuffed out beneath an artificial avalanche, and she knew that the man had to be removed from play now, before he could take more lives on a whim.

As fast as she could, she flew down to fight at Wolverine's side.

''It's Avalanche,'' she said.

''Saw him 'bout ten minutes ago,'' Logan responded indifferently.

''We can't afford to have him runnin' around,'' she urged.

''So stop him, Rogue,'' Wolverine said. ''Steal his powers, knock him off the building. You can take him.''

''I know I can take him,'' she said testily. ''But I don't want to steal his powers. I do that when there's no other way to win. Plus, I don't want to do it 'cause that means I get his mind, too, at least a little bit—''

She belted a man with walrus tusks and a long sharp tongue that she thought looked as though it could punch holes through steel beams.

''—I don't want to see that. Ever. He's a demented little sucker.''

''So what do you want with me?'' Wolverine asked.

''Fastball special,'' Rogue said simply.

Wolverine actually smiled, in the middle of so much bloodshed and destruction.

SALVATION

"I miss that Russkie," he said.

"We all do," she agreed. "So, you ready?"

"I'm a whole mess o' ready," he said, still smiling. "Give me a bull's-eye, Rogue."

Rogue lifted Wolverine up with both hands. In the old days, their former teammate Colossus had been able to do the manuever with just one. It was something they'd practiced in the Danger Room, and in the field, many times over.

Taking air, Rogue flew up and to the side of the building where Avalanche stood. When she was about level with him, she simply hurled Wolverine with all her might across the sky. He landed on Avalanche, and his adamantium claws flashed in the same neon rainbow that had glinted from Avalanche's armor a moment before.

She left Wolverine to his own devices, and returned to the fight. Seconds after her feet touched the ground, the Juggernaut was beside her.

"Saw that fastball special you 'n the runt pulled," he said gruffly. "Well done."

"What do you know about it?" she asked.

"The fastball special?" he said with a smile. "You're kidding? You've used it against me enough times. I should know what it is. Fact is, I've done that move with Tom Cassidy a few times myself."

"Thief," Rogue said, doubly amused at finding herself bantering with a hated enemy, and in the middle of a war, no less.

"Yeah," Marko agreed. "But a successful thief."

Rogue couldn't argue there.

The tide was turning in their favor, finally, and it felt good. Felt good, that was, as long as she didn't think about lives already lost, and what else they might have to lose before the day was out, if they intended to defeat Magneto.

CHAPTER 15

Over the years that she had spent with the X-Men, Jean Grey had grown from an immature teenager who was happy to be known as Marvel Girl, into a woman of strength, a woman in control of her destiny. She had always been relatively quiet—though she seemed a chatterbox next to Scott. She thought that, maybe, she had become so introspective because, as a psi, she was always listening to the constant telepathic babble in her mind.

Or it might have been Scott's influence. He was so serious.

In the end, it didn't matter what forces had shaped Jean Grey, made her the woman she was now. The only thing that mattered was how the day ended, who was still standing when it was over. That was all she could think of.

Her jaw was set in a hard line of grim determination, and though her teammates made comments to one another during battle, Jean said not a word. Through the psychic rapport that they shared, she could sense that Cyclops was on edge. As well he should be, she thought. They might not all survive the next few minutes, never mind the many hours till morning. But his anxiety was not going to get them through, and so she tried to counter it with the confidence she had in him. With the determination she had summoned to keep going.

Thank you, he thought, and she picked up the gratitude, acknowledged it with a small nod.

They would make it through. No other outcome would be acceptable.

Though she could not see most of her teammates, she touched briefly on all their minds. Iceman was in a dark, furious rage that was quite unlike him, as he battered Harlan Kleinstock with all his might. Wolverine was vaulting down the stairs of an office building, hurrying to get back into the fight. He had just taken Avalanche down, and hard, but he shut out her psi-scan when she tried to inquire further.

Bishop and Cyclops fought side by side, the heir to Xavier's dream and its far-removed descendant, grimly upholding the principles Charles had always espoused, willing to give their lives for that dream. That hope.

226

SALVATION

Ororo, lost in the power of the storm, thundering her judgment down upon the enemy with righteous anger, even a taste of which made Jean realize how the woman could once have allowed humans to call her goddess.

Rogue, tired of fighting. Inexhaustible, but nearly ready to drop. Jean wondered which of them would collapse from exhaustion first.

Finally, the Beast. She could actually see Hank, just ahead, through a screen of violent flesh. He was . . .

Hank, look out! she psi-shouted. Senyaka had moved in and was about to snag Hank around the throat with that terrible psi-whip of his. Hank turned in time, batted the Acolyte's hand away, and the two were one on one after that. Jean turned away. Senyaka didn't have much of a chance.

"Hello, little girl," a deep voice said.

When she turned, Jean was startled to find that the speaker was a woman, a huge, musclebound female whose eyes blazed with murderous intent. Arclight, Jean thought she was called.

"Such a pretty, flimsy, little thing," Arclight said. "But I'm still going to have to break you in half."

She moved in fast, hands up, fingers curled into a horrible set of claws. Jean didn't flinch, didn't turn, didn't run. Reaching out with her mind, she tore a phone kiosk loose from its moorings and brought it flying across the street to slam into Arclight's upper body and chest, driving her backward and to the pavement.

Jean wanted to move on, but a moment later, Arclight was up and after her again.

"Now you really did it, Red," Arclight snarled. "I'll enjoy killing you."

"I've seen *Caged Heat*," Jean said dismissively. "You didn't impress me then, and you don't impress me now."

Arclight roared. Jean turned and walked away. With every ounce of psychic strength she could muster, Jean picked up what was left of the Oldsmobile Bishop had stood on earlier, and threw it at Arclight. Pain spiked through her head, like a migraine, but she ignored it. The price of power, she thought.

The car slammed into Arclight, knocked her down, and

rolled over on top of her. She was not dead, Jean knew that she wouldn't be. But she wasn't conscious either.

Jean felt the tension exuding from all the X-Men. They had reached the end of their respective ropes. They'd crossed some lines that day, and she was sad to think that they would probably cross more before the night was through. It disturbed her.

Success! Professor Xavier telepathically shouted in her ear. Jean almost jumped a mile.

Professor? Charles?

Success, Jean, they've done it! They've taken the Sentinels away from Magneto!

Jean Grey smiled. Her eyes welled up with moisture. A single, ecstatic tear slid down her right cheek. She returned to the war with renewed vigor.

Nebulous hope had suddenly become tangible.

* * *

"No!" Magneto shouted.

Valerie Cooper thought he sounded like a petulant child. But whining toddlers were not capable of killing with a thought or a gesture.

Magneto had been paralyzed by Archangel's wing-knives, but his powers were unaffected. He didn't need to move to use them, could, in fact, propel himself wherever he wished to go using those powers. He seemed awkward, for a few moments, as he got his bearings, as he dealt with the crushing blow to his dreams of empire that Valerie had just struck.

But in a moment, he might well come into the Sentinel's command center and take her life in retaliation.

"Do you have any idea what you've done?" he cried in astonished fury.

A stupid question, really. Of course she knew. Now what she needed to know was whether or not he was planning to kill her. The Sentinels were on their way, she knew, to take Magneto down as she'd reprogrammed them to do. But he would have ample time to crush her to death in the immobile Alpha Sentinel's skull if he so desired.

Seconds ticked by, matched by her heartbeat. Magneto's

disorientation was leaving him. She could see it in the cold and silent rage burning in his eyes. Val looked away. She didn't want to see. She felt him moving toward her, and turned her body to the side. If death was coming for her, then . . .

"Val, let's go! Move it!" Archangel shouted at her.

Val snapped her head around to see Warren, silver wings almost invisible in the night air, hovering outside the shattered skull of the Sentinel, Gambit held in one outstretched arm.

"Here we go again!" she shouted, then ran to the blast hole and leaped through.

When Archangel caught her, he was already in motion, flying down and away from where Magneto stood in midair.

"Faster! Faster!" Gambit shouted, and though she didn't want to look, Val had to glance back at their enemy.

Magneto was not giving chase. Instead, he had toppled the crippled Sentinel and it was falling toward them, would crush them to death in seconds.

"Faster!" Val cried, joining Gambit's urgent call for speed.

Archangel knitted his eyebrows, gritted his teeth, and poured on the speed. Val thought for sure they had cleared it, but the thing was so tall it seemed to be chasing them rather than merely falling. Its head slammed into a mostly glass hotel building, barely missing them on the way down.

"He still comin', 'Angel," Gambit said. "An' he don' look too happy."

"I'm sure," Archangel said, and as Val watched, a smirk appeared on his face.

Then Warren started to laugh.

"What's so funny, Archangel?" she snapped. "He's going to kill us."

"Maybe," Warren replied, and tried to get serious, putting all his effort into flying.

"But, Val," he said, as the smile came back, "you should have seen his face."

Archangel burst into a fit of laughter, and they dived lower as he roared helplessly on. A second later, Gambit began to laugh too. A snicker at first, and then full-throated bellowing. Val was afraid Warren was going to drop them, or smash into a building. They were still losing altitude. Warren just couldn't keep going, not with the two of them in tow and the tears streaming down his face as he fought to breathe through a fit of giggles.

Val was about to tell them they were getting punchy, that Magneto was gaining. That they were going to be killed.

Warren was right, she hadn't seen Magneto's face when he lost control of the Sentinels. But the idea of it, and Remy and Warren's cackling, was enough to get her going too. She didn't know if she was laughing at Magneto, or at them.

"You clowns," she said between breaths. "You're sleep deprived and you're going to get us all killed."

They thought that was funny too.

Then they were going down.

"I just can't—" Warren huffed for breath "—can't keep going."

They hit the street too fast, Warren let them go a few feet too high, and Val and Gambit both stumbled and rolled before leaping to their feet again. Together, the three of them turned to face Magneto.

He was just behind them.

"You're pathetic," he said. "Particularly you, Worthington. Once, I thought you might have been of some value to me, but now I see you are as worthless as these others."

"God," Warren said in mock-seriousness, unable to get control of himself despite the danger. "I feel like I'm back in grade school."

Val watched as Archangel and Gambit made a halfhearted attempt at holding the laughter in, then both of them were bent over, holding their bellies as they howled.

"You dare laugh at me?" Magneto cried. "I have spared you one time too many I see. The time has come—"

"Oh, shut up!" Archangel snapped.

Val had been staring at Magneto in trepidation, but now her head swung around in shock. The humor was gone from Archangel's face, and quickly draining from Gambit's as the other X-Man watched the exchange.

"If you're going to kill us, then just do it," Warren said.

SALVATION

"I've been listening to your posturing and watching you feed off this world's fears for too long. You're the worst kind of leader, Magneto. You ignore your press, but believe all your own PR."

Archangel stepped forward, into the spray of light thrown by a street lamp. He spread his arms wide, and his wings out to their full span.

"Go ahead, then," Warren urged. "Strike me down with the wrath of the god you want us all to think you are. But when I'm dead, ask yourself one question. If your goals are so noble, why do you always leave corpses in your wake?"

Magneto opened his mouth to reply, took in the breath that would fuel his words, lifted his hands to launch the assault that would end all their lives.

Then he did something that Valerie Cooper would remember for the rest of her life.

He smiled.

"Bravo, Worthington," Magneto said. "I hope you feel your words are a fitting epitaph."

Gambit and Archangel had never been powerful enough to hold Magneto off for long, and now both were completely spent. In the next moment, they would all be dead.

"Mutant Target Designate Magneto, surrender yourself or face grievous injury during acquisition!" a robotic voice boomed.

Val looked up. They all looked up. Three Sentinels looked down at them. Several more were rocketing toward them across the night sky, their eerie running lights glowing in the darkness.

"Ah, a reprieve, then, Worthington," Magneto said coldly. "Another time, perhaps."

He turned, tore a signal lamp from the street corner with the wave of his hand, and send it flying. It tore through the lead Sentinel's face like a razor-sharp arrow, savaging the robot's operational equipment.

Then Magneto was airborne, headed south, and an entire fleet of Sentinels gave chase.

X-MEN: MUTANT EMPIRE

* * *

A winged man with a face and body reminiscent of a carrion bird dived from the sky toward Storm. She could easily have evaded him, or manipulated the winds around him to, very simply, keep him away from her. But exhaustion was starting to overwhelm her, and her patience was wearing thin. Yes, Jean had passed on that the Sentinels were no longer in Magneto's control. Yes, they had been joined by human and mutant reinforcements. Yes, they had a chance, now, at long last. A chance.

But after a couple of hours in the sky, using the weather to slowly chip away at their overwhelming opposition, providing Iceman with all the moisture he might want to replenish what he stole from the air, Ororo Munroe was nearly spent. She did not have a single ounce of extra energy to use in her own defense. Storm was forced to use the simplest, and most drastic, tactic to keep the twisted bird man away from her.

She nailed him with lightning.

Ororo was an elegant woman, with elegant tastes. She was the very model of courtesy, nobility, and self-respect. But she had once led the Morlocks, a tribe of underground mutant warriors. To do that, she had to become an uncompromising warrior herself. And there was nothing elegant in war.

The charred mutant plummeted from the sky, and had the good fortune to land on the roof of a nine-story building rather than the street far below. Broken bones would heal. Storm breathed a sigh of relief, but there was no question in her mind that she would do it again.

Below, the battle raged on, the X-Men the center of a chaotic conflict, the focus of a maelstrom of blood and hatred. The combatants had merged so completely that she could no longer really use her power to advantage. At least not at the center of the battle.

At the edges, there were still mutants struggling to get into the fight, to take their anger out on anyone who would oppose Magneto. The Blob was with this group. She was too high to hear his oafish boasting voice, but she could imagine what he might say to exhort his comrades into battle. Just as she imagined the rest of the team was, Storm was tired. Tired of fighting, and just plain worn out. She had no patience with any of them, but Fred Dukes least of all.

Her problem was that no wind she might summon, even hurricane force, could make Dukes leave the battlefield. If they knew that the Sentinels were no longer under Magneto's control, a lot of them might surrender, or flee, but Storm and Jean had discussed it telepathically. They wouldn't believe the X-Men. Why should they? No, Storm had to think of . . .

Then she had it. She'd used winds, rain, lightning, to fight the battle. They could be devastating. But she didn't need to destroy the Blob and his cohorts. Only to hurt and annoy them.

A moment later, hail the size of baseballs and hard as stone began to fall from the sky in a dense and destructive rain. The hailstorm only covered an area half a block long. Windows were smashed, cars and a newsstand pulverized.

All but the Blob ran for cover. After trying to escape the hail by moving closer to the fight and finding that the freak storm was following him, Dukes finally realized who was behind it. With surprising intelligence, he did not look up into the sky. Ororo assumed he didn't want to be blinded.

Finally, likely cussing a blue streak, he stomped away from the battlefield. She hoped for good.

Now, she thought, *time to see about the rest of Magneto's pawns.*

* * *

"Can't you fly this thing any faster?" Gyrich snarled at the helicopter pilot.

The man ignored him. He was about to tear into the pilot, when Colonel Tomko's hand landed on his shoulder from the back of the chopper.

"I'm not even sure why you're along for this ride, Mr. Gyrich," the Colonel said. "Why don't you just sit tight and let your nation's armed forces do their jobs?"

It was a jab. He knew it was. But he wasn't Tomko's commander on this one. There wasn't anything he could say now.

But Tomko had made a mistake, allowing himself to feel comfortable enough to insult Gyrich to his face.

Gyrich never forgot.

"What have got down there, Sanchez?" Colonel Tomko barked from the rear.

The pilot mumbled something into his headset, maneuvering between two particularly tall office buildings, then turned his head slightly to respond.

"Control says the media's flooding the city, coming in through all the routes the Sentinels had blocked. Except the GW Bridge, of course," the pilot said.

For a moment it didn't click, then Gyrich remembered that there no longer was a George Washington Bridge.

"All right," the colonel said, "see if we can't get to the battle site first and seal it off from the media. That's all we need, is a caravan of press from all over the world surveying the damage and getting in our way. We're lucky to have taken such comparatively little collateral damage so far. Let's try to keep it that way."

The pilot relayed those orders on his headset.

Gyrich scanned what he could see of the city. Tomko tapped him on the shoulder, then pointed out the window to the southeast.

There were tanks moving through the streets. It occurred to Gyrich that the cumbersome metal war machines were far swifter than he would ever have imagined.

Gyrich smiled.

"With the Sentinels out of the way, Magneto doesn't stand a chance," he said gleefully.

He had to repeat himself, at much greater volume, for Tomko to hear. The colonel made a face.

"Let's not forget who we're dealing with here, Mr. Gyrich," Colonel Tomko said. "We can do the rest, but without blowing up half the city, the X-Men are still the best chance at taking Magneto down. Maybe the only chance."

Gyrich glared at the colonel. Neither man spoke again until the helicopter touched down several blocks east of the Empire State Building.

SALVATION

* * *

Magneto rode the planetary energies he controlled, propelling himself faster and faster to outpace the Sentinels that pursued him. It was hopeless. The faster he flew, the faster they flew. When he had reached New York Harbor, and the ocean was beneath him, he turned to make his stand.

He was trying not to think. Trying not to deal with the blow that had been struck against his plans for Haven, plans for empire. And the best way he knew to avoid thinking, considering, analyzing . . . was to destroy things.

"Mutant Target Designate Magneto," the new lead Sentinel droned at a painful decibel level. "Surrender now, or face painful acquisition procedures."

Magneto warped the Earth's magnetic field around him, reached out with nebulous hands of pure magnetic energy, and tried to tear the Sentinel's head off.

Nothing happened.

The seven Sentinels who were first to arrive, all fired upon him at once. He erected a force shield just in time, but the brunt of their attack sent him reeling, falling, splashing in the salt water, cold even in July. Heavy body armor and helmet weighing him down, Magneto surfaced, gasping for breath, and a numbness came over him, body and soul.

With a burst of magnetic energy that threw the ocean water away from him, he rose, crackling, from the sea.

Eleven more Sentinels had arrived, and he knew that was all of them. The Alpha unit was out of commission, and he had disabled one other. Now he was out over the ocean with little at hand to be used as weapons or projectiles. And the Sentinels seemed to be made of some metal alloy mixed with a polymer that he could not easily grasp.

Which meant nothing, no hardship at all for Magneto. He merely focused his will and attention on the Sentinels, on the web of magnetic power that blanketed the earth, and how this unknown substance reacted to it. It might not, technically, be metal. But it certainly had metal in it. More than a trace.

That was enough.

The Sentinels attacked again, all eighteen of them blasting him with plasma cannons located in their palms. Some also fired solar radiation flares from their eyes. He dodged some, allowed others to be absorbed and dispersed by the much more powerful force shield he was generating.

He didn't want to think. But he could not avoid it. Without the Sentinels, Haven's future was in jeopardy. With the support of his Acolytes and other newly arrived followers, they might have enough power to keep the Mutant Empire intact, to repel invaders to build a new world. They might.

And they might not.

The Sentinels were useless to him now. As much as he regretted it, Magneto knew he had to destroy them.

As a new barrage of plasma beams buffeted his force shield, so intense that his entire body ached from the effort he made not to buckle under the attacks, he concentrated on the little metal that was part of the alloy used in creating the Sentinels' shell. Focused on it, reached out with curses on his lips, and began to tear the fleet of Sentinels apart.

The debris piled up in the ocean until it looked like Pearl Harbor after the Japanese attacked, hulking metallic useless beasts with ugly faces staring up at the darkness. Dead. Defeated.

Magneto turned back toward Haven, and the war.

* * *

"Move it, people!" Trish Tilby shouted, in a tone she knew combined the worst traits of high school teacher and drill instructor.

But it was effective. The press corps she had gathered around her hustled like crazy.

"Set up wherever you like, get the best angles, whatever. Just stay out of the X-Men's way. This thing is going to end fast when it ends, one way or another," she explained.

She sounded confident. She knew that. But inside, she was wilting. The fight had gone on too long. If the X-Men were going to win, they'd have had it all wrapped up before now.

SALVATION

With the Sentinels keeping the military out, Magneto only had to destroy the X-Men and it was over.

And the X-Men, from what Trish could see of them a few blocks north of the conflict, were looking pretty haggard. It was—

"Trish!" one of the CNN crew shouted behind her.

When she turned around, she saw a tank rolling down Seventh Avenue toward them. Seconds later, she identified a sound blossoming on the air: helicopters. Trish looked up in time to see three choppers rise up over the long block between Sixth and Seventh, about ten blocks south of their own position.

"Get me set up, now!" Trish ordered.

"You're ready to go, and mobile," a producer named Gayle told her. "You've got the feed to all networks."

Trish ran then. Forward a block and a half. Close enough to the fight to hear the grunting, the slap of flesh, the burning crackle of energy let loose on an unsuspecting enemy. That was as far as she wanted to get, and too close by far.

"Go," she said simply.

The camera came up, and she began to speak.

"This is Trish Tilby, reporting from the site of a new Civil War, a struggle fought not between blue and gray, but brother and brother nevertheless," she said.

"There are humans in the fight, mainly New York City police officers, and other brave souls banded together to protect their city. But the main conflict is between mutants.

"Some of you, watching this, have begun to think this is my story. The story of what I've been through in the past day or so. That's wrong. It's the story of America. Of what we've come to, tearing one another apart because of our differences.

"Those of you out there in the dark, watching me now, watching the fight raging behind me and hoping the mutants doing battle destroy one another, you should be ashamed of yourselves. The X-Men, and others allied with them, are out here fighting your battles, putting their lives on the line for your well-being, for your children's future.

"They would fight for themselves, but, you see, it is too

late for them. Too late to be happy, too late to live normal lives, too late for the simple pleasures of life. You, Mr. and Ms. America, have taken that away from them. So, while Magneto punishes you for it, while Magneto tries to do to you exactly what you so desperately want to do to him—erase you from the picture—the X-Men stand and fight for a dream that is so much like the American dream. They fight for ideals that most of America seems to have forgotten. For justice. For equality. For freedom.

"They fight for you. They may well die for you. The courage of fools, or the selflessness and benevolence of patriots? I guess the answer to that question is fairly subjective, but how you answer it, ladies and gentlemen, how you answer it may tell you something about yourselves that you'd rather not know.

"The military can only stand by and wait. It's the X-Men's show, now. It all rests with them. If Magneto isn't stopped here, he'll be in your town next, that I guarantee. And as you watch for the next few moments in silence, as you watch what they are suffering for you, ask yourself one very disturbing question: What in the name of God would we have done, what would our fate have been, if the bigots of this nation had been successful in destroying the X-Men, as they've been trying to do for years? What would we have done without them?"

Trish signaled with her left hand, which was out of the camera frame, and the cameraman panned away from her and settled on the quickly dwindling war.

It stayed there a long time.

The world watched.

Chapter 16

As staid as his well-deserved reputation painted him to be, Charles Xavier was not above childlike excitement. That was the very emotion he had felt when he realized that Valerie Cooper, Archangel, and Gambit had succeeded in their quest to take the Sentinels away from Magneto.

It was a huge victory, a priceless one. For several entire minutes, Xavier was able to put aside his anxiety over the continuing war, his political spin-doctoring of mutant-human relations, his constant monitoring of all the major parties involved.

The smile hurt his face.

When Gyrich had come over to deliver the good news, Xavier had forced himself to stifle the smile. As Gyrich walked away, he had thought it would return, but it did not. The reasons quickly became apparent.

In his youth, Charles Xavier had been a man of action; a soldier, an adventurer, so many things. After he lost the use of his legs, all of that changed. In his lowest times, he considered himself the worst kind of voyeur. Not that he eavesdropped on people's thoughts, or peeked in on the fantasies in their minds. That never interested him.

Instead, he lived vicariously through the X-Men, in so many ways. They did what, in almost every case, he could not. They went out into the world and fought for his dream. He did all he could, politically, financially, personally. He guided their every action. But it was the X-Men in the field, without their teacher, mentor, founder.

Sometimes, Charles Xavier, among the two or three most powerful men on the planet, felt completely powerless. Useless.

He might have asked Gyrich to bring him along, but the man would never have complied. Who wants to take responsibility for a man who cannot walk in the middle of a war zone? He might have forced Gyrich to take him, but that would have led to disaster.

In any case, that was not his role. Xavier was to direct, to command, to inspire, to plan. There were things he might have done to end the battle more swiftly, but his moral code would not allow him actually to undertake any of them. Under normal circumstances.

These were hardly normal circumstances. It was quite possible that, before dawn broke once more, Xavier would have broken even more of his own personal commandments, ignored his entirely subjective thou-shalt-nots in favor of safety, of life, of victory.

Part of his role was to see the big picture, to sense the danger the X-Men were in and try to guide them through it.

X-Men, beware, he thought, sending the message to each member of the team simultaneously. *The deciding moment of this war has come. Magneto is on his way to you now. Enraged as he is, he is more dangerous than ever. Do not let your guard down for a moment, do not allow relief to diminish your readiness for battle. For everything you have done up until this moment has been but a prelude to this, the final battle with Magneto.*

If you are not careful, he could destroy you all.

Message sent, and silently acknowledged, Xavier looked up at the night sky and breathed deeply. There was no pleasure in it, no relaxation of the grim set of his features. Only preparation for whatever might come.

For Charles Xavier had finally realized that he could remain on the sidelines no longer. The final battle with Magneto was his to fight. The X-Men might triumph without his help, but he feared that not all of them would survive.

Victory was his to earn.

He did not move from the spot where he had sat for hours in his wheelchair. Even so, Charles Xavier had gone to war.

* * *

Gambit and Val Cooper tore onto Fifth Avenue on another stolen motorcycle, with Archangel flying above. Mutants and humans alike were fleeing the field of battle—at least those that could still move under their own power. They seemed to sense that the end was near, and that none of them would have any impact over the outcome of the war for Manhattan.

"It's like Times Square just after midnight on New Year's Eve," Archangel said on the comm.

"Or when de sun come up de morning after Mardi Gras," Gambit agreed. "Nobody even want to look at anybody else, just get de hell out of dere and home to bed."

It had come down to the X-Men and the Juggernaut against those Acolytes who remained conscious and some of their more powerful allies. By the time Gambit steered the bike through unconscious bodies he hoped were still alive, Archangel was already in the thick of battle. It would be over soon, he knew.

Or it would have been, if they had been the last of the enemy. But there was still Magneto to deal with. Soon. Very soon. But not yet. They could still finish off the others and present a united front against Magneto when he did get there.

"Valerie, get off," he said grimly. "De toy soldiers are over dat way."

She started to protest, even as she got off the motorcycle, but Gambit was gone before the first words were out. She'd done her part. Now the X-Men had to finish the job.

Cyclops was blasting away at a mutant who looked as if he were made of rubber, but the surface of his flesh rippled and shone like crude oil. Whenever Cyclops took a shot at him, the mutant's body bent or opened to let the blast through.

Then he'd hit Cyclops again, hard, leaving a dark inky stain behind. It wasn't much more than one on one, it seemed, and Gambit moved forward to help Cyclops, figuring his presence would make the difference, change the balance of power. It was so close to being over.

There was a small sound behind him, creeping cat's paws, and he started to turn. Too late. Senyaka's burning psionic whip wrapped around his neck, choking off his air before he could take a breath. Gambit tried to get his hands on the whip, to use his power, to use the whip against Senyaka, something. It moved side to side, snakelike, avoiding his grasp. He kicked out, taking Senyaka in the chest. The hooded Acolyte let out a grunt, but the whip did not let go.

Gambit tried once more to get his hands on the whip, then

lunged for Senyaka himself. But the air was gone. Completely.

He went down hard. When his face hit the street, he barely felt it.

* * *

From above, Rogue saw it all.

"Remy!" she screamed, and shot toward him out of the sky.

Rogue had never worried for herself. She worried about consequences all the time, worried for her friends, worried for the world. But never for herself. She was nearly invulnerable. Anything that might hurt her very badly would likely also kill her. Nothing she could do about that.

But Gambit was not invulnerable. Not hardly. Sure, Remy LeBeau knew how to take care of himself. That had been his full-time occupation before joining the X-Men, covering his own hide. Things had changed. He knew family now. Rogue flattered herself to think he knew love as well. She most certainly loved him.

Down on the street, the man she loved, the sharp-tongued mystery man whose Cajun charm had won her over from their first meeting . . . Gambit was dying.

"No!" she cried, shot like a bullet to street level, and didn't slow down a bit before slamming into Senyaka.

Ribs cracked under her assault. She slammed through glass partitions and into a row of ATM machines. His cowled head clanged off the machines and he stumbled for a moment, unsure of where he was. A weak glow formed in the palm of his right hand, a feeble attempt to create his psionic whip. Rogue spun him around, and Senyaka's cowl slipped down.

She recoiled.

"My God but you're ugly enough, ain't ya?" she observed.

Rogue hit him in the gut hard enough to carry him off his feet and back out onto the sidewalk, then he rolled into the street. Senyaka held tightly to his belly, doubled over, and vomited blood in the gutter.

She went after him. As she reached to pick him up, a powerful hand grabbed her right arm, and she spun, lashing out at this new attacker.

Hank McCoy blocked her swing with the flash of one blue-furred arm.

"Ow!" he hissed. "Now, that's going to leave a significant contusion."

"Let go of me, Beast," she demanded.

"Apologies, Rogue, but no," Hank replied. "Another blow and you would have killed him."

She glanced back at Senyaka. The blood was coming from his nose as well, now. The Beast relaxed his grip, but she didn't go after her target again.

"In truth, he may yet die from the injuries you've given him," the Beast said sadly.

"Let him," she said, though she did not really mean it. She was no killer. Rogue said nothing as the Beast knelt to see what medical assistance he could give to Senyaka.

Across the street, Gambit lay very still. Rogue wanted to go to him, feel his pulse. That way she could breathe again. But she couldn't drive herself through the night. It had all become surreal to her suddenly, and touching Gambit's neck or wrist would bring them back to reality. If he were dead, she didn't think she . . .

"Oh, thank God," Rogue gasped.

She had seen his chest rise and fall. Even now, it continued to do so.

Rogue rushed to Gambit's side, knelt by his unconscious form. They'd all been through a lot the previous few days, but Gambit had had it even tougher than the rest of them. She ran her gloved fingers over the stubble on his chin, pushed his hair away from his face. She longed to be able to touch him, her own skin to his flesh. But the pleasures of such simple contact were denied Rogue forever. With her personality-, memory-, and talent-absorption powers, she could permanently damage anyone she touched.

It was the worst kind of isolation. And yet, with Gambit, Rogue had begun to feel a little less alone.

SALVATION

"You rest now, sugar," she said quietly. "You've done your part."

She kissed the fingers of her gloved right hand, then pressed the kiss to his lips. Rogue didn't even glance back at the injured Senyaka, at Hank McCoy, who was trying to undo at least part of what she'd done. It didn't matter. In many ways winning didn't even matter anymore.

The only thing that did matter was an end. Now, Rogue wanted nothing more than to go home, to bring Gambit back to Salem Center to heal.

She prayed that it would be over soon.

* * *

"You tried to kill my brother!" Harlan Kleinstock shrieked, more astonished than accusatory. "Oh, you're dead, man."

"Please," Iceman said, sarcasm like venom from his mouth. "If I'd wanted to kill him, I'd have flash-frozen the air in his mouth and nose, or freeze-dried his chest and just shattered it."

Harlan fired a blast of kinetic energy from his fists, but Iceman blocked it with a concave ice shield, deflecting it back at his attacker. Kleinstock was too angry to be impressed.

"Go down and stay down, pal," Kleinstock snarled. "I'm getting a little tired of you, of this whole thing. Give it up, will you?"

"Wait," Iceman said, flustered and angry. "You're tired of me? You're tired of me? Oh, that's rich!"

Bobby formed the moisture from the air into a battering ram of ice that tore Harlan Kleinstock off his feet, drove him back several yards, and slammed him into a brown UPS truck parked askew at the corner. Kleinstock didn't get up.

With a long sigh, Bobby sat down on the street corner, chin in his hands, not even bothering to look and see if his teammates needed help. He didn't think they did. It was almost over now.

"I'm going to Disneyworld," he said softly to himself.

* * *

When Ivan Skolnick spotted Colonel Tomko standing with Henry Peter Gyrich, he froze in his tracks. His human allies continued to swarm from the battlefield toward the growing ranks of the media on the sidelines. But that was not Skolnick's proper path and he knew it.

Approaching Tomko and Gyrich was the most courageous act he had ever performed. When he was only a short distance away, Gyrich looked up and recognized him. The man's eyes went wide and he glanced nervously at Colonel Tomko, then at a blonde woman behind him, who Skolnick recognized as Valerie Cooper, the mutant affairs expert. Then Gyrich turned his attention back to Skolnick's approach, and glared.

The look was an eloquently wordless threat. Skolnick ignored it. When he was ten feet away from Colonel Tomko, he snapped to attention.

"Major Ivan Skolnick, reporting, sir!" he barked. "Remanding myself into your custody, sir."

Tomko looked at him quizzically, then at Gyrich and finally at Cooper.

"Custody?" he asked. "What for, Major? You aren't in my command."

"Yes, sir, I know, sir, but you're the highest ranking officer present, sir," Skolnick said quickly, every word a sharp pain in his heart. His career was over.

"Major, I think you should—" Gyrich began.

"You overstep yourself, Mr. Gyrich," Colonel Tomko said, and Skolnick could hear the pleasure the colonel got from telling Gyrich off. He liked the sound of it himself.

"Colonel, sir, I was leader of Special Ops Unit One, orders to terminate Magneto," he said. "But I'm a mutant, sir—"

"What?!?" Gyrich nearly shrieked. "No wonder!"

"I turned on my own unit and joined Magneto's cause," Skolnick said, eyes on the pavement.

Gyrich was fuming.

"But you led the human resistance in this decisive battle, didn't you?" Colonel Tomko asked.

"Yes, sir," Skolnick replied.

"Were any of your unit hurt?" the colonel asked.

"No, sir," Skolnick said, "I wouldn't have harmed a hair on their heads."

"Colonel, this man should be court-martialed for treason," Gyrich said emphatically.

"You're not a military man, Gyrich," Tomko said. "It's none of your business. Besides, the major is hardly a traitor."

"But he—" Gyrich spluttered.

"He is a genius!" Tomko finished. "He used the fact that he was a mutant to construct an elaborate ruse, kept his men safe from harm by causing them to be incarcerated, and infiltrated Magneto's infrastructure in order to position himself to usurp Magneto when the time was right. If anything, he is to be commended."

"Commended?" Gyrich squealed.

"Mr. Gyrich, if you have a problem with my version of events, perhaps you'd care to discuss exactly whose orders SOU1 were operating under, in direct conflict with the President's very specific instructions?" Colonel Tomko said.

Gyrich grumbled something Skolnick couldn't hear. Behind him, Valerie Cooper had an enormous smile on her face.

"Good work, Major," Colonel Tomko said, and held out his hand.

Major Skolnick couldn't shake.

"Sir, I'm sorry, but it isn't the way you—" he began, trying to explain.

The colonel held up a hand, gesturing for him to be quiet.

"Major," he said patiently, "I don't know what you're about to say, and I don't want to know. I know what's going in my report, and I'm sure Gyrich's report will reflect the same. You'd do well by yourself and all involved to just keep quiet.

"You have something you want to say to your unit, Major, you say it to them in private. You hear me?" the colonel asked.

"Yes, sir," Major Skolnick responded, and offered a salute.

The colonel saluted in return.

All of it had gone away, like an awful nightmare. Well, not all of it.

The guilt was still there.

* * *

To Amelia Voght, Wolverine looked like some feral beast, a warrior out of barbarian times, a stone killer. As far as she was concerned, he was all of those things. His adamantium claws were nearly black with blood. Moonlight and neon glinted off speckles of crimson on Wolverine's face and chest.

Voght was terrified. The worst part was, she thought Wolverine could smell her fear.

"Come on, X-Man," she said. "Try me. If I can teleport your arms back to Avalon, those claws would make great trophies."

To her growing horror, Wolverine smiled. Voght wasn't sure—didn't want to be sure—but she thought she saw blood on his teeth. But no, she told herself, he wouldn't—She stopped herself. She didn't know for certain what Wolverine would or would not do, when pushed. And she prayed she wouldn't find out.

"Back off, or I'll take you apart," she warned, weakly.

"Threats don't mean much to me, little girl," he said, taking several steps toward her, stalking her. "You try to 'port my arms off, that means you gotta get real close. Before you lay a hand on me, your guts'll be painting the street."

Voght shivered.

"You'd best surrender, now, or we're gonna have to throw down. It's gonna be messy too," he promised.

She said nothing. Biting her lip, Amelia Voght considered all that she owed Magneto, all that his dream meant to her and to so many others. It had always seemed to her that Haven would be worth dying for, but here was her death now, taking another step toward her, and, by God, she didn't want to die.

"Let's do it," Wolverine said, and started for her.

Voght steeled herself. No matter how much she feared him, she wouldn't run. He was just another mutant. She'd beaten him before. If she had to kill him now, to save her own life, then that was the way it would be.

"Give it up, Voght!" somebody shouted to her left.

Wolverine slowed as Amelia turned to see who had spoken. Her breath slowly leaked out of her, and for several seconds, she forgot to take another.

It was the X-Men. All of them. Or nearly all, since Gambit was out of it. Jean Grey had spoken, and with her stood Cyclops, Rogue, the Beast, Bishop, Storm, Archangel, Iceman, and their unexpected ally, the Juggernaut.

Voght didn't know what to do. Then she knew there was only one thing she could do.

In a crackling flash, she teleported away.

* * *

"Quick, look around!" Cyclops ordered. "See where she turns up. It could be an ambush."

"Ain't nobody left to ambush us, Cyke," Wolverine snarled. "The party's over. I don't think Voght is coming back."

"Jean?" Scott asked, realizing that she would be able to sense Voght if she popped up anywhere near them.

After a moment, Jean shook her head. "Nothing," she said.

"Great," Iceman said. "Can we go home now? I'm going to sleep for about a year."

"Sounds good," Archangel chimed in. "Then we can go to Paris and sleep there for a few months."

"What's wrong with all of you?" Cyclops asked. "This isn't over. Hardly over. It's just begun. Remember what the Professor said?"

"Indeed," the Beast said. "But, then, where is *he*?"

They were all silent, then, as they tried to push their exhaustion aside and focus on the war still to fight.

"Well, I don't wanna look for him," Iceman said finally. "Maybe he figured it was done with, and went on home?"

Nobody thought that was very plausible.

Then Jean's eyes went wide, and Scott heard her voice, both as she spoke and telepathically.

"He's here," she said.

They all looked up at once.

"I don't think I'm ready for this," Iceman said quietly.

"None of us are," Cyclops admitted. "But we haven't come this far to lose. This is the real thing, the core of the fight. This is the battle the X-Men were created to fight."

"Then I humbly suggest we not screw it up," the Beast said calmly.

Nobody laughed.

* * *

Despite his intimate knowledge of them, despite all the times that he had thought them beaten and the X-Men had risen from the ashes to triumph over him again and again, despite all of that, Magneto was stunned to see them standing, nearly unscathed, amid the wreckage of several city blocks. Unconscious or semiconscious mutants littered the streets along with debris left behind by the battle. There were the dead as well, not too many, but some. Then there were those who were still walking, crawling, or dragging themselves from the battle-scarred streets.

The X-Men had survived. More than survived. They were triumphant. As far as Magneto could see, only Gambit had sustained any grievous injuries. The Cajun was not a factor. That left nine X-Men. And the Juggernaut.

Xavier's students stood ready, but made no move to attack. Magneto understood their trepidation. This was the final battle between them. He knew that. They must know it as well.

"Perhaps you feel as though you've won, X-Men," he called down to them. "You have not. You have merely prolonged the inevitable, merely made my life more difficult. Haven shall be. Once you are all destroyed, I will rid Haven of dissenters even if I must do it alone.

"It is almost too late for mercy, you see. Summers, Grey, McCoy, I appeal to your intelligence, and your instincts. You have thirty seconds to begin to withdraw from my empire. Then, sad as I am to say it, I will be forced to kill you all. You are just too much trouble to be allowed to live."

SALVATION

"Well, guys, it's been real, but I'm outta here," the Juggernaut said, and Magneto allowed himself a small smile. It was as he had expected.

"What?" Cyclops cried.

"Hey, Summers, no offense man, but I helped you out as best I could. I got you this far. But I didn't come here to die, okay? I'm gone," Marko explained.

"Cain . . . ?" Jean Grey asked.

"Sorry, Grey," the Juggernaut said with a shrug. "I'm not one of the white hats, okay? I'm not a black hat. Maybe I'm a gray one, but I don't think so. For me, it's all in the green."

There were several hushed exchanges, then the Juggernaut left and the X-Men turned their attention back to Magneto.

"Coward!" Bishop screamed as Marko walked away. None of the others would even look at him.

Cyclops gathered the X-Men closer to him and spoke softly to his team. Magneto wished that he could hear Scott Summers's words, better yet his thoughts, but he was no telepath.

Then, as he knew they would, the X-Men turned and attacked.

Cyclops let loose a barrage of optic blasts that did not injure Magneto but instinctively, he dodged. Faster than he would have given her credit for, Rogue was there. She could not harm him through his force shield, but the blows she rained upon it drove him lower.

Lightning tore from the sky and struck the sphere of energy that protected him, passing a terrible jolt of electricity into Magneto's flesh. He shook with it, and his body went numb a moment. Then it was over, but he didn't want to experience it again.

Bishop fired upon him with some kind of plasma weapon and Jean Grey tried to pry open his mind, to force him into unconsciousness. Bishop's weapon was laughable, and Magneto had taught himself how to defend against psychic attacks decades earlier.

Ice began to form within his protective sphere, and Magneto was amused by the audacity of Bobby Drake. He'd been a boy the first time they'd clashed, and Drake still had not learned his lesson. Magneto thought it might be time to teach him one. For now, he simply modulated his sphere to drop the ice out through it.

That was when Archangel launched dozens, perhaps hundreds, of his wing-knives. Two of them had paralyzed Magneto for minutes. Nearly a hundred might kill him, if they were allowed to get that far. But he knew their biometallic compound now.

With a gesture, Magneto turned the wing-knives away from him and sent them flying, his control over the metal moving them so fast, they were little more than a blur. The wing-knives slashed through Rogue's costume, and though she was nearly invulnerable, some passed through her skin.

Rogue fell from the sky and hit the pavement with a crack. She did not rise again.

Magneto tore Bishop's weapon from his hands with little more than a thought, then he reached out along the magnetic lines of power and did something he had wanted to do for a long time. He picked Wolverine off the ground by the adamantium in the Canadian mutant's skeleton, forced his claws out of their sheaths, and sent Logan twisting through the air following those deadly claws.

Wolverine plowed into Bishop, his claws slicing the future X-Man to bloody shreds.

"You bastard!" Logan screamed as he stood up. "You made me kill him! You're next, Magneto! Once and for all, you're next!"

Magneto forced Wolverine to turn his claws around, and drive them into his own chest, perforating heart and lungs. Wolverine fell.

Lightning struck his force shield once more, and Magneto jerked and writhed in pain for several moments. His guard slipped, and one of Cyclops's optic blasts slid through the field, tearing into his right arm. Then he knew that he wasn't the only one who knew it was the end. Either the X-Men would be destroyed, or Magneto would be dead. Even Summers knew that. He was using deadly force against Magneto.

Good, Magneto thought. If they were trying to kill him as well, it didn't feel so much like murder.

Storm, noble as she was, had annoyed him. She had hurt him for the last time. It was all too easy. Magneto snagged up a brown delivery truck that was essentially a steel box. In the web of his power, he flung it toward her.

"No!" Storm screamed. "Not again. Please, no!"

Thunder shattered windows for seven blocks, lightning flashed and struck at the steel prison that sped toward her. But Storm could do nothing. Magneto tore the truck apart, bending and warping it with his mind and then wrapping it around Ororo Munroe. He crushed her with it, and rather than set it gently down, Magneto merely let her fall.

Optic blasts hit his force shield again. Cyclops wouldn't give up. There were just the five of them left, the five original X-Men: Cyclops, Jean Grey, the Beast, Archangel, and Iceman.

Magneto knew he would have to kill them, or at least hurt them badly enough that they would be out of the war, permanently.

It saddened him, but it could not be avoided.

The X-Men had to die.

Chapter 17

"We've got to go in," Gyrich demanded. "We've got to take Magneto down now, while he's distracted!"

Colonel Tomko looked to Valerie Cooper, she assumed for some kind of rational response to Gyrich's raving. She didn't have one.

"Gyrich, you're out of your mind," she said, her tone as matter of fact as she could keep it. "The X-Men are in there, right now, trying to stop him. If we throw everything we've got at Magneto—and that's what it would take, if even that would do it—the X-Men are at ground zero. We kill him, and we'd be killing them too."

Gyrich glared at her. He didn't respond verbally, only with that hateful, arrogant glare. But Val didn't need words. She knew perfectly well what the glare meant, what the message was.

The first part of it was, *Stay out of it, Cooper, it isn't your affair.* But it was her affair. She was in it, no question, and she had the power, no matter how limited, to get in his way.

The second part was, *So the X-Men are in the way? So what? That's another near dozen mutants we won't have to be afraid of anymore.*

Val felt sick. Gyrich wanted to blow up several city blocks with Magneto and the X-Men as targets.

"You want them dead, don't you Gyrich?" she sneered. "And it isn't just because you're a bigot. It isn't just because they scare you. It's because your pride is hurt, because you couldn't take Manhattan back from Magneto. You couldn't stop the madman's bid to be emperor of the universe or whatever. It took mutants to do it.

"You think they're the scum of the Earth, you treat them like they're some unmentionable thing you've got to wipe off the bottom of your shoe, but they took the Sentinels out. They took the Acolytes down. And if we've got any hope against Magneto, it's in their hands.

"That burns you, doesn't it Henry? You hate them even more for that."

"Hatred has nothing to do with it," he said smugly. "It's

common sense is all. And if the X-Men are killed in the meantime, well, sacrifices have to be made. Victory comes at a price, Cooper. They know that.''

Val was fuming. She wanted to beat some sense into Gyrich, or at least enjoy trying. There was no doubt in her mind that she could do it too. But she wouldn't. Unlike Gyrich, she followed orders.

''Colonel?'' an overweight sergeant called from the front seat of a communications vehicle that had just arrived. ''I've got the President on the line for Mr. Gyrich and Ms. Cooper. He wants to talk to you too.''

Tomko's eyes widened, but he said nothing. She admired him. The man could roll with the punches, that was for sure. The chain of command had not been bent, but shattered. First he'd taken orders from Gyrich, out in Colorado. Then his Pentagon superiors had reasserted themselves. Now the President himself had stepped in.

''Ms. Cooper,'' the President said, when they had gathered to face his image on the vid-comm unit, ''I want to thank you for your assistance in this matter. So far, the X-Men's cooperation has kept loss of life and property damage to a minimum—though,'' he added, smiling slightly, ''I doubt the UN would agree with me. In any case, without them, we might truly have had to use the most drastic of measures. They disabled the Sentinels, brought the war down to Magneto against the rest of the world.''

''No argument, sir,'' Gyrich put in quickly. ''But they aren't going to be able to finish him off. I recommend that we—''

''Frankly, Mr. Gyrich, I'm not prepared to hear any of your recommendations at the moment. If I'd listened to you from the beginning, we'd be in a world of hurt right now,'' the President said.

''Colonel Tomko,'' he continued, ''you are to wait for the outcome of the X-Men's attack on Magneto. If they fail, you have authorization to use any means at your disposal to destroy him, regardless of collateral damage. Rely on Ms. Cooper as your consultant.

"Mr. Gyrich, you are to return to Washington immediately. The Director of Wideawake will be awaiting your arrival. Apparently, you have much to discuss, including what to do now that the Sentinels have been destroyed," he concluded.

"But, Mr. President, it isn't over here, I can't just—"

"Gyrich, in case you missed it, you've been relieved of any responsibilities in Manhattan at this time," the President said sharply. "You have your orders."

The screen went dark. Val tried not to smile. She needn't have worried. Gyrich stormed away immediately, boarding a helicopter that would start him back to D.C.

"That's one troubled soul," Colonel Tomko said, without a trace of the venom she might have expected from the man.

"The bad news is, he isn't the worst of them. The world is full of people much more radical in their views on mutant-human relations than Gyrich. All that hate is going to tear us apart," she said.

* * *

"Ms. Tilby, I'm—"

"Police Commissioner Wilson Ramos," she finished. "I'm pleased to meet you, sir, and very impressed with what you've done here today."

"Thank you," he said. "But we've no time for mutual admiration."

"What can I do for you?" she asked, slightly put off by his intensity.

"Gabi?" he said, deferring to an attractive girl standing just behind him.

"These men and women are mutants, Ms. Tilby," the girl—Gabi—said. "They came here because of what Magneto promised them, but when they realized what was happening, they turned on him and did everything they could to help the X-Men."

Trish admired the young woman, obviously one of the resistance fighters she'd heard about. She was courageous and yet obviously compassionate. But Trish thought Gabi seemed uncomfortable talking to her, and wondered if it was because she was a reporter. Reporters, she knew, had worse reputations than lawyers these days.

"What can I do for you, or for them?" Trish asked, quite sincerely.

Gabi hesitated, so Ramos stepped in.

"The military will take them into custody," Commissioner Ramos said. "Who knows what might happen to them, then? They just want to go back to their homes, back to the world they knew, no matter how flawed. Some of them have kept their genetic differences a secret, and now they only want to slip back into their old lives.

"I think they've had a hard enough lesson the past couple of days, don't you?" he asked.

Before Trish could answer, Gabi said: "Iceman told us we could trust you."

Trish smiled. It pleased her to know that, no matter what had happened between them, the X-Men still trusted her. She thought of Caroline, and of Kevin, who had both died because they were good people, people who didn't care about genetic differences.

"We've all suffered enough, I think," she said finally.

With Ramos assisting, she gathered around all the members of the media that she knew. Together, and using the police officers who had backed Ramos up in the war, they spent the rest of the night, and well into the morning, shuttling mutants back out of New York. An underground railroad for the twilight of the twentieth century.

When Trish first thought of the analogy, it saddened her greatly to realize that it was all too accurate. Hate never went away, it only changed to take advantage of the times.

Later, she would try hard to believe that wasn't true.

Sometimes, she could almost do it.

* * *

One by one, Amelia Voght teleported the original Acolytes back to space station Avalon in Earth orbit. Senyaka, the Kleinstocks, Frenzy, all of them were badly injured. They would heal, but not in time to make a difference in the final battle.

It was all up to Magneto now.

* * *

Years had passed since Magneto had first faced these five, the original X-Men: Iceman, the Beast, Cyclops, Jean Grey, and Archangel, who had been just Angel back then. He remembered the day well. He had been attacking the military base, Cape Citadel, when they came seemingly out of nowhere, offering a challenge he had never expected, from a man who had once been his closest friend. Surprise had been their advantage, as had his reluctance to simply kill them all, and Xavier as well, if necessary, to achieve his goals.

The stakes had risen since then, the consequences grown more deadly. The X-Men had grown in number, and become far greater warriors. But Magneto had evolved as well.

And they no longer had the advantage of surprise.

Cyclops continued to batter Magneto's force shield with his optic blasts. Magneto admired his persistence, but thought the man foolish. It was clear his beams were no match for Magneto's power. Although the constant attack was tiring him a bit, forcing him to constantly focus on his own defense.

The other four moved as one.

Jean Grey wrapped the Beast in her telekinetic web and lifted them both off the ground, rising toward the spot where Magneto hovered over the devastation. Iceman shot from the ground toward Magneto on a pillar of ice he was building beneath himself, then extended it into an ice slide that drove him forward. Archangel took to the air, diving and swooping back and forth, not giving Magneto an easy target.

The others were easy targets, though, and could be dealt with easily and soon enough. He turned his attentions to Archangel, who had already hurt him once. Magneto wasn't going to allow that again. As Warren Worthington tucked back his wings and dived, Magneto held up a hand, waiting for Warren to fire his wing-knives.

In that moment, Iceman flash-froze a huge block of ice on

the side of Magneto's force shield, disrupting the field as if it were a window of ice on the side of the sphere.

Jean Grey dropped the Beast, who bounded off the ice slide Bobby Drake had left behind, and smashed through the ice-window, scattering shards of jagged ice and slamming into Magneto's chest before flipping into a backward somersault and landing behind Drake on the ice-slide.

Archangel didn't fire his wing-knives. If he had, he was too close now for Magneto to do anything about it. But instead, Worthington dived in at extraordinary speed, banked in at an angle, and flew past the hole in Magneto's force shield before he had had time to repair the sphere. His right wing sliced out, through the break in the sphere, and cut Magneto's side in several places.

Blood poured. His concentration faltered.

"No!" he cried.

Even as he knitted his force shield back together, Cyclops took advantage of the opening, and fired a full-power optic blast through the narrowing gap. It slammed into Magneto's chest, and threw him backward and down. His concentration evaporated; he fell.

To one side, a row of windows exploded outward, powered by Jean Grey's telekinesis, and the shards rained down on him, lacerating his scalp, face, and neck. The rest of him was protected by body armor, but if he hit the street, he would most certainly be dead.

That would not do. His destiny was one of greatness, not the ignominy of such easy defeat.

Several yards above the asphalt, Magneto gathered the Earth's magnetic field around him and simply stopped his fall. He hovered there a moment, took a painful breath—Cyclops's last attack had broken several ribs and blackened his body armor—then lifted himself back into the air. His force shield knitted itself back together, the sphere of green electric energy even stronger than before.

"Hit him again, X-Men, before he is fully recovered!" Cyclops shouted from below.

"Not to worry, Scotty," Iceman replied. "We've got the bum on the ropes."

But Drake had always been a foolish young man. His ice making propelled him forward, up toward Magneto. He was cocky now, foolish. Iceman thought it was over. And it was.

For him.

Magneto gestured, and magnetic power arced from his fingertips, shattering the ice slide. Iceman fell. He tried in vain to form a new slide beneath him, but Magneto struck him again, and Drake fell, disoriented.

"Bobby, go limp!" the Beast cried from below. "I've got you."

"No," Magneto said softly, "no, you don't."

The Beast bounded across Sixth Avenue, trying to get under his falling comrade. Magneto wrapped his magnetic tendrils around a yellow cab, lifted it off the ground quickly, effortlessly, and dropped it on top of the Beast.

Hank McCoy died without screaming.

Bobby Drake crashed through the windshield of the cab. Inside, the warmth of his blood began to melt the ice from his body.

"Oh, my God!" Jean Grey screamed. "Hank, Bobby! Scott, he's killed them!"

Archangel screamed a curse, dive-bombing Magneto from above, apparently hoping for a replay of his earlier, successful attack.

It wasn't going to work.

"You are appallingly stupid, Worthington," Magneto said. "All of you. I never wanted you dead, don't you see? But you have backed me into a corner. You have put me in a position where killing you is the only logical option."

Archangel launched dozens of wing-knives.

Magneto reached out, focused, attuned his power to the strange metallic structure of Archangel's wings, and then he pulled. Warren Worthington screamed, wailed, shrieked, as his wings were torn from his back.

While Archangel fell, Magneto didn't even watch.

Only Grey and Summers were left, the loving couple in

SALVATION

whom Xavier had placed the future of the X-Men. They were to be the parents, both literal and figurative, of the next generation of X-Men. His heirs.

"You fought well," he said, almost kindly, as he floated down to street level to face them. "You had almost beaten me, there at the start. Teamwork has always been the X-Men's greatest weapon. But your time is done. In a way, I will miss you."

Grey was a beautiful woman, her red hair lustrous even in the neon-lit night. Her face was filled with loathing, but no fear. Her uniform in tatters, and yet she was still noble.

Summers limped slightly; blood ran from wounds on his chest and legs.

"If you don't fight me, I will make it as painless for you as possible," Magneto promised.

Grey and Summers bowed their heads.

The taxi slammed into Magneto from behind. His protective sphere held, but he was driven through the plate glass windows of a women's clothing store and trapped beneath the yellow cab with whatever remained of Hank McCoy that still clung there.

Grey and Summers had chosen their mode of death. They would die like warriors. He was glad. Proud of them, in some way. And never more sorry to have to kill them.

"Enough!" he cried.

Magneto lifted a hand, and the taxi levitated above him in a green glow of magnetic power. Cyclops and Jean Grey entered through the shattered wall. Summers continued to let loose with bursts of energy from his eyes, but they were growing weaker. Grey tried to use her telekinesis to wrest the vehicle from his magnetic grasp, but Magneto resisted her. She was greatly weakened as well.

With the taxi as his bludgeoning tool, he crushed them both.

When Magneto walked out of the shattered store, past the vehicle and the corpses of several X-Men, blood still ran freely down his left leg from the wound in his side. Every breath brought new pain to his broken ribs. But he was triumphant.

Compared to the X-Men, a battle with the American military would be simplicity itself. He was determined to remake Haven, and to hold it this time. His mistake from the very beginning had been to rely upon the Sentinels. He ought to have done it himself from the start.

He stumbled slightly.

"I hope you're proud of yourself," a familiar voice said.

Magneto looked up, held his chest in pain.

In the center of the street, amid all the debris, among the dead and injured, Professor Charles Xavier sat in his wheelchair. Alone.

"I'm glad you came, Charles," Magneto said, coughing slightly, the pain in his chest intense. He wiped his fist across his mouth and was astonished to find blood there.

"You're not doing so well, it seems," Xavier said calmly. "I doubt you're happy to see me."

"No, but happy to know I can destroy you, now that you've saved me the trouble of finding you," Magneto said.

"You were never a killer, Magnus," Xavier said. "Look around you. A man of your intellect, your courage—couldn't you have found another way than murder?"

"My dream, my destiny . . . its fulfillment is worth any price." Magneto coughed. "Haven will be a reality."

"Don't you see," Xavier pleaded, and at last the man sounded like the Charles that Eric Magnus Lehnsherr first met in Israel all those years ago. "Your dream cannot succeed. The best you can hope for is to rule a world that is in the process of self-destructing. Your dream will destroy the Earth, not only for humanity, but for all."

"I don't believe that, Charles," Magneto said. "We have been over this time and time again. I'm afraid, old friend, that we will have to agree to disagree. My way is the only way. You believe the same of your own dream, do you not?"

"The difference, Magnus, is that my dream does not require force, violence, oppression, and murder," Xavier said.

"Never mind the philosophical debate," Magneto said. "Only time will reveal who was right, and I intend to bend the future to my own whims. But let's talk about you, shall we? For a man about to die, for a man who has just seen his entire family killed, you seem awfully calm.''

"You just aren't paying attention,'' Xavier said. "I've never been more enraged, more disgusted, more disappointed. But it has nothing to do with the X-Men. In your right mind, you would never have committed such wholesale murder, especially of individuals you value so highly.''

Magneto frowned.

"You've gone mad, Charles,'' he said. "They are dead. Their corpses litter the streets around you.''

"No,'' Xavier answered. "You often dream of killing me, Magnus. Of killing the X-Men and so many others. But you aren't a murderer. You would avoid such things unless your hand was forced.''

Magneto faltered. He was confused. Xavier's words rang true. He had often felt driven to kill the X-Men, to kill Charles himself, a man who had once been his closest friend. But he never had. Had never intended to do so. Once, he had spent time with them, almost been one of them. In his own way, he cared for them, like an angry, impatient parent with naughty children.

But he had killed them. He had killed them all.

"I . . .'' he began, and faltered once more. He didn't understand.

"But, just in case I had misjudged you,'' Xavier said, "I couldn't possibly allow you the opportunity. The X-Men are, as you say, my family. I love them as dearly as any good parent.''

His mind was reeling, but Magneto knew what he must do.

"Enough of your hysterical babbling, Charles,'' Magneto said. "The time has come. I've got to kill you.''

"You're welcome to try,'' Xavier said.

Then he stood up, out of the wheelchair.

Magneto could not contain his astonishment.

"You—you're walking,'' he said in awe.

Xavier walked swiftly toward him, stepping around debris and the still forms of human beings. When he reached Magneto, he balled his right hand into a fist, and hit him.

Magneto fell, mouth still hanging open in surprise. He reached up to massage his cheek where Xavier had hit him. He looked up, saw Xavier glaring grimly down at him.

Then he understood.

"You're walking," he said, eyes narrowing with hatred as the full realization of what Xavier had done began to sink in. "If you're walking, that means we're—"

"On the Astral Plane, yes," Xavier admitted.

Everything went black a moment, and Magneto felt nauseous, his equilibrium shot. Then the world came back. He was standing in the middle of Sixth Avenue. Xavier was gone. Or at least, his body was gone.

Turn around, Xavier's voice said inside Magneto's head.

He turned.

A full-power optic blast hit him in the chest, driving him back. Lightning flashed from the sky, and only his own innate magnetism saved him from being electrocuted.

Cyclops hit him again, and this time he felt his ribs crack for real. A second bolt of lightning struck pavement not far from him.

A blue-furred hand grabbed him by the shoulder, spun him around. Magneto tried to put up a fight, tried to get his hands up, to concentrate, to defend himself.

He wasn't fast enough.

"You have wreaked enough havoc, stolen enough souls, for one day, Magnus," the Beast said.

McCoy hit him, hard, and Magneto stumbled backward into a yellow cab. He lashed out blindly, and the Beast was tossed away by a lance of magnetic force. The taxi began to feel warm beneath him, and when Magneto looked down, he saw that it was glowing with energy.

Explosive energy.

"'Bout time we got you on de run," Gambit said. "You in trouble now."

Magneto tried to run, but only managed a few steps before the car exploded behind him, throwing him into the air. At great velocity, he slammed into something hard and unyielding. Nearly delirious, he looked up to see that Rogue was holding him up by the shoulders of his body armor.

"See, sugar?" she said sweetly. "I didn't even have to hit ya to take y'down."

Then she let him go, and Magneto fell. And fell.

He hit something cold and slick, and began to slide. It was ice, he knew suddenly. Bobby Drake had saved his life. At the bottom of the ice slide, he rolled over, unable to get to his feet. A massive weapon was thrust into his face.

"Up," Bishop snarled. "Get up and walk before I incinerate your head just for the pleasure of it."

It was the disdain, the almost pitying disgust, that brought him back from the brink of unconsciousness. Mind beginning to clear, Magneto acted quickly.

Bishop's weapon exploded in his hands. Magneto reached for him, focused down and down and down until he could sense the iron in Bishop's bloodstream. He was going to just pull, just burst every blood vessel in the man's body.

Then he remembered Xavier's words, remembered his own misgivings about killing the X-Men. Bishop was a stranger to him, a recent addition to the team. He meant nothing to Magneto. But he meant something to Xavier, and to Xavier's dream.

"Kill me if you like," Bishop said, already weakened by Magneto's tampering with his blood. "But learn from the future I represent. Learn that you can't win by tearing the world apart."

Magneto was sickened by a sudden, terrible realization.

He preferred Xavier's dream.

The blood drained from his face and he let Bishop fall to the pavement. He preferred Xavier's dream. Xavier was right. No, not right, just more human. Xavier's dream might be preferable, he knew now that it was, but Magneto did not, could not, would not, believe that it would ever be realized.

Therefore, no matter what he wished for, Magneto knew that his own dream of the future was the only practical solution.

Still, he could not kill Xavier, the dreamer. He could not

kill the dream, for it represented something he had never had, not since the day his family was murdered.

The dream represented hope.

The X-Men were the living embodiment of Xavier's dream. He could not kill them.

Magneto turned to walk away from Bishop, and Archangel's wing knives slashed into him, paralyzing him where he stood. He fell to the street, bleeding, something broken in his chest, for real this time. Magneto was horrified by his sudden new understanding, of himself, of Xavier, or their eternal struggle with each other.

He had been defeated.

Haven was lost.

The empire was gone.

* * *

Wolverine saw Magneto go down, and knew it was his only chance. Maybe the last, best hope they would have to rid the world of the scourge of Xavier's dream. Magneto was the mutant bogeyman that humans told their children stories about. His actions had fed the flames of hatred for years. With him gone, they could begin the hard road to peace that Xavier had always talked about.

Logan was no optimist, but he knew an opportunity when he saw one.

"Wolverine, no, he still has his powers!" Archangel cautioned.

Ignoring the warning, he loped across the street, even as the other X-Men gathered around behind him. All of them. His friends, his family.

Wolverine leaped onto Magneto's chest. His claws slid out with a *snikt,* and he leaned down, breathing in Magneto's face, whispering low so only he could hear.

"It's over, now, bub," Logan growled. "You've given us all a world o' trouble, but the end is here. I'm gonna put you out of the world's misery."

He held Magneto by the throat with his left hand and lowered his right, claws pointed at Magneto's heart. Adamantium would slice through the tyrant's body armor like a razor-wire garrote through tender flesh. Then it would be—

"Back off, Wolverine," Cyclops ordered.

Logan wanted to ignore him, but Summers had that tone about him. He was a Boy Scout, sure, but he was something else as well. Scott Summers was good. Simple as that. Wolverine didn't like to take orders from him, didn't like knowing Summers was the boss. But all the things he loved about the X-Men, all the things that made the team so important to him, all those things were represented by Cyclops.

"He's gotta die, Scotty," Logan said, low, menacing. "If we let him live, who knows what he's going to do next? What then? He may win the next time."

"Magneto is paralyzed, Logan, but not without power," Jean Grey cut in. "Why hasn't he lashed out at you, tossed you away? I'd say he's waiting for you to decide what you're going to do."

Wolverine looked around at his friends, at his team, his family. Jean, so beautiful, so benevolent. Scott, every bit the hero, filled with impractical ideals and the guts to try to make them work. Ororo, his best friend, the noblest of warriors. Hank, brilliant and tender. Warren, lost and brooding. Bobby, who didn't think life was so funny anymore. Bishop, terrified of the future. LeBeau, injured, hurting, trying his charming best to hide how badly he needed the X-Men. Rogue, always alone, even with those who loved her most.

In the back, silent, stood Cain Marko. He had not participated in the final attack on Magneto. Xavier's intervention had made him back off. The Juggernaut hated his half-brother more than anything. He was a bastard, but even he had helped the X-Men to defeat Magneto.

Wolverine let out a long breath.

"I'm sorry," he said. "It's gotta end now."

Logan drew his arm back, prepared to drive his claws into Magneto's chest. Magneto's eyes flared with surprise and hatred, and Wolverine knew he had a heartbeat to act before Magneto lashed out at him.

"Attaboy, Wolverine," Marko shouted. "Perforate 'im!"

Adamantium claws touched Magneto's throat, but went no farther.

"Hell," Logan snarled. "If Marko's eggin' me on, it can't be . . ."

He looked into Magneto's eyes, saw the anger and the amusement there.

"Ah, hell," Wolverine said.

Then the power burst from Magneto and Logan was whipped up and back, tumbling to the pavement thirty yards away. He was up in an instant, and he ran back to help the X-Men if Magneto was on the attack again.

But Magneto was in no condition to attack. The paralysis was wearing off, but the tyrant was on his knees, coughing blood.

With a crackle of energy, Amelia Voght flashed into existence by her master's side.

"Lord Magneto," she cried. "You are injured."

"It will pass," he said, then hacked and coughed again, before spitting blood on the street.

Magneto looked up at the X-Men, gave a small laugh and grimaced with the pain of it. Then he turned to Wolverine and hatred altered his features.

"You should have killed me when you had the chance," he said. "Next time, Logan, I'll tear you apart."

"You don't look so hot, bub," Wolverine said confidently. "I'm not real sure there's gonna be a next time."

"Amelia," Magneto said, then turned to look upon Voght, almost tenderly, "let's go home."

The air crackled again, and they disappeared in a flash of phosphorescent light. Voght had teleported them back to Avalon.

In the midst of death and devastation, none of the X-Men said a word. When Wolverine looked around again, the Juggernaut had gone.

Finally, it was over.

EPILOGUE

Charles Xavier sat in darkness in his study. His thoughts were a burden, his dream, his mission, unforgiving. There would be no rest, no respite, though the X-Men had fought their most precipitous battle, and emerged the victors.

The war went on.

Xavier had monitored all that had happened after he had allowed Magneto to return to reality from the Astral Plane. He had witnessed Wolverine's attack on Magneto, had not interfered. That was his way, to let his people choose their own paths. Taking their choices away would alienate them from him.

He knew that Wolverine had done the right thing. In some ways, he was proud of Logan.

But there was another part of him that wondered, merely wondered, whether the world might not have been a far better place if Wolverine had given in to his primal urge.

Silently, Xavier vowed that the next time the X-Men faced Magneto would be the last. He would find a way to take Magneto out of the game for good, and he would do it himself, so none of the X-Men were left to feel responsible. It was the only way, he knew. The only way for the dream to come true, the only way to assure victory.

Charles Xavier had determined, not to kill, but in some way to destroy a man who had once been his best friend. What he had yet to consider, what he resolutely refused to consider, was what that decision would cost him.

* * *

On the observation deck of the space station Avalon, Eric Magnus Lehnsherr stood alone, gazing down at the planet of his birth with a heavy heart. He was no longer welcome on Earth. More than a man without a country, he was a man without a world. And he feared such would be the fate of all his kind.

Slowly, Magneto let out the breath he had been holding. He nodded slightly.

He had made one final effort to turn his dream of mutant

domination into a reality. The X-Men had opposed him, as he had known they would, but in the end, it was Charles Xavier who had won the day. Xavier had triumphed by doing the unexpected, by using his abilities in a way that Magneto had never imagined the man's delicate philosophical bent would allow.

So be it. There would be now an entirely new set of rules based upon this latest engagement. Magneto would put all his efforts behind turning Avalon into the sanctuary Haven had not been allowed to become. A massive headquarters in which to build a conquering army. It might take years, but when all was at the ready, they would strike.

It was only a matter of time. Indeed, the ascendancy of mutants, of *homo superior*, was an inevitable product of natural evolution.

Put simply, Magneto planned to speed evolution along.

* * *

Valerie Cooper sat in the Oval Office staring across the long desk at the President. It was the first time she had ever met with the Commander-in-Chief without anyone else present. Despite her bluster and natural confidence, she was nervous.

"You wanted to see me, sir?" she asked.

"Yes. Thank you for coming, Valerie," he answered.

"You are the President, sir," she joked.

He didn't smile. Not even a little. Val sat up a little straighter and erased the smile from her own face. Apparently, this was not going to be a cordial visit.

"New York is rebuilding, Valerie," the President said. "There wasn't as much damage as there might have been—I don't have to tell you what might have been, do I? But the cost of rebuilding has been estimated at anywhere between fifteen and two hundred forty-seven billion dollars."

Val blanched.

"I'd no idea," she said.

"And when you leave you'll forget I mentioned it," the President ordered. "If we're to keep peace between humans and mutants, avoid a civil war, such things must be downplayed as strongly as possible.''

"I understand," she said.

"I know you do," the President replied, with the first trace of warmth she had received from him. "What I want to know is, what happened to all the mutants who aided Magneto?"

"They returned with him to Avalon, sir," she answered.

"Not the Acolytes," he said. "What of the others, the recruits?"

"Well, we do have several dozen mutants in custody for treason, Mr. President," Val said. "But I don't know if they'll ever get to trial."

"That's not your problem," the President said sharply. "Those numbers are. There were hundreds of mutants, nearly a thousand according to some estimates, helping Magneto in Manhattan. What happened to all of them?"

Cooper felt sick. Most of Magneto's mutant allies had escaped. The President wanted to know where they went.

"Some left long before the military showed up," she explained. "Those that looked human melted back into the landscape of the city. Those who didn't had a more difficult time of it. The forty or so mutants who were captured all had mutations that were apparent. Not a single mutant who looked human was captured. I believe bias got in the way of our efforts sir."

There was more to it than that, but Val wasn't about to tell the President that Police Commissioner Ramos and Trish Tilby had helped many mutants escape. He just didn't need to know. She could be tried for treason if it were discovered that she knew of it. That was her risk, and she was comfortable with it.

"Ridiculous," the President said. "But I don't have a better explanation, so it will have to do. You may go."

"Thank you, Mr. President," Val said, and rose to leave.

"Oh, one last thing."

"Yes, sir?"

"It's over, now," the President said. "Everything returns to status quo. That includes your situation and your relationship with the Director of Wideawake and with Gyrich.''

"But, sir," Val protested. "Gyrich was a—"

The President held up his hand, and Val's protest faltered. He was the President, after all.

"Gyrich is my concern, Cooper," the President said. "I will deal with him as I see fit. It isn't your problem anymore, nor is it your business."

Val wanted to scream, to demand Gyrich's punishment.

She knew better.

The best she could do was make a silent vow to herself that she would watch Gyrich very carefully in the future. He was a dangerous man.

* * *

Scott and Jean stood on the terrace of the Xavier Institute. They stood in silence for quite some time, idly holding hands.

"They're doing well," Scott said, after a bit. "Most of the injuries have healed. We seem to be getting back up to fighting condition."

"Mmm," Jean mumbled noncommittally.

"What is it?" he asked, and glanced at her, concerned.

"Not all of our injuries were physical, Scott," Jean answered.

"I know that," he said. "But the apocalypse didn't happen, Jean. What with Trish Tilby's network coverage, the President's public appreciation, and Magneto's defeat, well, for the most part, mutant-human relations are no worse off than they were before Magneto decided to play emperor."

Jean didn't respond, only watching the stars with a growing look of concern.

Jean? Scott thought, knowing that she would telepathically hear him through the psychic rapport they shared. *What is it, sweetheart?*

It's us, Scott. All of us. We went to war. We got a glimpse of the future that Bishop fears so much, and it made us brutal, as brutal as we have ever been, even in the worst of circumstances.

"After all that's happened," she said aloud, turning to look at him finally, meeting his eyes, "I just have to wonder what impact it's going to have on each of us. Personally, I have been profoundly affected by the past few days. So many mutants responded so quickly to Magneto's promises, despite his terrorist tactics, that I have to wonder what hope there is for us. For the dream."

"Losing your faith? Is that what this is about?" Scott asked.

"God, no," Jean said. "I believe with all my heart in what we do. But I wonder who will take up the banner and carry on when we can't do it anymore. We could all have been killed, Scott. How can we be assured that the fight will continue, when all I want to do is gather up the next generation of mutants and bundle them off somewhere safe? They shouldn't have to live like this."

Scott pulled her close, and Jean let him. They stood like that a moment, the embrace more powerful than any words, any thoughts, they might share.

"If we do our jobs," Scott said quietly, "if we fight hard enough, maybe the next generation won't have to."

They kissed, then, a brief and tender kiss, filled with promise.

CHRISTOPHER GOLDEN is the author of a dozen novels, including *Of Saints and Shadows*, *Angel Souls & Devil Hearts*, the Daredevil novel *Predator's Smile*, a *Battlestar Galactica* novel, the Hellboy novel *The Lost Army*, the forthcoming X-Men hardcover novel *Codename Wolverine*, and, of course, the previous two books in the *X-Men: Mutant Empire* trilogy, *Siege* and *Sanctuary*. Golden has recently entered the comic book field with work on such titles as *Wolverine*, *The Crow*, *Thundergod*, and *Vampirella*. He has written articles for *The Boston Herald*, *Hero Illustrated*, *Flux*, *Disney Adventures*, and *Billboard*, among others, and was a regular columnist for the worldwide serivce, BPI Entertainment News Wire. His short story appearances include *Forbidden Acts*, *The Ultimate Spider-Man*, *The Ultimate Silver Surfer*, *Gahan Wilson's The Ultimate Haunted House*, and the upcoming *Untold Tales of Spider-Man*. Golden was born and raised
in Massachusetts, where he still lives with his family. He urges everyone to check out his WorldWideWeb page at http://www.oneworld.net/sf/authors/golden.htm.

* * *

RICK LEONARDI was born in Philadelphia. He started working at Marvel in 1980, and set himself up as one of their premiere fill-in artists, providing issues of *Daredevil*, *Uncanny X-Men*, *The New Mutants*, *Amazing Spider-Man*, *Excalibur*, *Spectacular Spider-Man*, and many others. He broke the trend by becoming the regular penciller on *Cloak & Dagger* and *Spider-Man 2099*. More recently, his work can be found in *Fantastic Four 2099*, *Sovereign Seven*, and the *Spider-Man/Spider-Man 2099* team-up, and he's provided illustrations for the books *The Ultimate Spider-Man*, *The Ultimate X-Men*, *Untold Tales of Spider-Man*, and the other two *X-Men: Mutant Empire* novels.

* * *

TERRY AUSTIN is the Eagle, Saturn Alley, and *Comics Buyer's Guide* award-winning inker of such comics as *The Uncanny X-Men*, *Detective Comics*, *Star Wars*, *Dr. Strange*, *Batman vs. Predator II*, and the prestigious *X-Men/New Teen Titans* and *Green Lantern/Silver Surfer* team-up books. He has also written issues of *Cloak & Dagger*, *Power Pack*, *Uncanny X-Men Annual*, *What If . . . ?*, *Excalibur*, and, most recently, the adaptation of *Star Wars: Splinter of the Mind's Eye*. His current complaints include his inability to get the theme song from the Saturday morning cartoon *Freakazoid* out of his head.

Marvel Comics

star in their own original series!

___ **X-MEN: MUTANT EMPIRE: BOOK 1: SIEGE**
by Christopher Golden   1-57297-114-2/$5.99
When Magneto takes over a top-secret government installation
containing mutant-hunting robots, the X-Men must battle against
their oldest foe. But the X-Men are held responsible for the takeover
by a more ruthless enemy...the U.S. government.

___ **X-MEN: MUTANT EMPIRE: BOOK 2: SANCTUARY**
by Christopher Golden   1-57297-180-0/$5.99
Magneto has occupied The Big Apple, and the X-Men must penetrate
the enslaved city and stop him before he advances his mad plan to
conquer the entire world!

___ **X-MEN: MUTANT EMPIRE: BOOK 3: SALVATION**
by Christopher Golden   1-57297-247-5/$5.99
Magneto's Mutant Empire has already taken Manhattan, and now
he's setting his sights on the rest of the world. The only thing that
stands between Magneto and conquest is the X-Men.

® ™ and © 1997 Marvel Characters, Inc. All Rights Reserved.